Praise for

VICTORIA DAHL

"Dahl delivers a fun, feisty and relentlessly sexy adventure in her first contemporary."
—*Publishers Weekly* on *Talk Me Down*

"Sassy and smokingly sexy, *Talk Me Down* is one delicious joyride of a book."
—*New York Times* bestselling author
Connie Brockway

"Sparkling, special and oh so sexy—
Victoria Dahl is a special treat!"
—*New York Times* bestselling author
Carly Phillips on *Talk Me Down*

"[A] hands-down winner, a sensual story filled with memorable characters."
—*Booklist* on *Start Me Up*

"Dahl has spun a scorching tale about what can happen in the blink of an eye and what we can do to change our lives."
—*RT Book Reviews,*
4 stars, on *Start Me Up*

Dear Reader,

A few years ago, my family and I moved from the mountains of Colorado to the coast of Virginia. If you and I are ever stuck together in an elevator, I'll happily tell you the horror story of that cross-country move, but for now, let's just say it was an *adventure*. Yes, an adventure!

Before then, I'd only seen the ocean a handful of times, but during our two years in Virginia we traveled up and down the coast and spent hours exploring the Chesapeake Bay and the Great Dismal Swamp. Every day was an exciting discovery (ever heard of biting flies?) and I loved it.

I knew that any story told in this setting would have to have some thrills, but I had no idea it would be quite so chock-full of them! A plane crash, a federal investigation, tabloid scandals, a runaway groom, the paparazzi, sunken treasure and lies, lies and more lies! Plus, of course, a steamy vacation fling on a nearly deserted island. And perhaps the strangest part of the whole story...there's a nice, normal, *average* girl at the center of it all. (This is reminding me more and more of that cross-country move.)

So how does a nice, normal girl find herself in the middle of an international tabloid scandal? I hope you don't mind the quick detour from the mountains to the beach to find out. After all, the wild coast of Virginia is perfect for adventure, and who couldn't use a few days in a beachside cottage? With a handsome treasure hunter. And ice-cold margaritas.

Enjoy!

Victoria Dahl

VICTORIA DAHL

Crazy for Love

HQN™

3 1907 00252 6811

Recycling programs
for this product may
not exist in your area.

ISBN-13: 978-0-373-77462-3

CRAZY FOR LOVE

Copyright © 2010 by Victoria Dahl

This edition published by arrangement with Harlequin Books S.A.

For questions and comments about the quality of this book please contact us at Customer_eCare@Harlequin.ca.

® and TM are trademarks of the publisher. Trademarks indicated with ® are registered in the United States Patent and Trademark Office, the Canadian Trade Marks Office and in other countries.

www.HQNBooks.com

Printed in U.S.A.

This book is for Bill, of course.
Thanks for always taking such good care of us.

Also by

VICTORIA DAHL

and HQN Books

Talk Me Down
Start Me Up
Lead Me On

Crazy for Love

CHAPTER ONE

CHLOE TURNER STARED DOWN into the black, roiling water, squinting her eyes against the cool spray. The wind ate into her skin. When the boat dipped into a trough, the water rose up, reaching for her, trying to pull her under. She drew her head back as if she could avoid the swipe of the watery paw. Before she could recover from the fear of that close call, the boat tipped up, climbing toward the crest of another wave. The storm had come out of nowhere. She suspected they were in big trouble.

A slender hand settled on her shoulder, offering faint comfort.

"I think we might die out here," Chloe murmured.

The hand smacked her arm. Hard. "Oh, for God's sake, Chloe. It's a frickin' ferryboat. Get over yourself."

Chloe tossed a glare at her best friend, Jenn. "We're in the middle of the ocean. In a storm."

"First of all, we're barely out of the bay. Second,

there's a nine-year-old kid a few feet away who's having the time of his life."

The boat rose on another storm-tossed wave, and Chloe's stomach dropped. When the boy hooted with excitement, she glared in his direction. "Idiot," she muttered.

Jenn smacked her again. "If a reporter heard you say that, you'd be screwed."

"They can't find me on a boat. Isn't that the reason we're sailing straight into the perfect storm?"

"Be nice or I'll call and alert them to your where-abouts."

Chloe shrugged and pushed a strand of wet brown hair out of her eyes. "I'll be tipped off when you put on makeup and turn on the cleavage show."

A smile pulled up the corners of her friend's mouth. "I did look pretty hot last Saturday."

Chloe smiled back. "You did. Especially when you put your hand in front of the camera and yelled, 'She is not an animal!'"

"Oh, God," Jenn groaned, using that very same hand to cover her eyes. "I still can't believe that. It was so chaotic."

"The good news is that a nineteenth-century London freak show called to offer me a stall. I get to keep half the coins the public pelts at me."

Jenn shook her head, the hood of her windbreaker

slipping back to expose her gorgeous blond hair. "You'll never get tired of that joke, will you?"

"Never." As Chloe's laughter faded, she glanced over her shoulder, as if she could still see the Virginia coastline behind her. "Do you think they followed us?"

"The photographers?" Jenn's eyes clouded with worry, but Chloe was already feeling silly. No speeding car had followed them from Richmond. No black van had screeched up to the ferry landing to disgorge a pack of paparazzi. Chloe might feel infamous and trapped by the notoriety thrust upon her by her ex-fiancé, but she wasn't hunted day and night. Not quite.

"No one saw us leave, Chloe."

"I know, I know. Sorry, it's just—" The ferry swayed forward and a loud thump vibrated up through her knees. "Oh, God!" she cried out, grabbing for the railing. "This is it. We're going down."

Mouth flat with obvious disgust, Jenn shook her head. "We're at the dock, you coward."

"Are you kidding me?" Chloe looked around, eyes widening at the dark shadow of the dock looming out of the mist. "We made it? Oh, my God, we actually made it!"

"You won't have to fight that kid for a seat on the lifeboat, so I'm pretty relieved, too."

"I totally could've taken him," Chloe murmured under her breath as she followed Jenn to the walkway. Jenn must've heard her, because she twisted around to give Chloe a narrow look.

Chloe had been a nice, happy person just a month before. The kind of girl who'd never joke about fighting a kid for a seat on a lifeboat. Hopefully, somewhere deep inside, she was still nice, but she'd taken so many brutal blows in the past few weeks that she couldn't feel anything but the dull pain of layered bruises.

But not right now. Not this week. Jenn had arranged this trip to get Chloe away from the insanity created by her broken engagement. They'd managed to ditch the paparazzi back on the mainland, and there was no roaring speedboat looming out of the mist to catch them.

Jenn had assured her that the tiny resort on White Rock Island didn't have any TVs, and the whole island was limited to fuzzy reception on old-fashioned antennas. This might be the one place where Chloe wouldn't be recognized.

The deckhands lowered the walkway to the narrow wooden dock. Drawing a deep breath, Chloe watched a spot of sunlight on the dock expand into a wide patch. When she glanced up toward the heavy gray clouds, the sun burst through like an omen of good days ahead. Her luck was changing. She was sure of it. Even the wind shifted toward the east, warming away the chill she'd caught earlier.

"Come on," Jenn called out, waving toward the short line of people filing onto the dock. At the end of May, the weather wasn't consistent enough to draw people to the little island. Today, for example, had brought forth a wicked thunderstorm, but now the clouds were shrinking and breaking up, and summer temperatures returned.

When Chloe set her foot on the dock, which rocked only a little less than the boat, she drew in a deep breath of relief.

Jenn slipped her arm through Chloe's. "Are you ready to relax?"

"Yes."

"The resort will pick up our bags. Let's grab some groceries and head over."

Sand crunched beneath their feet as they walked toward the buildings gathered around the tiny harbor. The resort was less than half a mile away, according to Jenn, and they could walk or ride bikes while they were here, which meant they'd have to be choosy about their groceries.

"You brought the margarita mix?" Chloe asked.

Jenn patted her gigantic purse, and a quiet clunk echoed from its depths. "Safe and sound."

"So we should be good with Lean Cuisines and doughnuts?"

"I don't see why not."

In the end they added a few more essentials to the list: chips and guac, Diet Coke, marshmallows, and some grapes to counter nutritional guilt. Half an hour later, they were on the porch of their seaside cabin, legs propped on the porch railing and iced margaritas in their plastic cups.

"This is going to be a great week," Jenn said brightly. Chloe wasn't so sure, but the longer she sat there, the more likely that seemed. The Richmond courthouse and Chloe's ex-fiancé were a whole world away. Maybe two. And Jenn had been right: their little two-bedroom cottage had a kitchen and a bathroom and a porch facing the waves, but one thing it didn't have was a television.

Better yet, her cell phone showed only one flickering bar, so even if a reporter did manage to get through, Chloe wouldn't be able to hear him over the constant crash of the waves. She was off the grid, and the idea melted her into the ancient gray wood of her deck chair.

Miracle of miracles, she was *relaxed*. More herself. But it didn't feel like she was becoming herself again, exactly. She was reverting to something more primitive. A feral cat sunning itself on the sand.

Her muscles gave up their tight hold on her bones.

Her joints loosened. Chloe slipped her sunglasses on and gave her body and soul up to the beach.

MAX SULLIVAN GRIPPED the boat's railing in numb hands and told himself that everything was okay. His brother was at the helm of his new boat—he'd turned out to be a quick learner—and the storm was subsiding. Max didn't need to rush over and take control. Elliott was fine. Still, he stared daggers into Elliott's back, willing him to turn around.

Finally, he did. "You want to bring it in?" Elliott called over the wind, tilting his head toward the wheel. "I'm not sure I'm skilled enough for this."

Max sucked air into his starving lungs and released his death grip on the railing. He hated being on the water. More than that, he hated being on the water during a high wind with a man who didn't know the first thing about boating. But that was the point. Max couldn't have let his brother learn the ropes by himself on the open sea. People died like that. So Max just offered his trademark grin and sauntered toward the captain's chair.

"Sure," he said. "I'll take her in."

"Her," Elliott repeated. "Right. Sea lingo."

Elliott had bought the boat to try to prove to himself that he wasn't a workaholic, but now he looked troubled by the idea of learning how to have fun.

"It'll be great," Max said as enthusiastically as he

could, considering that he was looking out at waves instead of solid ground. One careless move and the ocean would happily suck both brothers into its dark maw. Max was exhausted from constantly guarding against the danger.

Six weeks on dry land had sounded like pure heaven after three months on the southern Mediterranean searching for treasure. Max had the perfect damn life…and he hated it. Not that he was ungracious enough to let anyone else know that.

He glanced back to Elliott, who was starting to gather up their gear. Elliott was supposed to be learning, and Max knew he should call his brother over and guide him through docking, but he told himself it would be better to wait for nicer weather. Then again, if Elliott rocked the boat into a piling with enough force, the boat would need repairs and they could abandon this so-called vacation.

A wave swelled beneath them, throwing Max into the wheel as if in punishment for his fantasy. "All right," he muttered into the wind before waving his brother over. "Come on. I'll guide you through it. You shouldn't take her out in crud like this, but you never know what's going to blow in unexpectedly."

He talked Elliott through the danger of the narrow breakwater and into the marginally calmer waters of the tiny harbor. Five minutes later, his jaw and hands ached from tension, but the boat was safely tied in at one of the slips.

"Good work," he said to Elliott, instead of blurting out what he really wanted to say. *Why couldn't you take up golf like all the other high-level guys at the CDC?*

Elliott jumped onto the dock and Max handed the bags up to him so they could start the walk to their cabin. "How'd you find this place?"

Elliott shrugged. "Somebody on one of the boating sites recommended it."

"Looks nice." Max jumped up and they walked in silence for a while before he took another look at his brother's tight shoulders. "Elliott..." he started, wondering if he should mention the ex-wife. What the hell. "You're not doing all this just because of Rebecca, are you?"

Though Max had worried about offending him, Elliott didn't even look surprised, much less offended. "She was right."

"Aw, screw her," Max muttered. "You're a great guy. You know how many women would kill to marry a guy like you? You're totally stable. You're hardworking and honest and—"

"I'm not plugged in, I work too damn much and I'm boring as hell."

"That's bullshit."

"It's not bullshit."

Max scowled, shifting the duffel bag to his other shoulder. "You love your job."

"Yeah, I love my job, but it can't be everything. I always worked too much, but after the last flu crisis… I wasn't even surprised when she left, man. She'd given me enough warning."

Thinking of Rebecca, with her shiny black hair and bright blue eyes, Max shook his head. He'd first met her at his brother's wedding rehearsal, and his initial impression had been positive. She was lively, a real firecracker, only slightly overwhelmed by the stress of pulling off a perfect wedding.

Six months later, Max had returned from another long stint on the water and found that her liveliness had shifted toward restlessness and impatience with Elliott. Her hostile remarks about Elliott working on weekends had been interspersed with pointed observations about Max's work. Travel and excitement and weeks in exotic locations. She'd oohed and aahed until Max had been uncomfortable enough to leave early.

The truth was that life on the sea was utter boredom punctuated by moments of alarm. The tanned skin and windswept hair threw people off. But Rebecca hadn't been interested in explanations. She'd only been needling her husband. Max hadn't been surprised by the news that she'd left the day after their first anniversary. Apparently, Elliott hadn't been, either.

Max cleared his throat. "You're not trying to get her back, are you?"

Elliott surprised him by laughing. "Give me some credit. I know we weren't right for each other. I just don't want to make the same mistake again."

"You dating somebody?"

"Would I be spending a week at the beach with *you* if I were?"

"Hell, you've already admitted to being bad with women. Wasn't sure it would occur to you to bring a girl."

"Bite me," Elliott muttered.

"Again, better with a girl."

The punch to his shoulder hurt like a bitch. Despite spending sixty hours a week behind a desk, Elliott wasn't exactly a weakling, and they'd had plenty of practice whaling on each other as kids. Just as he had when they were young, Max laughed like it hadn't hurt and pushed his younger brother hard enough to make him stumble.

The sound and smell of the ocean still pressed in on him, but with his brother's laughter bouncing off the surrounding boats, Max decided maybe this vacation would be okay after all. But he'd stay on guard against disaster, just as he always did. The ocean had a way of serving up surprises.

CHAPTER TWO

"I THINK I'M DRUNK," Chloe murmured. The clouds had drifted away, and she was floating in a pool of sunlight and alcohol. "When did we eat lunch?"

Jenn rolled her head and looked sleepily in her direction. "We were on the ferry during lunchtime. We forgot."

"Huh. We should probably eat then, or this could get ugly."

"Uglier than being drunk at 3:00 p.m.?"

"Way uglier. Should I fire up the microwave?"

Jenn groaned in answer and shook her head. "Maybe we should eat some big cheeseburgers to celebrate the start of our vacation. There's a seedy bar just past the resort office."

Though Chloe's eyes had started to drift shut again, they popped open at the thought of bar food. "Really? We *do* want to start this week off on the right foot…"

"Exactly."

Just beyond the blond halo of Jenn's hair, Chloe spotted movement. Leaning forward a little, she slid her sunglasses down her nose and narrowed her eyes against the warm breeze. "Hello."

"What?" Jenn asked before her mouth opened wide in a yawn.

The approaching men had come fully into view now, so Chloe relaxed back into her seat and pushed her glasses up to hide her eyes. "I think we've got neighbors."

Jenn's nose wrinkled. "Not those gossipy old ladies from the store?"

"Not even close."

Her friend finally roused herself enough to roll her head in the other direction, and Chloe knew the moment Jenn spotted the two men, because she inhaled sharply enough to send a nearby seagull flapping away. The men were still too far off to have heard, but they were getting closer, obviously headed toward the cabin next door.

They both had dark brown hair and wide shoulders. Both wore cargo shorts that showed off strong calves dusted with dark hair. Brothers or cousins maybe, as the hard lines of their jaws were exact replicas, though one of the men was taller and had a dark tan that set him apart. The other wore cute wire-rimmed glasses and held his mouth in a far more serious line.

The tanned one turned his head in the direction of Chloe and Jenn, and he hesitated a bit over his next step, probably surprised to find he had an audience. Still, he didn't look the least bit uncomfortable as he jogged up the steps to the porch, the movement smooth despite the big duffel bag thrown over his shoulder.

Before the men had even disappeared through the door, Jenn's head whipped toward Chloe. "Holy smokes! Do you think it would be wrong to have a torrid affair with twins?"

"You think they're twins?"

"Close enough that I could pretend."

Chloe rolled her eyes, choking on laughter. "If you take both of them, who does that leave me with?"

Jenn sat up, dropping her bare feet to the floor as she took off her shades to meet Chloe's gaze. "Are you interested? I'll let you have both if you're serious."

"Why?"

"Because you need to cleanse Thomas from your palate."

Blood rushed to Chloe's face, though she didn't know why she felt shy.

"You need to," Jenn insisted.

"No one wants to date an infamous Bridezilla. I'm kryptonite to the male sex drive. After the first date, a man would expect to wake up and find me standing at the foot of the bed in a tattered wedding gown, rattling a pair of leg shackles."

"So this is the perfect place. No one here knows who you are."

Chloe shrugged and slipped her feet into her sandals. "Those guys aren't from the island. For all we know they could be paparazzi." She regretted her flip words when her friend's eyes widened with alarm.

"You think they're paparazzi?"

She glanced toward the cabin again, thinking of the healthy glow of the taller man. "No, I was just being rude. Those guys look way too healthy to be paparazzi. But as for dating…I just can't do that."

"So you're never going to date again?"

Despite the humiliation burning through her chest, Chloe had to smile at the worry in Jenn's voice. "It's only been a month. I've got some new trust issues, Jenn. That's what happens when your fiancé fakes his own death just to get away from you."

"Thomas was obviously enormously screwed up."

"Yeah, it seems so clear now." Chloe let herself relax back into her wooden deck chair. "He was nice before though, right? That wasn't my imagination."

"Yes, he was nice, but—"

"So there's another issue I'm trying to figure out. If he'd really been so nice, he would've at least called me after he faked his own death and humiliated me in front of the entire world, right? He's never even called. Though his mom left me a couple of messages this week. Maybe he talked her into calling for him."

Jenn cringed and swallowed hard, so Chloe forced a smile. "There's no hope for me, Jenn. I can't handle a pair of hot twins right now. You go on without me. Save yourself."

Jenn opened her mouth as if to argue, but after a moment, she took a deep breath and shook her head. "So I can have them both?"

"You're such a faker. You've only had sex with two guys in your whole life. *Individually.* I don't think you're ready for a threesome."

"Shut up. You're ruining my fantasy. And as you pointed out, fantasy is all I have most of the time."

That was true. Jenn, who was willowy and beautiful and outgoing with her girlfriends, became a nervous wreck around men. A threesome was definitely not in her future. In fact, she was blushing already, just from talking about it.

Chloe rolled her shoulders and stood up, amazed that her neck had lost the ache that had resided there for the past month. "We're both pitiful and hopeless, so we may as well have those cheeseburgers. The seagulls won't give a damn what we look like in our bikinis."

Jenn slipped on her flip-flops while Chloe grabbed her wallet, and they headed off across the sand, not bothering to pretend they weren't trying to look into the men's cabin as they passed. "They're probably a couple," Chloe murmured.

"I was serious about you going for it," Jenn said. "Not with both of them, but at least one."

"It's not going to happen."

"You need some fun, Chloe. I can't stand seeing you this way. Screw Thomas. Live it up. Be Island Chloe!"

"Island Chloe, huh?" She shook her head in resolute denial. Her life was crazy enough as it was. "It's not in me. Not right now."

"Just…keep an open mind."

Two minutes later they were standing in front of the rough gray walls of the bar, brushing sand off their feet.

"This place is great," Jenn assured her. "It's packed during tourist season. We used to swipe beers off tables and hang around on the deck."

Nobody was on the seaside deck today, but the locals probably got tired of ocean views and sun.

When they finally walked in, the first thing Chloe noticed was the arctic air-conditioning. She was about to suggest that they sit outside when she noticed something else. A lot must have changed since Jenn had worked on the island ten years before.

There were plasma-screen TVs in all four corners of the bar, and there was nothing static-y about the baseball games playing on any of them.

"Oh, no," Jenn breathed.

Fields glowed in vivid green contrast to the bright white uniforms on the closest screen. "The wonders of satellite," Chloe muttered, trying not to feel bitter, even as a familiar sense of panic boiled up in her chest.

"Chloe, I'm so sorry! I had no idea!"

"It's not your fault, and it's no big deal anyway. It's just a sports bar. Nobody here cares about me." And it was true, at least at the moment. There were only six customers in the place, and though heads turned in their direction, the games drew their attention again quickly enough.

Chloe let out a deep breath. Slowly. "Will you order while I grab a table on the deck?"

Jenn nodded and shooed her out as if there were a scrum of people at the door, all jostling for a seat outside.

Chloe spun and reached for the handle, but she froze with her hand wrapped around the cold metal. She didn't like the fear creeping along her spine, didn't like the panic making her fingers shake. Over the past month, she'd turned into a coward who jumped at every shadow and couldn't even trust people enough to eat dinner near them. The mere sight of a working television squeezed her stomach into knots.

She didn't want to run outside. She hadn't been in a bar with a girlfriend in…forever.

Fear turned to rage for a brief, shining moment, and Chloe spun back to face the bar, determined not to run…just this one time.

No one was watching her. Not even Jenn.

She let go of her death grip on the door handle and took a deep breath. Thomas's stupidity and cowardice had turned her into a paranoid freak. Or, if she were feeling fair, the twenty-four-hour media culture had turned her into that freak, but Chloe wasn't feeling the least bit fair.

But she was feeling wonderfully anonymous, so she put her chin up, ignored the icy air-conditioning and took a seat at the nearest table. One baby step at a time, she'd find a way to start a new life for herself. After this was over, she'd dye her hair and get a new apartment and walk through life as if her name hadn't become synonymous with psycho-bitch. But for now, she'd have a drink in the bar and not look over her shoulder while she was doing it.

Baby steps.

TRYING HIS BEST to ignore the incessant sound of rumbling waves, Max prodded the hot coals in the grill he'd set up on the sand.

"Hey!" Elliott called from the porch. "You sure you don't want me to do that?"

"I got it," he shouted back. Elliott lived in a high-rise condo in D.C. He likely didn't understand the dangers of wind-whipped fire. If Max didn't man the grill himself, he'd just stand on the porch, arms crossed, watching Elliott to be sure he didn't let the flames get too high. It was more relaxing to simply take control of the situation.

"All right," said Elliott from right behind him. "I've got beer duty covered, though." He handed Max an ice-cold Corona and stood a little too close to the grill for Max's comfort. Max shifted toward his brother to edge him farther away.

Jaw set as he stared out at the waves, Elliott moved a few inches to the side. Jesus, he looked even more miserable than Max felt. Max rolled his shoulders and put on his smile.

"Say," he said, slapping his brother on the back, "there are women on this island."

The creases in Elliott's forehead deepened. "I think wild vacation flings are more your kind of thing."

"Mm," Max grunted, aware, as he always was, that the persona he'd crafted for himself fit him about as well as an extrasmall wet suit. Fun-loving, carefree adventurer. It couldn't be further from the truth. But the wild woman part? That struck a little closer to home. "Yeah, well, I thought you were trying to add some spark to your life."

"That last girl you dated sure threw off sparks," Elliott offered, his mouth finally curving up in a smile.

"Don't remind me," Max groaned.

The smile twisted into a full-on grin. "What was her name?"

"Genevieve."

"Right, the infamous Genevieve Bianca. She…"

"Hey," Max cut in, "weren't we talking about *you?*"

"What's the point? Your life is a hell of a lot more interesting. It always has been."

"The fucking plague is interesting, too." Max deserved the laughter he got in response. *Interesting* was a mild word to describe his love life.

His woman problems had started out innocently enough. He liked to take care of things. To make sure the details of life were addressed. To make sure that *people* were taken care of.

There was no mystery about the origins of this neurosis. Their father had been an irresponsible, selfish bastard with no interest in taking care of anyone but himself. As the older son, Max had found himself stepping into that role. But something about the responsibility had gotten stuck deep inside him like a barbed hook. He couldn't ignore it, even when any rational person would be able to walk away. The need to guide people out of trouble was a painful tugging in his brain. And women in trouble...

Christ, his love life had been a goddamn catastrophe from the moment he'd turned sixteen. Everyone thought he was attracted to bad girls. The truth was, they were attracted to him, and he was pathologically unable to turn his back on someone in trouble.

Nine months ago, in an era he liked to refer to as post-Genevieve, Max had taken a vow of celibacy. No more women, no matter how vulnerable and needy they were. He was strictly hands-off. Life since then had been perfectly lonely. As isolated as he could manage. He'd loved it.

In fact, he felt a stark envy for Elliott's life. His quiet apartment. His office filled with papers and books and computers. His complete lack of any hint of drama. Elliott would never believe it, but Max would switch places with him in a heartbeat. Let Elliott deal with a wild, globe-trotting heiress like Genevieve. Max would live like a monk.

A monk who still took pleasure in watching the approach of two pretty women walking across the sand. "See?" he murmured. "Women."

Max took a swig from his beer and poked at the coals while Elliott did a double take. When the women looked in their direction and both smiled at the same time, Max did a double take, too.

They were nearly the same height—about five-six, he'd guess—but the similarities ended there. The blonde had long wavy hair and delicate features. The brunette was curvier, but wholesome-looking, like a hybrid of Ginger and Mary Ann from *Gilligan's Island*. Both Ginger and Mary Ann had been staple fantasies in Max's early teen years. He was intrigued.

No, you're not, his stern inner voice assured him.

Turning back to the grill, he grabbed the pack of hot dogs to keep himself busy. A vacation fling was the last thing he needed.

But his brain replayed the image of wind-whipped hair and swaying hips on an endless loop in his brain. That brunette looked peaceful, and Max craved peace the way a pirate craved treasure.

Perhaps a deserted island wasn't the best location for a man who'd sworn off booty.

CHAPTER THREE

JENN GRABBED ANOTHER ROCK from the pile and added it to the fire ring with a worried glance toward the other cabin. "He's watching you," she whispered to Chloe.

"He's probably watching you," Chloe answered with a distracted frown. "But I thought you wanted him to watch me," she continued. Jenn watched her scoop up a handful of sand and let it drift through her fingers.

"Now I'm suspicious."

"Hot guy checking me out? I don't blame you."

Jenn rolled her eyes. "Shut up."

Chloe just sifted more sand, her brow furrowed.

"Aren't you having fun?"

"What?" Chloe glanced up and her face cleared a little. "No, I'm having fun! This is great. Very relaxing."

"Relaxing, huh? I was hoping we'd make it all the way to Funtown."

Chloe laughed, but Jenn regretted her words as soon as they left her mouth. "Funtown! God, I haven't heard that in forever. I never see Anna anymore. Maybe we should've invited her, too."

"Mmm," Jenn answered, trying for nonchalance, wishing she hadn't mentioned anything associated with Anna Fenton. "You know how busy she's been with her job. I hardly see her anymore, either."

"She could've gotten off work if she'd wanted to. Her dad owns the damn hotel chain."

"Yeah..." Jenn's heart thundered in her chest as the weight of her lies pressed down on her. She shook her hair back, hoping to shake off the worry, as well. This vacation was meant to be fun, and she assured herself that everything would be fine. "I think he's grooming Anna to take over the kingdom or something."

"Too bad. It would've been nice. Like revisiting college. You two could've shared a room, and I would drop by at inconvenient times to sprawl on your bed and mope about boy trouble!"

"That does sound vaguely familiar."

"Well, we'll have to all get together again soon. After the trial. She can help with my makeover. I need her to tell me which era is back in style. You're as hopeless as I am."

"I just go to Ann Taylor and let them sell me stuff." Jenn rolled the last stone into place and dusted off her hands. "Anyway—"

"Why did she decide not to go to culinary school?

I haven't talked to her since she was looking at applications last November."

Jenn wanted to drop the subject, but she didn't want to look suspicious, either. "She didn't decide. Her dad told her that working in the kitchen was a good experience for a woman who was going to own a dozen luxury hotels someday, but she'd become a chef over his dead body."

"Oh, yikes. I had no idea. How's she taking that?"

"Okay," Jenn answered with a forced smile. Chloe had never been as close to Anna as Jenn was, thank God, or there would've been no way to cover up this disaster. "Anyway, what's the big deal? I'm not enough for you?"

"You're enough for me. Plus, she probably wouldn't have been able to relax without cell access. But it sounds like she needs a vacation as much as I do."

Jenn pushed up from her knees to dust off the sand. "I saw a bunch of driftwood at that first dune. I'll be right back." Even though Chloe lay back on the cooling sand as if she didn't have a care in the world, Jenn breathed a sigh of relief as she hurried off.

She wasn't cut out for deceit and never had been. As a kid, when she'd lied to her parents, all it had taken was one stern look from her dad to break her, forcing a weeping confession. Now the tears seemed to push behind her eyes, waiting for a chance to escape.

But it was too late to confess. There was no point. Chloe needed to move on and Jenn was going to help her do just that.

Anna couldn't understand that. She'd tried to convince Jenn that this time on the island would be a great opportunity to clear the air, get the truth out. Jenn had pretended to consider it, but, in reality, she wanted the truth buried under a hundred feet of earth where air would never touch it.

Jenn stole a look over her shoulder at Chloe stretched out on the sand, the slanting rays of the setting sun gleaming over her. Chloe deserved to be happy again. Jenn was determined to make that happen, even if it meant lying for the rest of her life.

Speaking of happiness… She used the excuse of bending down for wood to angle her head toward the other cabin. Sure enough, that guy was staring hard at Chloe, forehead creased in thought.

Jenn frowned at him. What could he be thinking about? Did he recognize Chloe? The whole point of this stupid getaway had been to hide Chloe away from prying eyes so she could take a deep breath before the charges were filed, because that was going to be a complete nightmare. Hints were starting to come out that Thomas had done more than just fake his own death…

Jenn wanted to give her friend a little peace before the trauma. And maybe all that other talk would just die down.

Clutching the wood to her chest, Jenn hurried back toward the cabin, keeping her eye on the man next door. He was still frowning at Chloe.

Crap. She wanted Chloe to have a good time, but what if Jenn pushed her toward this guy and he really was a reporter?

Before Jenn could intercept him, he stood and stepped onto the sand.

CHLOE OPENED HER EYES to find a man standing over her, profile orange in the rays of the setting sun.

"Hello," the man said.

She propped herself up on her elbows. "Hello, yourself."

"My name's Max Sullivan. My brother, Elliott, and I are staying next door."

When he extended a hand, Chloe shook it, then gave it a little tug to hint that she wanted up. Max pulled and she jumped to her feet with hardly any effort at all.

"I noticed," she said. "It's nice to meet you, Max. I'm Chloe. This is Jenn." She gestured toward Jenn, who was rushing forward with an armful of wood as if she were planning to storm a castle with a battering ram.

He glanced over his shoulder, then dropped Chloe's hand and swung toward Jenn, saying, "Hey, let me help with that."

Chloe felt a twinge of unwarranted disappointment when he hurried toward her friend and swept all the driftwood out of her arms. He was probably interested in Jenn, like so many men were. But, sadly, Jenn was a waste of adorable blondness as far as Chloe was concerned. She was shy around guys, and only got more anxious the more attentive they became.

But maybe she liked this guy. Oh, well. Easy come, easy go.

Jenn's face pinched into worry as Max smiled at her.

"This is Max," Chloe said hurriedly. "One of our next-door neighbors. He came over to say hi."

"Hi," Jenn offered quietly.

Max winked and carried the wood to a spot about ten feet from the fire ring, dropping most of it on the sand before he carried a few pieces toward the pit. "So what are you ladies doing out here in the wilds of Virginia?" he asked as he began rearranging stones.

"Nothing," Jenn said loudly. "Just relaxing."

Okay, she wasn't normally *that* nervous around guys. Chloe shot her a questioning look, but Jenn ignored it.

Their neighbor scooped more sand out of the pit until the bottom was wide and flat and dark with moisture. "Elliott and I are out here fishing." He tossed five small pieces of wood into the hole, then added one large one to the top before reaching toward the lighter Chloe had left there.

"That's not going to make a very big fire," Chloe muttered. The man shot her an amused smile as if that answered her complaint.

"What do you do for a living?" Jenn blurted out.

His brows rose, drawing Chloe's attention to his dark brown eyes. Nice. When he began to twist up one of the supermarket circulars she'd brought out as kindling, her focus moved from his eyes to his wide, strong hands. Very nice. "I work on the water," he answered.

"Doing what?" Jenn's eyes narrowed suspiciously.

"I'm an officer on a research vessel."

"Where?" she prodded.

Chloe frowned at her rudeness until Jenn made a picture-taking gesture behind Max's back. Chloe rolled her eyes and shook her head. No way was this guy with one of the gossip rags. He looked healthy and muscular, not like a man who spent 90 percent of his life huddled outside the doors of L.A. night-clubs. Also, he didn't have a cigarette dangling from his mouth.

Max was hunched over the fire, coaxing a weak flame to grow to something that would take hold of the wood.

Chloe cleared her throat. "I really don't think that's going to keep us warm once the sun sets." Little fingers of fire worked over the tiny bits of driftwood, inching slowly toward the larger piece.

"You can add more later. It'll burn better if you start small."

"Are you some sort of beach party expert?"

"I've had my fair share of sand down my shorts," he drawled, finally glancing up from his task. Those brown eyes crinkled when he smiled, and Chloe felt her insides melt at the sight. Was he flirting with her? Or had he looked at both women with the same amount of warmth?

She couldn't be angry if he was just spreading his luck around. After all, they'd discussed the men as interchangeable parts just a few hours before.

His gold-streaked hair curled onto his brow on a gust of wind, and Max dusted off those big hands and shoved it back, his arm muscles making interest-ing shadows as he moved. She sat down and help-fully patted the ground next to her, happy when he dropped down and propped his arms on his knees. "What kind of research do you do?" she asked.

"We, um…" His smile edged toward sheepishness. "We locate and map out previously uncharted shipwrecks."

"Here?"

"No, we're usually in the Mediterranean."

"What kind of wrecks?"

He laughed, a deep chuckle that spoke of good humor and friendship. "Mostly the kind that have gold in them."

"Oh!" Chloe gasped. "You're a treasure hunter?"

Even Jenn gave up her suspicious glare and looked surprised at that.

"We prefer to think of ourselves as researchers bringing long-lost artifacts out of the depths and back into the world where they belong."

"Ah, so you give all the loot to museums?"

That smile again. Wow. "We do our best to find dives in international waters, but even we wouldn't keep the historically significant artifacts for our own profit. For the most part."

Chloe laughed, but when his gaze fell to her mouth, a little shiver of nervousness jumped through her stomach. The thick piece of driftwood crackled weakly as the fire finally latched on to it. Chloe used it as an excuse to look away. "We'd better move back,

Max. That inferno could jump out of control at any moment."

"My point exactly." But in acknowledgment of her mockery, he grabbed the last piece he'd brought close to the pit and laid it carefully on the fire, angling a challenging look in her direction. The twisted piece of driftwood was half the size of the other.

Good Lord, this man was quirky. And cute.

"So what do you do for a living?" he asked, turning his head toward Jenn, the original interrogator.

"I'm a CPA."

Eyebrows raised, he turned back to Chloe.

"Me, too," she said.

"Wow. Accountants. That's…sexy."

"Yeah, right," she laughed. "That's the first I've heard of it. How about you, Jenn?"

"Definitely a first."

"Come on. Number-geek girls? That's hot."

Chloe shook her head, flabbergasted. "That's the worst pickup line ever! You have to at least say something we *might* believe. Just because we're accountants doesn't mean we're desperate."

Max leaned back, a frown twisting his mouth. "That's not a pickup line! Jeez. Do you think every strange man who wanders into your private party uninvited is just trying to pick you up?"

Laughing, she shook her head.

"Maybe I just saw you in your bikini and thought

'There's a girl who'd want to talk baseball over beers.' Did you ever consider that?"

"No," she managed past a wide grin.

"Pickup line," he muttered in mock bitterness.

When her giggles subsided, Chloe thought about buttoning up her shirt. She was wearing shorts, but felt suddenly, hotly aware that her stomach was exposed from her navel all the way to her blue, halter-style bikini. But that would be too obvious as she was still casually propped up on her elbows, so Chloe arched her back a tiny bit to smooth out any unfortunate creases. The skin on her stomach sizzled when his eyes drifted down before he cleared his throat and looked at the fire.

"Anyway, now that I've successfully played caveman—" his hand tilted toward the flames before he pushed to his feet "—I'll leave you to your evening."

Chloe looked up at him, wondering if he was a little over six feet tall or if her perspective was throwing off her estimate. Aw, who the heck cared? The faint apprehension winding up her gut was a far more pleasant sensation than the one she normally felt. Chloe decided to go for it. "We've got marshmallows. You and your brother are welcome to help us roast them if you think we're not up to the task."

His gaze flickered down to her stomach again.

He seemed to consider her offer carefully before answering. "Well…there is a fine line between pleasantly burned and marshmallow conflagration."

"So true."

"I'd hate to leave and then find out later that everything went horribly wrong."

Chloe smiled in a way she hadn't smiled at a man in a long time. "Exactly."

He matched her friendliness with a spectacular smile of his own. "All right. I'll grab Elliott and some beers and be back in a few minutes. Thanks."

She maintained her smile as he walked away. It wasn't hard. He presented a very nice picture in retreat. Without looking away from Max's ass, Chloe asked, "What the heck's wrong with you, Jenn?"

"I saw him watching you from their porch. I worried that he'd recognized you. He could be a photographer, you know."

"If he brings his camera back with him, we'll know for sure."

"A reporter then," Jenn insisted.

"Look at him. Have you seen even one newspaper reporter who looks like that? He looks exactly like a man who's spent months on a boat in paradise."

"That's true."

"Thanks for trying to watch out for me, sweetie. You're the best friend in the world. But I'm starting to think your original plan was a good idea. Vacation relaxation helped along by some illicit island love, remember?"

Jenn's face finally brightened. "You know what? You're right. He's not a reporter. And he's hot. You should go for it. Absolutely. Get your groove back."

"Was he really watching me?"

"Yes."

"Like, in a good way? Or in a 'I wonder if her dismembered limbs will fit into my duffel bag' way?"

"He was frowning, actually, so I was wondering what he was thinking. But maybe he was just coming up with awful pickup lines."

Chloe waved a hand before scrambling up to her feet. "He probably thinks I look vaguely familiar but can't place me. I get that a lot these days. Luckily, there's no one around to clue him in…unless his brother recognizes me. But whatever." She took a deep breath. "I'm Island Chloe, right? The girl without a care in the world?"

"Yes!" squealed Jenn, pumping her fist into the air in victory. "Funtown, here we come!"

"Maybe just a short trip." Chloe lifted her chin high. "And now I am going to go put on some clothes, so I can stop holding in my gut."

CHAPTER FOUR

DARN IT, THIS GIRL WAS CUTE. Max took a swig from his beer, his gaze rising up to the swirl of stars above, but fully aware that she was only inches away. He couldn't count the number of nights he'd spent staring up at the Milky Way, surrounded by the sounds of lapping, rolling water, but he'd never been quite so relaxed.

Chloe was like a softly pulsing beacon beside him, sending off waves of warmth and peace. It would've been the perfect evening if not for the damn fire they kept feeding more wood to. At this rate, it would be morning before the embers cooled and Max could stop worrying enough to get some sleep.

"Another?" Chloe asked, holding out the bag of marshmallows. Max shook his head, and she set the bag back on the cooler before licking the last of the sticky mess from her fingers. He watched her mouth carefully. Her tongue glinted sparks of firelight when she licked.

They'd pulled chairs down to the sand, so he was

separated from her by the wide wood armrests of the old beach chairs, but that was probably a good thing. As attractive as he found her, Max still didn't plan on getting involved. But she kept licking melted sugar from her fingers, eyes closed as if she enjoyed the task...

"Castellan," he heard the other woman saying to Elliott. "Jenn Castellan."

Max made his eyes give up their vigil on Chloe's fingers and turned toward the blonde. "That's a Spanish name, isn't it?"

"It is." Her smile looked more relaxed, too. As if they'd all fallen under a drugged spell. "I know I don't look it. But my grandfather came straight from Spain to America. We're all blond and blue-eyed Spaniards."

"Funny," he said, "Chloe's the one who looks like she could have Spanish blood. What's your last name?"

Her gaze shifted for a moment, fingers folding together for a brief squeeze before she picked up a stick and started poking at the fire. "It's Turner."

"Turner. That sounds perfectly English."

She took a deep breath, as if she were waiting for something, but after a few seconds, she melted back into her seat. "It is. Nearly 100 percent. Embarrassingly boring."

"We're all Irish. Sullivans on one side, McKillops on the other."

"So how'd a nice Irish boy like you get into treasure hunting? No work at the police station?"

Elliott laughed, raising his beer toward Max in a mini-toast. "Max was always out there getting into some sort of trouble. He likes to be in the middle of everything. I'm just happy he found a way to turn it into a job."

Her knee bumped into Max's, drawing his attention back. "You were a troublemaker, hmm? Somehow I'm not surprised."

"That's me," Max said as if it were true, smiling as Elliott launched into a tale about Max volunteering to lead an illicit weekend trip to a beach during his senior year of high school.

"He made up some story about helping out a youth group and talked our neighbor into giving up his van for the weekend. Max fit ten people into that van, six of them girls, of course. And they all camped out on the beach for three nights. I was green with envy, always a little too young to tag along."

Lifting his own bottle up, Max offered the expected self-satisfied smile. Though it really had been a good weekend. There'd been ten seat belts in the van, and Max had scoped out a legitimate seaside campground with running water and bathrooms. Then he'd conveniently forgotten to bring the hard liquor he'd promised to score. Everyone had made it home safe and sound, and Max hadn't gotten his girlfriend pregnant, though he'd worried about that for weeks afterward, due to the warnings on the condom labels about storing them in the heat. The van had definitely been hot as hell.

"Six girls?" Chloe asked. "And four guys?"

"Hey, we were in high school. It was all innocent fun."

"God, you are so full of shit."

He laughed because it was true, and felt even better when he saw his brother laughing with Jenn. "So are you girls just hanging out on the beach for the week?"

"Mostly," Chloe said. "But the wind's supposed to be calm tomorrow afternoon, so we're going to try diving."

Max's heart lurched as if it had been hit with a stick. "Diving?" he croaked.

"Yeah, I'm sure there's nothing out here that rivals what you see overseas, but we've never tried it before, so we're going to do the pool certification before lunch. What the heck? The seas are supposed to be calm, and we'll probably be the only ones on the boat. It should be fun."

Fun? Good God, no one seemed to regard diving as what it really was: a journey into an environment utterly hostile to human life. "Who's the dive instructor?"

She shrugged. "We found a brochure at the grocery store."

His heart lurched again, slamming into his chest wall as if it wanted him to do something about this ridiculousness. *A grocery store.* Unbelievable. His skin prickled with icy sweat, but Max tried to talk himself down.

You don't even know this girl. If she's dumb enough to sign up for a dive with a stranger, it's none of your business. This is not your responsibility.

But she was so sweet and peaceful. A good soul. And how was she supposed to know how dangerous diving could be?

"You know," Max heard himself say, "Elliott's only been diving a couple of times. Would it be weird if we signed up? I don't want to crowd you or anything, but you're right. Forecasts call for calm seas tomorrow, but God knows what the weather will be like later."

She shrugged. "It's not a private dive. If you two want to come along, feel free. But surely there's nothing out here that would interest someone with your experience."

"Diving is addictive," he lied. "I can't live without it. It'll feel good to get the gear on."

Chloe set her beer down and leaned forward, a

sparkle in her eye that could've been a reflection of the fire, but looked more like mischief. As if she knew a secret. Max held his breath. She got close enough to whisper.

"Fishing is just too darn boring for you, isn't it?"

"Yeah." He sighed on a rush of air. "Yeah, it's hard to stay awake in that little boat."

She laughed, stirring the air against his ear. "I'm not a big fan of excitement, but I probably shouldn't tell you that."

No. No, she shouldn't tell him that, because Max felt himself leaning toward her, an unwilling shift of his muscles. She didn't like adventure. Despite that welcome news, he wasn't going to kiss her, not in front of his brother and her friend, but his body wanted closer to that oasis of calm.

Her eyes sparkled again. She glanced down, her gaze touching his lips. Firelight danced over the soft skin of her cheek, as if it were mocking him, touching her where Max couldn't.

Aw, damn. In public or not, he was about to kiss her. And he was already too involved, inserting himself into her life for no good reason at all.

No. He wouldn't do it. One dive trip, and then he'd cut the unwelcome threads he'd already tied between them.

Max grabbed the bag of marshmallows as if that

had been his goal all along. "Honestly," he said, popping a sugary puff into his mouth. "I'm a pretty boring guy."

Her eyes flashed suspicion. She didn't think he was telling the truth, but for once in his life, he was.

JENN WATCHED ELLIOTT SULLIVAN'S EYES as he spoke about his work. He dismissed it as boring, something she wouldn't want to hear about, but she found it fascinating. He'd done an internship at the CDC labs in Atlanta during college, and he'd gone to work as one of their scientists as soon as he'd graduated from medical school. Just that would have widened Jenn's eyes with amazement, but he hadn't stopped there.

After working for five years on studying flu vaccines and antiviral drugs, Elliott had moved up to the D.C. offices to work with the CDC branch of Health and Human Services, preparing for and fighting global outbreaks of the disease. He was like a modern-day superhero, working every day to save lives.

He paused as if he'd finished a point, and Jenn realized she'd been too busy staring to hear what he'd said. A blush rose up her face. He was waiting for an answer and she didn't know what to say.

Elliott's face fell. "But enough of that—"

"You're amazing," she blurted out. "I mean…what you do? That's amazing."

"I…" He shifted, taking his glasses off and putting them back on. "It's just a lot of paperwork."

"But it's…" She wouldn't tell him it was like being a superhero. That would be ridiculous and geeky and all the things she normally was with a man. And she didn't want to be ridiculous with Elliott. He was serious and smart. Jenn took a deep breath to calm her nerves. "What you do is so important."

"Ah, well. So is maintaining the sewer system."

He said it like it was a joke he'd heard before, but Jenn laughed in shock. "What?"

"Actually the sewer workers are more important. If cholera made a comeback, no one would be worried about the flu."

"You're hilarious!"

"Really?" he asked, then shook his head. "I'm thinking you don't get out much."

"That's true," Jenn agreed, "but you're still funny."

It was impossible to tell if he was blushing. The firelight bathed them all in warm yellows and golds. But he did look embarrassed as he leaned back in his chair and tapped his fingers on the armrest.

Jenn's heart pattered in her chest. He was out of her league, of course. A successful scientist. A serious man with an important job who happened to be cute, too. She had a sudden urge to ask if he was married. He wasn't wearing a ring, but sometimes that meant nothing. She couldn't just ask, though. That question was loaded with all sorts of hints and suggestions.

Now she didn't know what to say, and he seemed lost in thought, probably happy she'd stopped talking. But what if—

"Maybe it's all those accountants you hang out with."

"What?"

"Maybe you've spent so much time with them that you find bad science jokes funny."

"Ha! Maybe. But I'll have you know I work on international auditing. We're like the 007s of corporate accounting. Last year's seminar was in Hong Kong."

"Wow!" he exclaimed, and suddenly Jenn felt ridiculous. He'd probably been to Asia a dozen times. He probably traveled all over the world for his work.

She was so awful with men. She always had been.

"So—" Elliott started, but Jenn jumped up to her feet.

"Pardon me for a moment. I'll be right back."

It was her dad's fault, she thought as she walked toward the cabin stairs. He'd been a high-level salesman, selling multimillion-dollar pieces of equipment to factories all over the globe. A slick talker who thought that the world revolved around him. And he'd traveled for weeks at a time, gone more often than he was home. Jenn had suffered a bad case of hero worship for her handsome father, desperate to be close to him whenever he was home, yet unable to think of anything to say that could engage his interest. Of course, it didn't matter who was talking. Her father had a habit of starting a story right in the middle of another person's sentence.

He was good at talking. And really, really bad at being a father. Or a husband.

She rushed onto the porch and through the door, relieved once she was alone. She was fine around her girlfriends. Completely normal and just as interested in men as they were. She could talk the talk, joking about having sex with hot strangers, but she failed miserably at walking the walk. Once she became interested in a man, her brain stopped working properly. Horrifying, not just because it was embarrassing, but because she was smart and independent and capable in all areas but this one.

Needing a few minutes alone, Jenn slowly washed her hands to get the last of the marshmallow off them. She stared at the mirror, hating the delicate features that often attracted the wrong kind of man. Wolflike men who looked at her and saw weakness and vulnerability. Elliott Sullivan didn't seem like that kind of man, which was why he wouldn't make a move. He probably liked strong scientist women in intimidating glasses and trim lab coats. Women who could talk nucleotides and DNA strands during postcoital conversation.

Jenn looked like one of those gangster molls from the twenties whose preferred method of communication was breathless, high-pitched exclamations of alarm.

Also, she'd clearly had one too many beers.

Disgusted with herself, Jenn dried her hands and turned off the light. But on her trip back through the living room, she spotted a green light blinking from the coffee table, like a bomb about to go off. Heart sinking, she picked up her cell phone and stared at the little message icon. Crap.

News from the outside world, and there was no chance it was good. Jenn called up the message and told herself everything was fine as the beep sounded in her ear.

"Jenn," a hushed female voice said. "It's Anna."

Crap. Jenn pressed a hand to her forehead.

"Things are getting crazy here. I really think the mature thing would be to tell Chloe the truth. The reporters and police... This isn't just about you. Or her. She needs to know, and I think you're making this worse by hiding it from her. Chloe is an adult.

She'll be fine. I know she will. Just… Call me back, all right? You may be able to live with this, but I can't."

Jenn hit a button to cut off the message then deleted it with a shaking hand.

She wasn't going to tell Chloe a darn thing and she'd be damned if she'd let Anna anywhere near her with that kind of talk.

The e-mail icon blinked also, so Jenn took a deep breath and opened the folder. She let the breath out on a rush when she saw the in-box. Nothing from Anna. Just a link from Google Alerts.

Stupid of her, but she'd set up a Google Alert for Chloe's name, and even though every hit drove her crazy, she couldn't stop looking at them. This one linked to a slang dictionary site. She knew what it would say. She knew it would throw her into pained fury, and still she looked.

"To pull a Chloe," the dictionary entry said. Jenn's shoulders fell as she read the words that would forever define her best friend as the worst kind of lunatic bitch. "To become a Bridezilla so demented that the groom would rather jump from an airplane than jump into the marital bed. Based on Chloe Turner's disastrous engagement to Thomas DeLorn."

"Oh, God," she whispered, pressing a hand to her aching head. The lying was killing her, but she could do it. She had to do it. Because the whole world had turned against Chloe.

Some people—people like Anna—believed those stupid clichés about the truth setting you free. What she didn't know was that the truth sometimes beat you down and chewed you up and ruined your life.

Chloe didn't deserve that. She'd been through enough. And Jenn wasn't about to let the ugly truth ruin such an important friendship.

To be very sure that didn't happen, Jenn turned on Chloe's cell phone and checked the messages on that one, too. Sure enough, Anna had called and asked Chloe to call her back. Jenn deleted the message and blocked Anna's number, her heart burning as she did, then she went back outside to have one last beer. She might not make it to Funtown tonight, but maybe she'd at least get some sleep.

CHAPTER FIVE

"WHAT'S HE DOING?" Jenn asked as she brought her breakfast out to join Chloe on the porch.

Chloe watched Max Sullivan carefully, trying to puzzle him out, but also trying very hard to predict what each of the muscles of his chest would feel like beneath her fingers. "I think he's...digging a hole?"

When Chloe had come out, two small boys had been playing on the beach, digging furiously at the sand as if they'd been commissioned to break through to China. A half hour later, only their necks and heads had been visible, and that's when Max had jumped in to help them out.

What had his brother said? *He likes to be in the middle of everything.* Even digging a fort with two five-year-olds.

"Does he know them?" Jenn asked.

"I don't think so."

"Well, I guess you shouldn't be too flattered that he's tagging along on our dive trip, huh?"

Chloe reached over and gave Jenn's shoulder a

halfhearted shove. "Meanie. So tell me about the other Sullivan brother. He's a little reserved."

"He's sweet."

"Really? I was going to guess stern."

"No! He's serious, yes, but really nice."

"Mmm-hmm." Chloe nodded sagely. "Nice enough to get it on with? Because you were looking at him last night like he was a big old hunk of man candy, darlin'."

Jenn's face blazed scarlet. "I was not! Oh, God, I was. He's so sexy that I can't even think when I'm looking at him."

"You should— Wait." Chloe tilted her head toward the open window behind her. "Is my phone ringing? I thought I'd turned it off."

"Oh!" Jenn started to spring to her feet, but her plate was still on her lap and it tumbled down to the porch, misting her legs with powdered sugar.

"I got it." Chloe stepped over her and walked inside. She didn't know why she was looking for the phone in the first place when it was as likely to be a reporter as anyone else. But answering the phone was a Pavlovian response, she supposed.

She found it on the coffee table and glanced at the number, which sent an immediate shock through her system. DeLorn Limited. It was Thomas's mother... or Thomas.

Stomach clenching into a ball of cement, Chloe pushed the button and croaked out a hello.

"Hello, Chloe," the voice said. Though Mrs. De-Lorn's deep voice was nearly the same timbre as her son's, her old-school Virginia accent immediately gave her away.

"Mrs. DeLorn," she said a bit breathlessly. The woman ruled over her empire with an iron fist, but somehow Chloe had always liked her. And strangely enough, Mrs. DeLorn had liked Chloe. "You look a bit like my younger sister," she'd said the first time they'd met. And because her sister had died as a teenager, Chloe had seemed to fill a place in the woman's heart. They'd been close. Or so Chloe had thought. "It's been a long time."

"I'm sorry, my dear. This has all just been so tragic. You know I had to take to my bed when we first got the news about the crash and then… Well, my word. I don't know what to say. I honestly don't."

Chloe could believe that. And she hadn't exactly reached out to Mrs. DeLorn, either. Her heart softened a little. "I know you must be feeling pretty low."

"Oh, you can't imagine," she said. "But how are you getting along, Chloe? I suppose the investigators have been hounding you day and night?"

"Um." Was *investigator* some old-fashioned word

for paparazzi? "The press has been giving me a hard time, yes."

"Oh, the press. Yes, they are awful, awful people. They scurry around outside our office building like cockroaches. I wish I could squash them all under my shoe and be done with them."

"Yuck. Well, I'm sorry to hear they're bothering you, as well."

Mrs. DeLorn abruptly changed the subject. "Do you remember that trip we took to the Cherry Blossom Festival this spring?"

"Oh, of course."

"We had such a lovely time and the hotel suite was so nicely outfitted."

"Yes." Did she just want to stroll down memory lane? The trip had been nice, but not exactly the highlight of the year. Chloe had lobbied for returning to Richmond that night so she could sleep *with* her fiancé instead of in the bedroom next door to his.

"Well, I'm sure you remember...Thomas was going on and on about that all-terrain vehicle he wanted for this fall's quail season and I gave him a little extra to help him out."

"Um. Okay." Chloe made a face at a watercolor painting of seabirds that hung on the wall. What the hell? Maybe all the stress was proving too much for the old lady.

"You remember that?"

"I remember him talking about the ATV, yes."

"And when you two dropped me off at my place?"

"Yes?" Chloe asked shortly, belatedly remembering that one of Mrs. DeLorn's pet peeves was one-word sentences. *We've lost all the elegance of our language,* she would complain. Which maybe had something to do with Thomas's strange tendency to speak in full sentences during sex. *Oh, yes, Chloe, I love how it feels when you do that.*

She managed to choke back a laugh, but her amusement was made worse by Mrs. DeLorn's irritated huff. "Well, I was only calling to remind you of the money I loaned Thomas."

Chloe couldn't hide the incredulous shock in her voice. "Mrs. DeLorn, I don't know anything about that. Are you trying to imply that I share part of the debt? Unfortunately, I'm kind of high and dry right now. I put a lot of money into the wedding. I'm sure you remember?"

She'd never been rude to the woman before, but she couldn't believe this was the conversation they were having after her son had turned Chloe's life upside down. When Mrs. DeLorn had left those messages, Chloe had expected some sort of plea for forgiveness on behalf of Thomas. What the hell was this?

There was a long enough pause that Chloe was

left wondering if Mrs. DeLorn had hung up, but then she finally made a little humming sound in her throat. "I'm so sorry about that, dear. You know, why don't you let me take care of those bills?"

Chloe pulled the phone away from her face to look at it in shock. When she pressed it back to her ear, Mrs. DeLorn was still talking. "—Always been generous with both of you when you needed help. I won't begrudge you a little cash any more than I've begrudged Thomas all the gifts I gave him."

What in the world? She was tempted to just agree, but it felt a little like being bought off, so Chloe thanked her for the offer and told her she'd consider it once all the bills were sorted out. Thomas owed at least half of the deposits, after all, if not all of them.

Then she hung up the phone and stared at it for a little while longer.

"What was that all about?"

She spun to see Jenn standing in the doorway, legs still streaked with white. "I think Mrs. DeLorn is losing it."

"That was Mrs. DeLorn?"

"Why do you look so freaked out? You don't even know how weird she was being."

Jenn's shocked look quickly turned to nonchalance. "What did she say?"

"She was just talking about some money Thomas

owed her. It was strange as all hell. So what's Max doing?"

"Still digging."

Chloe tossed her phone back on the table and went out to watch the show.

MAX SULLIVAN WAS HOT on land, but on a boat… on a boat he approached nuclear levels of hotness. Chloe watched him with the complete freedom offered by her dark sunglasses as he spoke with the diving guide. He looked perfect out here, hair tossed by the sea wind, sun glinting off the golden hairs on his strong arms. His mouth widened with a laugh as he slapped their guide, Jacob, on the arm and shook his head.

A few words drifted to her ears, but she couldn't make sense of them. Names of dive sites or harbor towns, she assumed. The guide's eyes took on a starry look of admiration as he shot questions at Max.

Ten minutes of excited conversation later, with a couple of miles of sea behind them, Chloe half expected the guide to turn and ask if they'd be willing to skip their lesson so he could dive with Max Sullivan. Instead, he shook Max's hand and gestured generously toward the tanks lined up against the side of the boat.

Max knelt down and began picking up tanks and

shifting them around as if they weighed nothing. Chloe knew they were heavy. Just as she'd suspected: utter hotness.

His strong hands cradled the tanks, turned knobs and ran over every piece of equipment. Chloe watched, heavy-eyed, relaxing into the fantasy of him so thoroughly checking her over. The boat rocked. Chloe sighed.

He hadn't made a move last night, and she'd been surprised at that. At one point, she'd been sure he was about to kiss her and then…nothing. A couple of beers, some nice conversation and way too many marshmallows. On the one hand, he'd invited himself along on this trip. On the other, he looked far more interested in the diving equipment than in her. Not a good indication that they were headed toward a fling.

The guide shouted something that was snatched away by the wind. Max straightened and gave him a thumbs-up and a big grin as he shouted something back, but she caught the way his mouth twitched to a frown when he crouched down and tapped on one of the tank dials. Was something wrong?

Chloe glanced at the other two. Elliott wasn't paying any attention. He was watching Jenn from the corner of his eye, and Jenn was too busy staring out at the waves and pretending not to see Elliott.

The frown remained on Max's face. He peered

closer and eased a knob open in a slow circle. What if there was something wrong? What if there was a tragic accident and things went bad down there? Chloe pictured her face splashed all over cable. On every magazine cover and Web site. She'd die in the prime of the scandal, and no one would ever remember her for anything else. She'd be Chloe the Bridezilla for eternity.

She jumped up and rushed across the boat.

"Hey!" she said breathlessly. "Is everything okay?"

When Max raised his face, he was wearing a blinding smile. "Sure, everything's great!"

"Why were you frowning?"

"What?"

"You were frowning. At that tank."

He stood and wiped his hands. "Just concentrating, I guess. The tanks look good." He moved his hand toward a clipboard tucked into a pocket of the boat. "He keeps good records." When he glanced down at the board, the frown flitted across his face again before he replaced it with a smile.

Chloe grabbed his wrist. "Listen. The lesson in the pool today was fun. And I wanted to have a tiny adventure out on the sea, but I don't want to go this way, okay? I don't want to be on the news and on the... Sorry, I don't mean to freak out. It's just..."

She took a deep breath and tried to channel Island

Chloe. This was Max's job. Something as easy as pie for him. It wouldn't be cool to hyperventilate and pass out in a puddle of urine or something.

"Chloe—"

"Whew," she said with a laugh. "Sorry. Being surrounded by all this water makes me feel insignificant. And fragile. But you know what you're doing, so just tell me that this guy is okay, all right? I'll be fine."

He wrapped his free hand around the fingers clutching his wrist in a death grip. "Diving is inherently risky. Things can go wrong. But I talked to the guide about the dive this morning while you were finishing your lesson. We decided to do an easy dive—only thirty-five feet down. The wreck is wide open on the sea floor, so there aren't any spaces to get caught in. And I wouldn't let you near that water if the equipment wasn't safe. Okay?"

"Okay." Her fingers didn't loosen, despite the warmth of his hand on top of hers.

"I don't recommend finding a dive guide at the grocery store, but you lucked out."

"Okay," she said again. Her hand didn't relax, but she purposefully flexed her fingers. No panic attack. Not this time. She'd only had one actually, but the idea of having another was enough on its own to spiral her close to an attack. Evil, vicious circle.

Max's hand let go of hers and rose up to cup her

chin. Warmth edged over her jaw and calmed her down. "Hey, we'll stick together, okay? I could do this in my sleep. But—" he said hastily as Chloe opened her mouth to protest "—I won't."

"Ha."

His hand slipped away, fingers trailing down her throat so briefly that she couldn't tell if it had been an accidental touch. His smile disappeared. "Or you could just change your mind."

When the boat hit a wave and bounced beneath her, Chloe let go of Max and reached for the railing to catch herself. Max didn't even budge. He was like a pirate, accustomed to life on the high seas, impervious to waves and sea spray and unstable footing. She wished his faded blue tee was an open-collared shirt that could whip around in the wind and reveal his chest.

The roar of the motor dropped down to a low grumble and the boat slowed. "Almost there!" the guide shouted.

Chloe set her shoulders and forced a smile. "I'll be fine. Jenn's really excited. And so was I until that little freak-out. It'll be fun. It must be like a whole other planet down there."

His eyes crinkled. "That's exactly what it is. Want some help getting your wet suit on?"

"Do you ask all the girls that?"

"It's my job."

"Oh, really?"

He tipped his head in concession. "Almost."

Chloe said, "I think I can handle it on my own," as she sauntered off. Or as close to sauntering as she could manage as the motor died and the boat began to rock in the gentle waves. She gave up when her thigh slammed into the railing, and took the last two steps just hoping that Max wasn't watching.

He wasn't. Max Sullivan was too busy getting ready to dive. The first step appeared to be shucking his baggy swim trunks and T-shirt to get down to the tighter layer underneath.

"Holy ass cheeks, Batman," Chloe muttered, not caring that she had just taken a seat next to the man's brother. Chloe didn't care about anything at that moment but the sight of Max's thighs outlined in tight Lycra. He was wearing a suit that looked like a Speedo crossed with bike shorts, painted in blue and black deliciousness onto a Greek statue with the ass of a Roman god. Or something like that.

Elliott, seemingly oblivious to her stunned expression of lust, grabbed his duffel bag and walked over to join his brother. When he pulled his shirt over his head, Chloe jabbed Jenn in the ribs.

"Ow!"

"Turn around, you idiot!"

"I think the— Oh, my gosh."

The guys both sat on one of the cushioned benches

and began easing the wet suits up their legs. Chloe and Jenn should have been getting ready, too, but they just sat, openmouthed, staring at the peep show. The Sullivan brothers happily obliged them by carrying on a serious conversation.

"We shouldn't be watching them like this," Jenn murmured.

"What are they going to do? Call the cops and report us?"

"Still—"

"Shut up. I can't concentrate with you—"

"Ladies!" the guide boomed, stepping into their line of sight. "Get a move on. It's time to get wet."

It sure as heck was. Chloe toed off her tennis shoes and tilted her head to see past Jacob's body. Max had his suit up to his waist now. But his chest was still bare.

His chest was tanned, sculpted muscle, sprinkled with golden hairs. Not big, bulging muscles, but the muscles of someone who did physical work every day, hefting tanks around and lowering boats into the water and swimming and climbing and—

"Miss Chloe—"

"Oh, all right already," she grumbled, begrudging the interruption even though Max was zipping the suit up to his neck. She whipped off her shirt and eased her shorts down without standing up. She was an accountant, after all. The heaviest thing she lifted all day was her coffee cup. Her figure was fine, but it wouldn't stand up to close scrutiny when being squeezed into a Neoprene sausage casing. All sorts of rolls and gatherings were bound to appear.

Max wasn't watching, thank God. He was busy fitting his brother with a tank and talking rapidly as he adjusted the fittings. As a matter of fact, Max didn't glance over once. She hadn't wanted to be watched, but she'd expected at least an interested once-over of her bikini.

Elliott's gaze drifted over to Jenn's petite body more than once, even as his conversation with his brother continued. But Max didn't take his eyes off the gear, and Chloe suddenly realized that she'd better get all the adventure out of this dive that she could, because there wasn't going to be much excitement back at the beach.

Party animal or not, this guy wasn't that interested in Chloe Turner. Her kryptonite powers were securely in place.

CHAPTER SIX

CHLOE CARRIED A COUPLE OF BOTTLES of water and the last two doughnuts out to the darkened porch. There was just enough light squeezing past the curtains to see the chairs, but not enough to interfere with their view of the stars.

"Your phone is beeping," she said, plopping down into the seat.

"It's probably just the battery," Jenn answered, her voice a little hoarse. The return ride had been bumpy, and Jenn had turned faintly green. She was exhausted, but Chloe was still pumped up from excitement.

The dive had been amazing. Absolutely like being on a different planet, as if they were the first people to ever see it, even though the dive site was well-known and heavily trafficked. The wrecked ship had been a steamer from the early twentieth century. It had so intrigued her that she hadn't begun to notice the fish until five minutes in. Then suddenly they'd become visible to her, sliding in and out of holes and arches. She'd even spied an eel poking its head out cautiously.

Amazing.

And she'd been able to relax and enjoy it all because Max had hovered a few feet above her, moving whenever she'd moved, like a floating guardian angel. He hadn't explored the site for himself at all, as far as she'd seen.

Frowning, Chloe took a big bite from her doughnut. Something wasn't adding up. So far, she'd heard several stories about Max being some sort of overgrown good-time guy, but she'd yet to see him instigate any sort of adventure, aside from playing in the sand with a couple of kids.

On the dive trip, he'd made no effort to enjoy himself, he'd just watched and given the occasional thumbs-up to her excited gestures. And the beach fire… He'd deliberately inserted himself into the scene, but instead of building up a ridiculous bonfire as was the instinct of every other man on earth, Max had kept subtle control of the flames at all times. And though the men had fit in an early-morning fishing trip right at sunrise today, Elliott was the one who'd suggested it. So Max didn't respond to fire, diving, flirtation or fishing.

Maybe he was just bored. Maybe beach bonfires and easy, shallow dives held no excitement for him anymore. But he hadn't looked bored, he'd looked *tense*. And that tension had had nothing to do with her, even when she'd wanted it to.

For God's sake, the man hadn't even glanced at her in her bikini. Not until after the dive. *Then* he'd finally relaxed. *Then* she'd caught him watching her past sleepy lashes as she'd stripped out of her tight wet suit.

Yes, after the dive, Max had been all quiet, good humor and jokes, and "Oh, it's too bad we won't be able to fit another one in on this trip," offered in a suspiciously cheerful voice. The rest of the group had been exhausted and disappointed that the day was over.

Chloe finished off her doughnut and glared at dancing glimmers of moonlight on the sea. Warning sirens were blaring in her head, and after her recent troubles, Chloe was inclined to heed them.

"I'm so tired." Jenn sighed.

Chloe looked over to the faint outline of Jenn's profile. Her eyes were closed, her forehead creased. "Are you okay, Jenn?"

"I'm just sleepy," she said quickly, eyes popping open.

"Are you sure? You seem a little tense."

"No!" Jenn yelped, making Chloe jump. "I mean, I'm fine. You're the one who's been thrown under the bus by life."

"Ouch."

"I just mean, whatever I might worry about, mostly it's you. What Thomas did to you..."

The words prompted Thomas to make an appearance inside Chloe's head like a looped video. He was laughing at a joke, pretending to be the perfect fiancé. Even now, she couldn't see the selfish, panicked thoughts that must have been turning behind his eyes for months. The truth was unavoidable, but her 20/20 hindsight wasn't kicking in. He'd seemed fine. Would he look different now?

She hadn't seen him since the day before the crash. Hadn't talked to him. What was he supposed to say, anyway? "Hey. Sorry I faked my death in order to escape your love."

Acid burned in her stomach, but, strangely enough, nothing else hurt very much. Could love wear off that quickly? And if it did, had it really been love at all?

Chloe shook her head, afraid to poke too intently at that question. "The whole point of coming here is to not think about it. Just for a few days. If I can manage that, you can, right?"

"Yeah." Jenn tilted her head, looking in Chloe's direction. "I just don't want you to be hurt any more."

"What's going to happen? What can be worse than finding out that your loving fiancé would rather give up everything in the world than marry you? He jumped out of a plane, Jenn. He abandoned his house and his family and his job and he jumped out of a fucking plane in hopes of never seeing me again."

"Chloe…" Jenn sounded like she might be crying.

"Come on, sweetie. I'm sorry. It's okay. Thomas was obviously a coward. I knew he was a mama's boy, but I should've seen something more than that, right? I should've seen something long before he faked his own death. So part of this must have been my fault, too. I'll get over it someday. And right now, I'll just pretend that I'm great because this is a beautiful place and I'm happy."

"Are you? I'm so glad you like it here. And maybe, after we get back and the hearing's over, things will get better."

"Yeah, the press can't possibly be interested for much longer." Chloe's vision had fully adjusted to the dark, and now she could make out the pale, sugary circle in Jenn's hand. "If you're so upset that you can't eat that doughnut, you should give it to me. I'd hate for it to go to waste."

"Here."

"Jenn—"

"I'm awful company. I'm tired and the waves gave me a headache, so I'm going to bed. I'll be more fun tomorrow, I promise. Why don't you go see your new boyfriend?"

The coyness in her friend's voice pushed a hesitant smile onto Chloe's face. "Come on. He hasn't even pretended to *accidentally* touch me."

"I've seen him shoot you a few hot looks. And then there's your lustful staring."

"There is that."

"Wander over and see him. He looked wide-awake when we got back."

Chloe shrugged. She was thinking of wandering over, but she couldn't decide if she should go in the hopes of luring Max into a make-out session or solving a mystery. Maybe both? The light of his front window beckoned.

Yeah, maybe both.

Jenn stood. "I'm turning in. Go get some nookie for me." She pressed a kiss to Chloe's head.

"Get your own nookie," Chloe said, but Jenn just shook her head.

It was only ten o'clock. The boys were going to be awake for a while yet. Taking a bite of the last doughnut, Chloe craned her neck, trying to see if they were on the porch or not. A slightly darker area of shadow on the porch might've been one of the men, or it could've just been a chair.

She thought of Max frowning down at those dials, thought of the way he'd checked the hoses and tanks over for long minutes before any of them had splashed into the water.

He was none of her business, really. She'd only been single for a few weeks. Even under normal circumstances, that would be too soon for anything, even a fling. But at least the puzzle of Max Sullivan was taking her mind off her own problems.

Chloe dusted off her hands and headed for the men's cabin.

Aware of the crabs that scuttled frantically around from the moment the sun set, she stepped carefully across the sand, trying not to cringe every time her foot touched something hard.

"Hi," a deep voice said. Though she could only make out the outline of a man, she recognized Elliott's voice. The clink of dishes drifted through the window behind him. "Max is inside."

"Thanks. I just wanted to ask you to keep an eye on the cabin for me. If Jenn comes looking for me, tell her I'm going for a little late-night swim."

Glass crashed inside the cabin, and before the last pieces had fallen to the floor, Max jerked the door open from inside. "Hey!" he said brightly.

"Um, is everything all right?"

Elliott started to stand up, but Max waved him down. "Everything's fine."

Right. Fine. "Okay… I was just going to take a swim, so if you could—"

"Care for company?"

Despite her plan, Chloe couldn't keep the doubt

from her voice. "You want to go swimming? Right now?"

Dish towel still in hand, Max leaned against the doorjamb, pretending casualness. "Sure," he said, the straight line of his shoulders giving away his tension. "If you're going to be there." Enough light filtered from the living room that she could see his flirtatious smile. He aimed it right at her, oozing charm.

Oh, my God, Max Sullivan was a total faker.

Chloe smiled up at him, letting her expression melt a little. "Sure, Max. That'd be great."

His shoulders dropped half an inch on his next breath. He tossed the towel aside and jogged down the stairs to join her. Some of her analytical detachment faded as he drew closer. She remembered the way his thighs had flexed in those Speedos, as if the muscles were barely contained by his skin.

Man.

"It's a little cool to swim, isn't it?" he asked, pausing to wait for her to turn and start their walk. It had taken him all of one second to try to change her mind.

"I like it. It feels…*thrilling*. Tossed around by the waves in the pitch-black."

"Mmm. Well, sure, I like to swim at night, but I have a special connection with the sharks who swim after dark, too. It comes with the profession, you know."

"Sharks?" she asked, just as he'd wanted her to.

"Yeah. They like to hunt at night."

"I'm sure it'll be fine."

He nodded. "As long as you're a strong swimmer. The riptides can be a real bitch this time of night."

"Oh, sure. I'm pretty strong."

Her feet finally touched damp, packed sand. She turned and followed the waterline, watching Max's large feet make hollows in the sand next to her.

Max audibly sighed. "So tell me more about your job," he said.

She tossed him a smile. "I'm an accountant at a big accounting firm. What do you want me to talk about? Spreadsheets?"

"Okay, then. Tell me about your family."

"I have a mom and a dad and a big sister. I grew up in Richmond in a house with an honest-to-God white picket fence."

"No way."

"Yep. It was perfectly boring. No scandals. No drama. My sister and I aren't close, but we get along fine."

"Boring is nice."

"Hmm. I detect a not-pleasantly-boring child-hood."

"Nah, it was fine. There was no white picket

fence, but I was hardly Oliver Twist. So why did you decide to become an accountant?"

So he didn't want to talk about himself? Well, she didn't particularly feel like talking, either. "I like numbers. And puzzles. I like figuring things out." Turning to face him, she smiled and began to walk backward toward the water, wondering what he'd do. She pushed down her shorts and tossed them up to the dry sand.

"Are you coming?" she called as she backed into the breaking waves and slipped her shirt off, as well. The wind touched her belly, warm air rubbing against her like a cat, and she hoped he was checking out her red bikini, since the blue one hadn't thrilled him.

"Of course." Max's voice oozed cheer.

Chloe threw her shirt onto the sand and walked in deeper, smiling at the sound of Max's splashing footsteps behind her. The water was up to her knees. She wasn't the least bit surprised when he started talking.

"In Greek mythology, Amphitrite was the wife of Poseidon and the queen of the sea." He was beside her within two seconds. She kept walking. "But in the beginning, she wasn't simply Poseidon's wife. Amphitrite *was* the sea. The ruler and the goddess and the sea itself. One day Poseidon saw her playing in the water, and he was overwhelmed by her beauty and power."

"Oh?" The water lapped against her upper thighs. She stopped to gaze out at the beautiful moon reflecting off the water.

"Chloe." His fingertips touched the flat of her shoulder blade, tentative at first, then his touch grew heavier, fingers spreading, palm touching her skin. His hand curved around her shoulder, holding her and pressing his heat inside.

She froze, afraid if she shivered, he'd move his hand.

"You're beautiful. You look like part of the sea itself tonight." His hand kept her still as he circled around to stand in front of her. A wave pushed him closer. "Natural. Peaceful."

She knew he was going to kiss her, and she knew he was only kissing her to keep her from swimming, but she didn't stop him. She wanted to be kissed. Only Thomas had kissed her in the past three years. She wanted those memories erased by someone new.

Max's mouth curved in a charming, crooked smile. His eyes fell to her lips and lingered as if he were savoring the moment. But…something was off. His gaze wasn't heavy-lidded. It wasn't soft. Sharp thoughts turned behind his eyes.

Chloe wanted to be kissed, but more than that,

she wanted to be *wanted*. For real. With no lies to dilute that wanting.

He lowered his head, edging his mouth close to her ear. "I can think of better things for a sea goddess to do on a dark beach than go swimming."

She put effort into keeping her voice light and coy. "Oh, yeah?"

"Yeah." He stepped forward, and the press of his leg moved her back a step. She knew she was being manipulated, but when his lips brushed her temple, the warmth still sent sparks racing down her neck. Not fair.

When his hips nudged her, Chloe took a step back in frantic defense. *Totally* not fair. His mouth curved in triumph, as if he were thrilled he made her nervous, but Chloe was convinced his thrill had more to do with her migration toward the sand. When she planted her feet, sure enough, his eyes narrowed.

"Come up to the beach," he murmured. "I want to show you something."

"Really? Is it in your pocket? Because that sounds a little creepy."

"Oh," he said. Then, "No!" as he started to laugh. "No, not that. Jesus. I was talking about the moon." But even past his laughter, he was moving her backward. The waves only reached her knees now.

"I just thought…" His hands slipped down

her shoulders to her upper arms. "We're finally alone...."

God, this would be so lovely if he wasn't faking it. She could just close her eyes and pretend...

Max dipped his head, easing a centimeter closer to her mouth. "So I thought maybe..."

"Oh, God, you're really going to do this, aren't you?"

His chin jerked back a little before he eased back into his role. "I sure am," he said with a slow drawl.

"It's not fair, Max."

"Hmm?"

"You're going to make out with me just to keep me from swimming!"

This time his whole body jerked back when his chin drew in. Chloe gave him a disappointed push to help him along.

"What?" he huffed.

"You don't want me to swim at night, so you're pretending you want to make out!"

Panic flashed in his eyes, but Max assumed an incredulous expression. "That's ridiculous. What are you talking about?"

"I'm talking about you being a freak, Max."

"Hey!"

Shaking her head in disgust, Chloe spun away

from him and waded toward the sand. "I thought you *liked* me."

"Wait…" His splashing tossed water high, making her shiver when the drops struck the small of her back. She'd felt confident and playful a moment before, but now she was left vulnerable in her swimsuit, exposed to a man who didn't find her attractive.

She made it to the waterline and looked around for her shirt.

"Chloe," Max said behind her. She jerked away when his fingers curled around her elbow. "Chloe, I do like you. So why are you calling me a freak?"

"Give it up, already. I'm on to you, okay? I see what you're doing."

"What?" He threw his hands up. "What am I doing?"

Though he tried to hold her gaze, Chloe turned away to search the beach for her shirt. Humiliation was a familiar enough feeling that it only stung a little when she realized how close she'd come to letting him distract her with his fake kisses. Even now she wished she'd kept her mouth shut. Or just opened it for him, actually. She could be rolling around on the sand with her hands wrapped around those big biceps right now.

"Last night, you weren't interested in me or in

Jenn, were you? You were checking on the fire. That's why you came over."

"Chloe," he said, his voice warm with indulgent laughter. "Come on."

"And the *diving?* You didn't want to go diving. You didn't even look at that wreck."

This time he didn't respond. Finally spotting her shirt, Chloe sprinted over to grab it and shook it hard to be sure there were no crabs nesting in it. She jerked it over her head, then glanced back to find him standing five feet away, hands open as if he'd paused midgesture.

He inclined his head, and his hands completed the circular motion. "Of course I wanted to go diving. I love diving. It's what I do. Sorry, I must've gone into work mode. I guess I'm not used to diving on vacation anymore."

"Max."

"What?"

"You're a big fat liar! You didn't want to have marshmallows, and you didn't want to go diving, and you definitely didn't want to make out on the beach tonight."

"I… It's…" He looked dumbstruck. His big, sexy shoulders drooped. "It's no fun to make out on the beach. The fucking sand is a hundred times worse than a rug burn."

"The *sand?* What's the sand got to do with anything?"

"You said I didn't want to make out with you. That's not true. I just didn't want to do it here."

She ignored the stab of ugly hope that hit her belly. Slick talk. "So why'd you follow me out here?"

He snapped his mouth shut.

"Why did you want to come with me?"

"It seemed like a fun idea." There was a tiny note of question in the last word, as if she finally had him on shaky ground, but he clearly didn't mean to give up the truth. She'd had enough of lying men.

Chloe shook her head in disgust. "I need to find my shorts," she growled, bitterly aware that a phrase like that should be uttered under much happier circumstances. "Good night. I'm sure I'll see you tomorrow."

Wishing she'd brought a flashlight, Chloe walked along the waterline, squinting into the darkness. Where the hell could her shorts have gone? Had she missed the sand completely and they were even now floating toward Europe? The perfect end to a shitty evening.

She finally spotted the shorts and hurried to grab them. No wonder they'd been hard to spot. The pale gray material blended right into the sand. As she checked them over carefully for clawed animals, Max's voice emerged from the darkness.

"I didn't want you to drown."

Chloe frowned and turned toward him, shorts clutched to her stomach. "What?" She couldn't make out his features in the ten feet of darkness between them, but she could see that he'd stopped walking and stood with his hands shoved into his pockets.

"I didn't want you to drown. Or get eaten by a shark."

"Okay." He was talking, at least, but she couldn't see the logic. "So you came along to keep me from drowning. Why couldn't you just say that?"

The edge of his jaw looked hard as rock now. "Because people don't like to be told what to do."

"Max—"

"People don't want to hear that swimming at night is idiotic. In fact, if you tell someone they've got a really stupid idea, they become determined to prove you wrong."

"So you made it seem like a great idea instead?"

"I just thought I'd find a way to distract you."

She narrowed her eyes at his words and took a step forward. Now she could see his mouth set in a flat line. "What about the beach fire? You didn't really come over just to flirt, did you?"

"Your pit was too close to the sea grass. It needed to be deeper, and I wanted to be sure you didn't build it so high it would stay hot all night long."

"I see. I suppose I can understand being haunted by Smokey the Bear. Lots of people have a fear of fire." She crossed her arms. "So what about the diving?"

He took his hands out of his pockets, then put them back in before rocking back and forth on his heels.

"Max?"

"What about it?"

"You didn't want to go."

His mouth tilted at an incredulous angle. "I asked to go."

"Jesus, Max!"

"What do you want me to say? I'm a professional diver. You actually think I don't like diving?"

"You did *not* want to dive with us, so why did you go?"

"Because diving is incredibly dangerous," he bit out. "And you were diving with a guy with unknown credentials. *Who picks a dive guide off the grocery store bulletin board?*"

Whoa. Well, he wasn't being charming anymore. Chloe told herself that was progress.

"Sorry," he muttered, kicking at a clump of wet sand. "I didn't mean to raise my voice. I don't know what got into me."

Chloe suspected she knew what had gotten into

him. Panic. But now she was getting truly angry. "So you didn't want to dive?"

"No."

"And you didn't want to toast marshmallows?"

"No."

Great. Another guy pretending to like her. Just fucking great. She was cursed. "Well," she snapped, "I'm not going swimming, so you can go now."

"It's dark out here. I wouldn't want to—"

"Just go! I absolve you of any responsibility, okay?" Wrapped up in her righteous anger, Chloe wasn't expecting any response from him. She certainly wasn't expecting him to shout again.

"It doesn't work like that, damn it!" He took a deep breath and lowered his voice. "You can't absolve me of responsibility, Chloe. If I leave you out here alone in the dark and something happens to you, it'll be on me, because I left knowing it wasn't right."

She shook her head. "I'm an adult. You're not responsible for me. I can do whatever I want."

"That's the problem!" His hands flew wide, gesturing around him, as if drawing attention to the whole world. "You can do anything you want, so I have to make you want something else."

Her breath left her on a rush, leaving behind a painful void in her chest. Chloe pressed her palm to her heart. "That's just cruel, Max."

Though he'd been glaring in the direction of the lights of the cabins, Max's head swung toward her. "Cruel?"

"You pretended to like me just to...just to get control over my beach fire!"

"That's crazy. I was never pretending to like you."

"Oh, I'm sorry. When you inserted yourself into my entire vacation, I guess it was stupid of me to assume you were flirting!"

"I *was* flirting," he said simply, as if her voice hadn't taken on the edge of hysteria. "I like you. It's just hard for me to stop...thinking." He crossed his arms and uncrossed them while Chloe tried to take in what he meant to say. He *liked* her?

He ran an impatient hand through his hair. "Do you want to go for a walk? I need to walk."

"Why?"

"I've never had this conversation before." He strode toward her and took her hand to tug her along the edge of the water. "It's nice tonight. Let's walk."

He seemed to need to burn off some energy, and for once, his charm wasn't on display. Max looked nervous and unhappy. And his fingers were wrapped tight around hers, distracting her more than even his most charming smile could. She kept pace with him, letting the occasional wave sweep over her toes, but he didn't drop her hand.

"How could you have never had this conversation?"

One shoulder rose in a suspiciously casual shrug. Now that they were walking, he seemed disinclined to talk. Ironically.

"Max? Do you want to talk or is this walk just another one of your ploys?"

He stared straight ahead. "How did you see it?"

"See what?"

"How did you see what I was doing?"

"Well, I was kind of looking forward to hanging out with an international party boy, but then there didn't seem to be much partying going on."

He drew in a breath as if he meant to say something important, then let it out again, slowly. His fingers shifted, sliding in between hers. "You don't seem like the type of girl who likes party boys."

"Ha! No, I guess I'm not. That's why I was intrigued. New experiences."

"I'm sorry if I'm a disappointment."

"I don't know *what* you are. I can't figure it out."

Max finally smiled, his teeth flashing white in the moonlight. "Boy, are you selling yourself short. You're the only one who's ever called me on my... issues."

"I can't be the only one."

"Believe me, you are."

"But you can't take responsibility for every single person you meet, right?"

"Mm," he hummed, "of course not."

"Max." She stopped and used his hand to force him to turn toward her. "Do you take responsibility for every person you meet?"

"No!" he said with a laugh. A charming, warm laugh exactly like one she'd heard from him before. When he was being a big, fat liar.

"Look, we're on an island. We don't know each other. After the end of this week, we'll never see each other again. So you may as well tell me the truth. When will you have the chance to spill your guts without any consequences? Don't think. Just tell me."

He hesitated.

"Tell me."

"Yes!" he said on a rush of air. "Yes, I feel responsible for everyone I meet."

"But... That's crazy. How can you do that?"

"I can't. It's..." His wide shoulders slumped. "Chloe, it's exhausting."

"Oh, Max." She sighed at the utter weariness in his voice.

"It *is* crazy. I know that. I see that, but I can't stop it." As he spoke, she could hear herself in his words.

The desperation and tiredness and helplessness she'd been feeling for weeks. It was all there in his deep, rich voice, coming from this confident man with strong shoulders that looked like they could carry the weight of the world. And did, apparently.

"Max." She sighed, her fingers tightening in his. Forgetting for a moment that he might not even be attracted to her, Chloe leaned toward him, pushing up on her tiptoes, feeling the sand give way and squeeze through her toes. She felt all this, but his mouth was all she could see, all she could think of. His mouth and the sad curve of his lips, and the slight, surprised parting when she'd almost reached him.

At the last second, just as doubt reared its ugly head, he finally moved to meet her. That sad mouth didn't feel sad at all. It felt…comforting. Warm. And definitely interested.

For two heartbeats, his lips simply pressed hers gently, but then Chloe felt the faint rush of Max inhaling, and his arms curved around her.

A brief moment of shock sizzled through her. Shock at being touched by a man who'd never touched her before. But when the surprise wore off, his hands were so solid and hot against her back, and she was no longer on her tiptoes. Max was holding her, his lips parting to taste her.

Chloe opened for him, and the first taste of Max

drew a little sound of approval from her throat. An embarrassing sound, surely, but Max's tongue rubbed against hers and she didn't have time to be embarrassed. She was too busy being happy.

Oh, God, she was kissing a gorgeous man who was nearly a stranger. Chloe, who'd always been a good girl. Who should've been on her honeymoon this very week. She was rubbing her tongue *into* this man as he deepened the kiss and pulled her closer.

There was nowhere to put her arms but around his neck. And nothing to do with her hands but slide them into his hair.

And suddenly, despite everything, the night was perfect. The ocean rushed gently behind her, the wind danced over them, and they both held on tightly as they kissed and tasted and licked. If he was faking his interest, he was doing a damn good job of it. His hands moved restlessly against her back. He pulled her closer, until their bodies lined up. My God, he felt like one solid wall of muscle against her.

She was so focused on his chest and hips and thighs, Chloe hardly noticed the downward path of his hand. It felt cozy and right when he touched the small of her back, then a bit more exciting when his palm slid over her hip. She kissed him harder, caught up in the excitement of exploring hands and big shoulders.

But when he ventured farther south, his fingers

curved over her ass, and Chloe remembered that she wasn't wearing pants.

"Oh!" she gasped as she turned her head to the side. She meant to slow things down. She really did. But then Max's lips touched her neck. His mouth closed over the very sensitive, secret spot just below her ear. And he sucked.

"God," she groaned, knees shaking to uselessness. He'd found the chink in her lust armor. His teeth scraped the skin and he pulled her hips more tightly against his.

No, he definitely wasn't faking. And she still wasn't wearing pants.

"Max, I… Oh, that feels good. We should… Oh, I think we should…"

"Yeah," he murmured, as if she'd said something intelligible. "Yeah, we should."

Before she could ask what he meant, Chloe found herself being lowered to the sand. "You don't like the sand!" she gasped, trying to decide if she was excited or panicked.

"I do now," he murmured just before his mouth took hers again.

This was better. Way better. Now he was snug against her side, controlling the kiss, one knee resting atop her bare thigh, and Chloe decided it wasn't panic welling up inside her. It was sweet, hot lust pooling beneath her skin like a fever.

Max kissed her, his hand framing her jaw with gentle fingers. He kissed her again as his fingertips trailed down her neck before he turned her face to the side and sucked beneath her ear, already confident she'd like it. She did.

A minute before, she'd been thinking she should stop him. But now his body pressed heavy against her side and filled her up with recklessness. Her fingers curled into his arm as his mouth licked at her pulse.

"Max," she breathed, the sound of his name giving her a thrill. Two days ago, she hadn't known him, now she was holding her breath as his hand inched lower.

"God, you taste good," he whispered, his words slipping over her skin.

"You *feel* good," she said, running her hand all the way up his solid biceps. The muscles flexed beneath the skin, rewarding her for her exploration. "So good."

His leg slid more snugly between hers and Max kissed her again. Finally, his hand slid down and cupped her breast. Despite her anticipation, Chloe shivered in surprise.

This was like high school all over again. She felt just as excited and scared and uncertain. Goose bumps spread over every inch of her skin as his thumb brushed her nipple. Her hand shook against his wrist, as if this were her first time.

But it wasn't her first time, and she knew exactly how rare it was to feel such sweet, heavy heat flowing through her veins. Max might be a virtual stranger, but the chemistry between them was unbelievably hot.

Chloe angled her mouth to take his tongue deeper. She rubbed her leg against his and moaned at the tightening of his fingers. Max made a low sound in response, and a subtle shift of his body made her suddenly aware of the press of his arousal against her hip. All the nerves in her body flared to brighter life.

He was excited. For her. For *her.*

Yes, this was like high school, when male attention had been unexpected and flattering to an average girl. The insistent, impressive length of his cock was a hot brand against her hip, and there was hardly any barrier between them. His baggy swim trunks and the paper-thin material of her bikini. They were practically naked.

"Max." She sighed, curling both her hands into his hair to drag his mouth back down to her neck. In a move she would later admire for its smoothness, he kissed his way to the other side of her neck, requiring a slow shift of his body in order to reach her favorite spot. A few breaths later, Max was sucking just where she liked and his body fully covered hers, all their parts lining up perfectly.

So perfectly that Chloe groaned in sharp pleasure.

"Jesus," Max whispered, rocking against her. Balancing his weight on his elbows, he slipped his hands into her hair to hold her head, then he began a leisurely exploration of all the sensitive spots on her neck.

Eyes open, Chloe stared at the swirl of stars above her. Pleasure spun through her body. His mouth trailed heat while his cock pressed her clit. Chloe couldn't stop herself from moaning his name.

He whispered her name back to her. As if she were desirable in ways she'd forgotten she could be. In ways she'd never been with Thomas. That thought scared her, so she pushed it away and edged her knee higher up on Max's thigh.

His weight lifted, and she was just about to whimper in disappointment when one of his hands touched her waist before sliding to her belly. His fingers were shockingly hot on her bare skin.

Oh, God, he was about to slide his hand into her bikini bottoms and feel how wet he'd made her.

Her nerves sang with anxiety…and desperate arousal.

"Can I…?" he murmured, but his hand was already slipping beneath the delicate fabric, feathering over sensitive skin.

Chloe could barely breathe. She arched her neck, twisting her head to the side to draw cooler air than the heat that shimmered off his skin.

"Chloe," he said again, just as he touched her.

"Oh," she breathed, not quite registering the flash of pale yellow that moved across the sand a few feet away.

His fingertip circled her, and she whimpered with lust, just as another flash of yellow shifted in front of her.

She blinked, drawn away from her focus on Max and his hand. A crab? She would've been scared if she'd had room for that in her head, but she was too full of what Max was doing, now sliding two fingers up and down just where she needed them. "Oh, God, yes," she whispered.

"Yeah," Max answered.

But the crab sidled into view again, clear and bright as if... Oh, no. Light flashed in her eyes.

"Chloe?" Jenn called out of the darkness.

"Ack!" she yelped. She moved to knock Max's hand away, but he'd already slid it free. He had just enough time to shift his weight to the side before the light found a steady home on Chloe's face.

"Chloe!" Jenn called out happily. Her footsteps

hurried closer before they came to an abrupt stop about ten feet away. "Oh. I…"

Chloe closed her eyes in mortification, but she clearly heard her friend's loud swallow.

"I'm sorry!" Jenn said.

Chloe shook her head. "No, it's fine, we were just…um…"

"Your mom called, and it sounded important, and Elliott had a flashlight, so…"

Opening one eye, she saw the dark shape of a man next to Jenn. "Oh, hi, Elliott."

Max's muffled curse reminded her that while this was embarrassing, it was also a little bit funny. "Maybe," she whispered, "we should get up."

"I was hoping for a minute," he muttered back.

"A full minute?"

"Ideally, yes."

She was still laughing when he pushed himself to his knees.

Elliott cleared his throat. "Maybe we should just—"

Chloe shook her head and took the hand Max offered once he got to his feet. "What did my mom want?" Walking toward Jenn, she swiped sand off the backs of her legs, then looked up to find two sets of eyes focused low on her body.

Still no pants. Right. "Uh… We were swimming." Jenn's gaze rose to Chloe's shirt, which was clearly not wet. "I, um, found my shirt, but… So about the phone call?"

"Oh." Jenn cleared her throat and cut her eyes toward Max. "She was calling about something to do with your cousin Tiffany."

"Is she okay?" Chloe asked, even as Jenn's reluctant tone finally registered in Chloe's brain. Reluctant, because she obviously didn't want to discuss it in front of the men. Which meant it had something to do with Thomas and the scandal.

The scandal Chloe had completely forgotten about during her walk with Max. Wow. "I'll call when we get back to the cabin," she blurted out, trying to cover up Jenn's awkward silence.

"Yes!" Jenn said.

Max's hand touched her back. "I hope everything's all right."

"I'm sure it's fine." She forced a smile at his doubtful look. "My cousin is always up to something."

"Oh, I see. I hope it's nothing then."

Elliott cleared his throat for the third time. "We'll head back." When his hand touched Jenn's arm, she jumped and he jerked away.

"Sorry. Yes, let's head back." The two of them took off as if they'd just accidentally stepped into an extraordinarily uncomfortable situation.

"Uh, okay," Chloe called. "I'll be there in a minute!" Her friend disappeared into the darkness, and Chloe quietly added, "after I find my pants."

CHAPTER SEVEN

OKAY, SO THE CELIBACY THING wasn't working out so well.

Max's heart was still pounding and didn't seem interested in slowing its pace, overwhelmed as it was with three strong emotions. Lust, for a good start, and shock at having been discovered rolling around in the sand, and then there was the anxiety of having his secrets revealed.

He watched Chloe's dark profile as she stared in the direction of the bobbing flashlight, and his pulse didn't slow at all. "We'd better go," he said. "You need to call your mom back."

Crossing her arms, she turned toward him. "We didn't finish talking about your problem."

"I thought we wrapped it up pretty well."

"No, we just made out instead."

"Exactly." The flash of her smile drew him closer, and Max slid his arms around her body and lowered his lips to hers. His heart turned over at the taste of her, but Chloe pulled back.

"Was all that about distraction, Max?"

"You totally distracted me, yes."

"No, I mean were you trying to distract *me?*"

"Chloe, for God's sake, did it feel like I was playing you?"

When she touched her hand to his chest, it felt like a caress, but he knew it was a sign that he should keep his distance. "You said no one's ever noticed your control issues. Which means that you must be pretty damn good at fooling people, right?"

Fooling people. Tension wound around his stomach and squeezed. Yeah, she was right to be wary. He'd acted his way through countless relationships. "You're right. I'm good at fooling people. Really good at it."

"What about girlfriends?"

His fingertips felt numb and his jaw close to cracking. "I don't want to talk about that." It was sick, what he did, taking needy girls home like stray dogs. He was weary and exhausted from the constant vigilance.

"Why don't you want to talk about it?"

"Because it's ridiculous and it's over. I haven't dated in months. I decided to…" Oh, shit. That wasn't something you blurted out to a woman on a first date, even if the date had been based on fear of sharks and drowning.

"What?"

"Don't you want to call your mom back?"

He couldn't see her roll her eyes, but he was pretty sure it was happening. "Avoidance much, Max? All right, I'll let you off the hook. Let's go."

He'd wanted to stop the conversation, but he also didn't want this little bubble of peace to be gone, so Max reached for her elbow before she could step away. "That wasn't an act and I wasn't trying to do anything but kiss you, Chloe. I swear. I've been thinking about doing that since the moment I saw you."

"Sure fooled me."

"You said yourself that I'm really screwed up."

"True."

"Come here."

She turned easily, swaying into his chest and wrapping her arms around his neck. Kissing her pushed away some of the awful tightness in Max's chest. Whatever he'd done before, whatever lies he'd told, what he wanted from Chloe was real and good. *She* was real and good.

So he kissed her and held her and let himself forget the mess he'd made of his life. For just a few more minutes.

CHLOE SQUINTED AGAINST the brightness of the cabin lights, caught for a moment in the doorway like a deer facing imminent death.

"Did you two take the long way home?" Jenn asked.

A blush flared to hot life on her cheeks. "I had to find my pants."

"Uh-huh. You sure are bad at coming up with excuses. The explanation is supposed to make you look more innocent. Not less."

"Shut up."

"So…?"

Chloe grinned nervously. She couldn't help it.

Jenn gasped, "You did it?"

"No! I mean we did something, but not *it*."

"And?" She made a hurry-up gesture.

"And what?"

Jenn grabbed an empty water bottle and aimed it threateningly at Chloe's stomach. "Don't hold out on me. You're the only link I have to the world of real sex. Is he as delicious as he looks?"

Chloe sauntered over to the couch and dropped into it. "Elliott is pretty delicious-looking, too. Why don't you find out for yourself?"

"Don't tease me," she groaned. "You know I can't."

"Why?"

"He's a serious guy, Chloe. I'm sure he dates serious women. And I'm…not."

Chloe twisted around to glare at her friend.

"You're an accountant. It doesn't get much more serious than that."

"You know what I mean." She waved a dismissive hand.

Chloe would never understand this about Jenn. She was beautiful and smart and funny...and she had no self-confidence whatsoever when it came to men. "He was seriously interested in your body."

Jenn dropped onto the couch beside Chloe. "You think I should?"

"Should what? Get it on with Elliott Sullivan? Yes! Are you thinking about it?"

"I don't know." Jenn began to nibble on her thumbnail, a sure sign of nervousness. She was definitely thinking about getting it on with Elliott.

Chloe let her think for a good long while before she interrupted. "So my mom?"

Jenn's nose wrinkled. "Your cousin did another interview."

"Crap."

"It's going to air tomorrow, but your mom watched it online tonight."

Chloe picked up her cell phone and looked at the bars. Two bars tonight. Just her luck.

"Hi, Chloe," her mom said before the first ring had finished. Her voice was heavy with sympathy.

"Hey, Mom. So Tiffany is talking to the press again."

"I'm so sorry, baby. I don't know what's wrong with that girl."

Chloe rubbed her eyes. "She's nineteen and she likes to be on TV. And she's a selfish brat. How bad is it?"

Her mom's deep sigh didn't promise anything good. "She says you wouldn't let her be a bridesmaid because she was too short."

"That's ridiculous! She's only two inches shorter than me!"

"Tiffany claims you wanted the bridesmaids to ascend evenly from your maid of honor to your tallest friend."

"Tiffany used the word *ascend?*"

She was glad to hear her mom laugh. "No, she described a stair-step pattern. And then she claimed you tried on over a hundred dresses before making a choice. And that you threw a bouquet at the florist when she made a mistake."

"As if she'd know. I've hardly talked to Tiffany in the past six months. But I'm sure as hell going to talk to her now."

"Honey, if you do that, she'll—"

"I know, Mom." Chloe sighed. "She'd tell the press I was abusive and insane. I get it."

"I'm sorry, hon. Try not to worry about her, okay?"

Chloe let her head fall back on the couch. "She didn't know about this vacation, did she?"

"No. I didn't say a word to her mother. How's the trip, by the way?"

"Good," Chloe answered. Then, with more honesty, "Great."

"You sound much better. Try to have fun and give Jenn my love. I promise I'll call if there's anything else. If you don't hear from me, everything's fine, all right?"

"Got it, Mom. I love you."

Chloe hung up and tried not to cry. Her poor parents. Retired and living in their small house with its tiny yard, and the press was still stalking them, just because she'd spent a week there before she'd found a place to live. A place that didn't belong to Thomas's mother. The press had trampled her father's rosebushes and driven her mother to wear a head scarf and dark glasses every time she stepped outside.

Chloe slung her arm over her eyes and groaned. "Tell me again that I wasn't a Bridezilla."

"You know you weren't."

"I did cry at the dress shop," Chloe whispered.

"They screwed up the hem, and you got overwhelmed. You weren't a bitch."

She took a deep breath, but the lump in her throat didn't budge. "I must've been. I must've been a bitch to Thomas. I must've been an obsessed, type A ice queen with a scary attitude, or none of this makes any sense."

Jenn's arms wrapped around her waist and she snuggled her head into Chloe's shoulder. "That's not true. You're sweet and kind. And maybe a little bit type A, but just a little. Don't cry."

But she was already crying. "My life was so normal."

"I know."

"What did I do?"

"Aw, Chloe, you didn't do anything wrong. It was Thomas! He… He must have gotten cold feet."

"When men get cold feet, they don't jump out of a plane and hide out at a beach resort in Florida! I don't know what I did!"

Jenn made soothing noises and rubbed her back until Chloe stopped sniffling. "Thomas was a mama's boy. You knew that. He didn't know how to stand up to his mom, and apparently he didn't know how to stand up to you, either."

"But I don't even know why he wanted out."

"Does it matter?"

Did it? Chloe took the tissue Jenn offered and wiped her tears. He'd wanted out. Badly enough to chew off his own foot to escape the trap. How was she supposed to excavate a logical, thoughtful reason from a mess like that? "Maybe it doesn't matter. I'm sorry I get so weepy."

"I'm sorry about your cousin."

"It wasn't that. I think your vacation just worked a little too well. I kind of forgot all that craziness for a while. I let my guard down and it snuck up on me when I talked to my mom about Tiffany. And… and I'm kind of freaked out that I've been able to forget Thomas so easily. When I was making out with Max… How could I enjoy that so much if I was in love with Thomas just a month ago?"

"You don't have to feel bad about that. You don't owe him anything after what he did!"

Chloe crumpled the tissue in her hand. "No, but if I'm already getting over Thomas after a month… then we really shouldn't have been getting married, right? Thomas was right."

"Thomas wasn't right about *anything*."

"He—"

"Look, Chloe, I knew him, too. I've known him almost as long as you have, and I've spent time with him and…Thomas was nice and smart and handsome, but he was weak. And he was a *liar*."

She took a deep breath. And then another. "Yes. He was a liar."

Jenn's hand touched hers. "So if you're moving on, I'm happy about that and you should be, too."

"Okay."

"So tell me about making out with Max Sullivan."

The tears had taken something dark with them. Chloe felt lighter than she had in a long time. Maybe even months. So she smiled and told Jenn exactly what had happened on the sand. By the time she went to bed, her eyes were swollen, but her sides ached from laughter. Not a bad trade-off, really.

CHAPTER EIGHT

THE WAVES SLAPPED the sides of the boat as the wind pushed spray above the bow, and Max's heart pounded. Another day on the water. Another day of making sure his brother didn't sail into a storm or flip the boat or wreck them on the rocks.

But this time Max's heart wasn't pounding with anxiety. It was pounding because Chloe Turner was lounging on one of the captain's seats, her feet balanced against the railing as she grinned into the wind. Her red bikini glowed like a siren in the sun, alerting him to what they'd been doing the last time he'd seen it.

Wow.

"Slow down as you come up on these buoys," he said to Elliott without taking his eyes off Chloe's belly. His fingers tingled at the memory of that soft skin. "Keep the red on the starboard side and the green on the port. That's left."

"Got it."

She turned to look out at the water, her thighs

flexing with the movement. God, he had to touch her again, soon.

This celibacy thing was backfiring. His mind was swimming with the taste of her mouth and the firm push of her nipple against his palm and the slick heat of her sex beneath his fingers...

"A little slower," he murmured. The pitch of the engine didn't change, so Max sighed and pulled his gaze from Chloe's body. "A little slower!" he called out, and Elliott gave him a thumbs-up and cut the speed.

The water was rougher today, so they'd decided to take the boat all the way back to the protected waters of the bay. A forty-five-minute trip, but what the hell. Chloe was there, totally relaxed, sending him secret winks every time he made a move to control the situation.

God, she was hot.

"Does this look good?" he asked Elliott, gesturing toward a little curve of the shoreline. What he meant was *Stop here*. But asking for input was a much more effective way to maneuver people. When Elliott nodded, Max said, "I'll drop the anchor." The engine cut off and a faint ribbon of peace washed over him with the silence. The sound of water was more muffled here in the protected confines of the bay. The most prominent sound was the trilling of birds and the rattle of insects and the soft laughter

of the two women who'd asked if they could accompanying the men on their fishing trip.

Max took a deep breath and let the anchor fall.
Then he turned toward Chloe and her bright grin.
She clearly enjoyed being in on his secret, and Max
felt lighter than he had in years.

Chloe was... Chloe was an oasis.

Perhaps that was an odd metaphor in the middle
of a warm bay, surrounded by lush greenery. But
there was nothing peaceful for him here. Nothing
but Chloe.

"Hey, Max!" she called out, the corner of her
mouth edging up. "Can we take off our life jackets
now that we're stopped?" She'd already pushed the
boundary by leaving only the top buckle buttoned,
but since she'd exposed her stomach, he hadn't com-
plained. Much.

"Shush," he called. "I told you the Coast Guard
has eyes and ears everywhere. After that incident
with the admiral's twin daughters, he's out to get me
on any trumped-up charge he can. The life jackets
stay on."

"Oh, the *twin* daughters. Right. Got it."

"Welcome to my crazy world."

Laughter danced in her eyes. "You got a rod for
me?"

He raised an eyebrow and grabbed a fishing rod

as an excuse to go sit next to her. "Have you ever fished?"

"It's been a long time. My dad used to take me out when I was little, but he took care of all the details. The worms and the…fish."

"Right." His knee brushed hers, just as it had the night before. He looked down at the creamy skin of her thigh. What would've happened if they hadn't been discovered? She'd just been starting to make the best sounds. If he'd—

"So are you going to take care of it for me?"

"Hmm?"

"The worms?"

"Oh, sure. The worms. We use squid strips, actually. But I'll bait the line if you like."

"I like."

He showed Chloe what to do, glancing up to see that Elliott was doing the same for Jenn. Chloe looked familiar with the rod and reel, so he stepped back to wipe off his hands and let her cast. The movement pitched her body forward, and Max cringed and reached for her. His mind spit out a charming line as he pulled her back against his chest. *I was looking for an excuse to touch you,* it said. Then, *Maybe you need a little more hands-on instruction.*

Max stayed still, one arm wrapped around her waist, the other hand holding her elbow. And he realized that he didn't need to find a charming line to lull her. He could just…say it.

He took a deep breath. "Could you not lean out like that again?"

She turned her head enough that Max could see her profile as she watched him from the corner of her eye. "Okay."

"Because it makes me think you're going to fall out."

"Surely the water's not so deep here."

"No, but that doesn't matter. You could hit your head or get caught up in vegetation you can't even see." Max held his breath, waiting for her to snap at him, to say something like, "Yeah, I'm not an idiot." Or "I can take care of myself."

But Chloe nodded. "Okay. I'll be careful."

"Thanks," he said lightly, even though his heart was struggling to pound out of his chest. It was so much harder to be honest. If you were charming, people couldn't throw it in your face. If you were funny and flirtatious, they *wanted* to indulge you. But simply taking a deep breath and stating your thoughts aloud…Christ, that seemed like an outright invitation for rejection.

But Chloe was still smiling, and when she leaned her head a little closer to his chin, Max brushed his lips across her temple.

"Mmm." She sighed, as if there weren't two life

vests propping their bodies far apart. But for Max the life vests were a conduit to the pleasure of this stolen moment. He rested his mouth on her soft hair and breathed in the scent of her as a prickle of electricity scattered over his skin. They were on the water in a boat that dipped and bobbed in every wave, but he could relax and breathe her in because she wore a life jacket and had agreed to be careful.

"You're not going to rat me out?" he whispered.

"Never. It wouldn't be nearly as fun to tease you if it wasn't a private joke."

Max realized the arm he'd wrapped around her waist was pressed against an expanse of warmth. An experimental swipe of his thumb revealed the sweet texture of her bare skin. Chloe's muscles jumped a little. He did it again and kissed her cheekbone.

"I couldn't sleep last night," he confessed, "thinking about you."

"Worried about your secret?"

"Chloe, pay attention. I'm coming on to you. I was thinking about you on the beach, letting me get to third base."

"Ooh." The parts of her face he could see turned pink. "Is that third base? I forget."

"That's about as third base as it gets. Your lack of knowledge makes me think you were a good girl in high school. Were you?"

Her blush deepened to a color close to red. "Maybe."

Max's entire body heated in immediate response. He dipped his head to kiss her ear, then carefully pressed his teeth to the delicate lobe, loving the way she shivered against him. Max spread his hand wide over her hot stomach. "Chloe Turner, I think you're the sweetest girl I've ever gotten to third base with."

The muscles of her stomach flinched. "That was in high school. I'm not sweet anymore."

"Liar. You're sweet. And soft. And peaceful."

"That's not—"

"And smart enough to see through my act."

"Well, I—"

When he opened his mouth on her neck and sucked gently at the flesh, Chloe's words died a quick death in her throat. Max found her sharp gasp immensely satisfying. He edged his pinkie finger beneath the waist of her bottoms, thinking of what she'd let him do last night. Thinking that this wasn't the time or place, but she'd been so damn hot for him, and he really wasn't going to touch her like that here on the boat, but maybe just for a second...

A high-pitched squeal pierced his head, and Max jerked Chloe a foot back from the railing, just in case someone had spotted a shark. A splash followed the squeal, and he was already kicking off his flip-flops as he spun into lifesaving mode. But Jenn and Elliott were both still on the boat.

"I've got something!" Jenn called, bouncing up and down on her toes.

Max cringed at the movement, but tried to turn it into a smile. "That's great! If you want to play Captain Ahab, you've got to get some leverage. Take a seat and brace one foot against the side of the boat. Some of these guys can be monsters."

She laughed over her shoulder, eyes bright with excitement. Max saw the exact moment his brother got hit over the head with the cartoon anvil of a bad crush. Elliott's face registered a moment of stark, painful shock as a ray of sunlight struck her wind-blown hair.

Max paused in his rush across the length of the boat. He should let his brother take care of Jenn. If Max left them alone, maybe the awareness he'd noticed between the two of them would develop into a flirtation. Maybe his brother really would relax and have a good time. Maybe he'd have a wild affair with a gorgeous woman and let go of this idea that he wasn't cut out for a relationship.

Max dropped his outstretched hand and took a deep breath, but then the boat bobbed up, and Jenn lurched toward the low railing, and Max leaped forward, covering the last five feet in a blink of an eye. He and Elliott grabbed her at the same time, but

Elliott merely aimed an irritated glance in Max's direction. Max could feel his own face frozen in fear.

"Look." Jenn shook off their hands and tilted her head toward the water. "It's tiny. I can handle it."

Worried that she was about to lean out and try to snag the line, Max reached for the net, but his hand knocked into Elliott's arm as he did the same thing. This time Elliott glared.

"Right," Max murmured, feeling like a dick. "Sorry." He stood and moved away from Jenn, staying close enough to Elliott that he could keep an eye on him as he swept the net out to scoop up the little roundhead she'd caught.

As soon as everyone was settled happily back into the questionable safety provided by the railing, Max backed away and resumed his place at Chloe's side.

"Elliott thinks I'm flirting with Jenn," he muttered.

"Even after you were over here feeling me up?"

"He thinks I'm a player."

"Are you?"

Surprised, Max met her serious gaze. "No!"

She raised an eyebrow. "So why would he think that?"

"I'm not… Okay, I admit I can be flirtatious, but I am *not* a player."

"You don't have to lie to me, Max." She turned back to look at the line bobbing in the water. "It's no big deal, all right?"

"I'm not lying!" When the bird chatter died out for a few seconds, Max realized he'd shouted. He glanced over to a puzzled Elliott and a suspicious Jenn and offered a friendly wave. "Sorry." Chloe, on the other hand, was smirking at the water. He leaned in close and whispered. "You're the first woman I've touched in nine months."

The smirk faded from her lips, but Max's heart was dropping. Had he just said that? Aloud? *Way to play the desperation card, Max Sullivan.* "It's nothing weird, though. I just decided that celibacy was… I mean, not *celibacy* celibacy. Just…"

"Celibacy?" she squeaked.

"No!" To offset another shout, he offered Jenn the flash of a sick smile over his shoulder. "Forget I said anything."

She shifted and tried to cross her arms, but the fishing rod and life vest interfered, so she just edged away from him. "So…you're sending mixed signals here. Flirting with me and then telling me you're celibate."

"But I'm going to have sex with *you*," he insisted, just before the roar in his ears warned him that this was getting very bad, very fast. His pulse pounded, pushing a headache to life behind his eyes.

"Really?" Chloe drawled.

"Oh, Jesus."

"Am I going to like it?"

"I didn't mean it like that."

"Uh-huh."

He ran a hand through his hair, aware of the drop of sweat snaking down his neck. "I meant that I really wanted to, even though I told myself it was a bad idea, and I couldn't stop thinking about you and that red bikini. And your eyes!" he added belatedly. "And you're such a normal girl. You're not glamorous or... Um."

"I'm starting to believe you really aren't a player, because this is the worst seduction ever."

"Oh," he said, unwilling to let another full word pass his lips. He'd just blurted out the most insulting things he'd ever said to a woman. And, of course, he'd said them to the nicest girl he'd met in years. How had this become such a disaster? "I'm so sorry."

She shrugged one shoulder. "Lucky for you, I'm one of the few women in the world who actually revels in being called normal. I'll even take average at this point."

"Chloe," he managed. That one pained word was all he could get out before he slowly lowered himself to the bench seat behind him. Suddenly, he didn't care about the dangers of being on a boat in open water. He didn't care that Elliott was leaning out way too far to slip the squirming fish back into the water.

Today Max Sullivan had discovered that he only had two speeds: fake and charming or freakishly awkward. Jesus. He'd spent so many years pretending to like women he didn't care for that he couldn't manage the most basic interaction with a girl he really did.

Chloe dropped into the space beside him and pressed her knee against his. "Max?"

He shook his head.

"You know what?" When she took his hand, her fingers felt beautifully delicate sliding between his. "In all honesty, I'm totally going to have sex with you, too. So it's a good thing you're onboard."

Max narrowed his eyes at her. "Is that a joke?"

"Well, the 'onboard' part was a joke, but maybe not a good one, if you have to ask. But I wasn't joking about having sex with you."

"You must have been."

"No. I haven't been celibate, but I've been monogamous, so I understand that it feels…awkward."

"By awkward, I assume you mean the ridiculously stupid shit that keeps spilling from my mouth?"

She inclined her head graciously, but he caught the smile that hovered on her lips.

"You have a boyfriend?"

Her head popped up, alarm flashing through her eyes. "No! Of course not. Not anymore. What kind of girl do you think I am?"

"The kind of girl who'd consider having sex with a complete jackass like me."

"Ha!" She smiled. And then she smiled wider, and Max felt the world flash around him. In that moment, he knew he wore the same expression that Elliott had worn minutes before. Damn.

Chloe's hand squeezed his. "I guess I'm a bad girl then, Max. A very bad girl."

Oh, Jesus. A stupid smile took over his lips and wouldn't give up. He wondered if there were little hearts spinning around his head. She was very obviously not a bad girl, but what could be sexier than a good girl looking to get dirty?

He apparently had no gift for smoothness unless he was lying, so Max kept his mouth shut and said nothing. Instead, he held Chloe's hand and enjoyed the comforting feeling of the rough orange fabric of their life jackets rubbing together in the wake of each wave.

THE ANCIENT BIKE SHE'D borrowed from the resort made Jenn happy. The springs under the giant seat squeaked every time she turned a pedal, the tattered reed basket rustled in the wind and she had no idea where the clanking sound was coming from. But she felt free and daring as she flew down the narrow road, her hair tugging itself out of its braid with every gust of ocean breeze.

She felt like a kid again, strong and carefree. She'd been allowed to run wild at certain times of her childhood. After her father would leave on one of his three-week-long trips, her mother would usually take to her bed for a few days. Jenn had been responsible for bringing her mom tea and toast in the mornings, but the rest of the day had belonged to Jenn. She'd loved it. She'd been grubby and tan and as brave as any adventurer as she'd explored her neighborhood and the woods beyond.

Then she'd grown old enough to realize what her mom and dad always fought about the night before each of his trips. His other women. His other life.

Jenn shook off the memories and pedaled harder, passing the harbor and continuing on toward the older homes beyond. Utilities were expensive here, and most of the yards were adorned with clotheslines of snapping towels and clothing. She rode along the main road for a long time, thinking of nothing. She didn't turn around until the houses disappeared and drifting sand turned the road into an obstacle course.

Her thighs ached, but for once, her heart didn't. As she headed back toward town, she passed a cottage with a hand-lettered sign in the window: "Monthly Rentals! Inquire Within."

Her pedaling slowed for a moment as she considered the idea of quitting her job and spending the summer at the beach. She could work at the resort again, or at a restaurant. It wouldn't quite be running away, not what Thomas had done. Jenn wasn't engaged; she didn't even have a boyfriend.

If she wanted to leave her life behind and escape, no one would be hurt. Frankly, she'd be better off on her own. So far she'd managed to make a mess of every important relationship she'd ever had.

As if he were a harbinger of another disastrous turn, Elliott appeared on the path ahead, stepping out of a shop, head bent as he looked over a newspaper in his hand.

He was a good forty feet in front of her, and obviously absorbed in his reading. Jenn slowed, frantically looking around for the escape of a side street. But the ancient brakes of the bike squealed and startled Elliott, who glanced over the rim of his glasses and took a step back.

She'd been made.

"Jenn," he said, as if he weren't the least bit surprised to see her. With the paper in hand and the creases in his brow as he watched her over his glasses, Elliott looked every inch the scientist. Jenn's heart shuddered with nervous excitement.

Having rolled to a stop in the middle of the lane, she put her foot down and just stood there, afraid to go closer. But Elliott wasn't as affected by her presence as she was by his. He folded the newspaper under his arm and strolled forward.

"I was hoping to run into you," he said. "Max invited you and Chloe over for dinner tonight, but I thought they could use some privacy. Maybe we could go out. I hear there's a good restaurant a few lanes over. We could take a walk."

The first thing that hit her was alarmed joy. Elliott Sullivan was asking her out. The second thing that hit her was alarmed arousal. They'd be alone.

Then she realized that the motivation wasn't a desire to spend time with her, but a desire to give his brother some privacy. As quickly as her heart had leaped into her throat, it sank too low in her stomach.

Elliott cleared his throat and glanced up the road. "You're probably tired after the fishing trip."

She was tired. It was the perfect excuse to say no, but then Elliott would have to spend the evening alone and she'd be stuck in her cabin feeling guilty. "I think a walk and dinner would be lovely. Thank you."

Did he want to spend time with her? Or was she just the third-wheel friend who had to be paired up with someone? Still, even that third-wheel friend got lucky sometimes. And she did need some stress relief.

Jenn pedaled off, trying to decide if she should be anxious or excited. She finally settled on both.

CHAPTER NINE

CHLOE RAN THE BRUSH NERVOUSLY through her hair one last time. She was going to do this. She was going over to Max's cabin for the sole purpose of having sex. Her previous sexual experiences had always been in the context of a relationship. A new relationship, maybe, but it had always been sex with the expectation that it would lead to something else. This was leading nowhere. Max worked on the other side of the world, and she was about to enter into the maelstrom of a scandalous trial.

Yet it didn't feel meaningless. She liked Max. He made her feel warm and tingly, and not just below the waist.

Jenn stepped up to the mirror to put on her lipstick.

"Are you sure you're not mad?" Chloe asked.

"No. I'm happy for you. Just be careful and use a condom."

"Thanks, Mom. You too, by the way."

Jenn's face blazed to immediate scarlet. "We're just going to dinner."

"Why?"

"Chloe," Jenn said sharply, obviously trying to put an end to the conversation. She bit her lip, her eyes darting nervously to the mirror as she patted her hair.

Chloe relented and smiled. "Have fun at dinner."

"We're walking to a place on the other side of town, so…we'll take our time."

"Okay. This is weird, right? Maybe Max and I will just have dinner, too."

"Sure! That's why you dug out your one matching set of bra and panties."

"Shut up. It's a vacation. I was going for comfortable."

"Oh, you achieved that."

"Be nice, Jenn, or I'll bring up the fact that you put on your nice underwear, too. Are you thinking of expanding your sex portfolio? It could use a new addition."

"Shut up. He only asked me out because Max wanted to make you 'dinner.'"

"Elliott likes you."

Jenn shook her head. "Don't say that. I'll just get more nervous."

"Then he doesn't like you at all, and I hope you two are able to tolerate each other long enough to get through the evening."

"Thank you."

One hug later and Jenn was on her way, which meant it was time for Chloe to go, too. Max had promised steaks and wine on the porch, but they both knew what was really going on. Hell, they'd stated it out loud, and Chloe was suddenly very sorry about that conversation. Funny enough on a boat in mixed company. But now?

Crap.

Hands shaking, she tugged the hem of her skirt down a little, thankful that she had packed a nice set of underwear. But if this turned into more than one night of fun, Max was going to be exposed to her "Super Hottie!" panties. Or the Tinkerbell ones.

"Definitely Super Hottie," she muttered to her reflection. Her lips were glossed and her legs shaved. There was nothing to be done about her curvy thighs or slightly chubby cheeks. It was time for sex.

"Okay." Her face radiated pale uncertainty, so Chloe said it a little louder. *"Okay."*

Just as a tiny glimmer of confidence took hold, a knock echoed through the cabin and she jumped and grabbed for the sink before she tipped over.

She'd told Max she'd been a good girl in high school. The truth was that she'd always been good. Always. And look where that had gotten her. Screwed over, knocked around and left on the side of life like roadkill. She was a laughingstock and an infamous bitch, and she didn't even know what she'd done to deserve it.

Whatever she and Max did tonight, she'd worked hard to earn it. She was going to grab this bull by the horns and enjoy the ride.

Smiling at her naughty pep talk, Chloe snapped off the light and walked toward the screen door.

"Hey, there," Max said, the words slow and deeply friendly.

"Hey, yourself."

Max pulled open the door, and before she had a chance to feel awkward, he leaned in for a not-quite-innocent kiss…and Chloe remembered why she'd decided to have sex with him.

His tongue was a hot, rough slide against hers. He tasted minty and sweet, and the way his hands curved over her bare shoulders… Chloe swayed into him, letting her weight settle against his chest.

"I've been wanting to do that all day," he said.

An embarrassingly breathy sigh escaped her mouth.

Max grinned and wrapped his hand around hers to lead her down the steps to the sand. He wore shorts and a button-down shirt with the sleeves rolled up, exposing the tanned skin of his arms. But his feet were bare. Chloe found herself staring at them, at the long bones and wide strength and tan toes.

Lust warmed her belly before spreading out

through her limbs, like a flower blooming beneath her skin. Lust inspired by a man's *feet*.

"Chloe?" Max ducked down to draw her gaze from the ground. "Are you okay?"

"I am, actually."

They'd reached his porch, and Max grabbed two glasses of wine from their perch on the railing and gestured toward the steps.

Chloe took a seat and glanced toward the grill. It looked suspiciously inert. Neither smoke nor heat waves shimmered from the air holes. "Is the grill still heating?"

"Oh, I…thought I'd cook on the stove tonight."

"Why?"

"Why?" Max looked over his shoulder toward the door, then back to the grill. "Um…"

Sipping her wine, she watched as thoughts turned behind his eyes and wondered what he was trying to hide.

He thought for a long moment, his shoulders tightening to rock before he finally answered. "I don't like the grill."

"You don't like this grill?"

"No, I don't like grills at all. You can turn a stove on and off. A grill stays hot for hours. There are… sparks," he finished weakly.

"Really?" She tried her best to keep the laughter from her voice. Tried and failed.

"An hour from now a kid could be flying a kite on this beach and stumble right into the grill. How am I supposed to keep from worrying about that?"

"So it's not just water. Or open fires. Or sharks."

"No."

In the middle of an amazed laugh, Chloe caught her breath and sat up with a sudden jerk. "Wait a minute."

Max leaned slightly away from her. "What?" he asked warily.

"How many phobias do you have?"

"I don't have any phobias at all. I'm cautious and protective. That's all."

"The little boys you helped dig in the sand? Tell me that wasn't some weird sand castle phobia!"

Max scoffed. "Of course not. I'm not a freak, Chloe."

"So you just like playing with kids?"

"No, I was trying to keep those boys from killing themselves. Do you know how many kids have been suffocated by collapsing sand tunnels in the past twenty years? A kid is way more likely to be killed by a sand collapse than by a shark attack, but no one pays attention to that."

"My God," she whispered. "How do you know that?"

He shrugged. "I don't know. I saw it on TV

somewhere. I just wanted to let them know that if you were going to dig a sand pit, the walls had to slope out from the bottom or else they'd fall down."

"Oh, Max. Do you worry about *everything?*"

He shrugged again, and that was answer enough. He must be worn down. He had to be, but it was hard to see the exhaustion past the healthy glow of his tan. Maybe he was even more tired than she was.

"Are you hungry?" he asked.

She reached over to touch his jaw, then rubbed her thumb against the little hollow beneath his bottom lip. His eyes closed. Funny that he thought she was calm and peaceful. Everyone thought the same thing about him. And together…together it might even be true for both of them. "No, I'm not hungry," she murmured.

His sleepy brown eyes opened, alive with interest. "No?"

She was still shaking her head when he leaned in to kiss her. And kiss her again. A moment later, Chloe heard the muffled clink of her wineglass hitting the sand at the foot of the stairs. His shirt was crumpled in her fists as she tried to pull him closer, closer.

Her life might never be peaceful again. Once she left this beach, her world might continue to swirl around the drain until she lost herself completely.

But here, with Max, for a moment, all was well. *She* was well.

Though both her hands were wound into his shirt and Max's fingers braced her head for his kisses, they weren't nearly close enough. She didn't want to know where he ended and she began. She wanted to forget there could be space between them.

Chloe stood and eased a leg over his knees, her skirt rising easily with the movement.

"Mmm," Max murmured as his hands slid down to cup her ass. Before she could settle on his knees, he pulled her closer. Not that she objected. She wouldn't have been bold enough to simply settle onto his lap, but if he was issuing an invitation… Chloe pressed herself against his arousal with a sigh.

"Jesus." He sighed. "You feel amazing."

"Maybe you've just been really celibate."

"Ha. Maybe you've been torturing me in that red bikini."

She arched her back and pressed into him. "Surely you've seen a lot of girls in bikinis."

Max's mouth was hot as fire when it touched her neck. Wet fire that sucked at her skin and sent rivers of desire sluicing down her body. "Are you still talking?" he muttered against her pulse.

"No," she groaned. "Not talking. Just… Oh, man, I want to fuck you."

He jerked against her just as Chloe realized what

she'd said. "Oh." She slapped a hand over her mouth. "Oh, God!"

"Chloe Turner," he scolded, choking on laughter. "What did you say?"

"Nothing!" she squeaked. She would've wiggled away, but his arm was tighter than ever around her waist as his grin stretched impossibly wide.

"Are you trying to kill me, Chloe? You know I've been celibate. I don't need that kind of dirty talk going on while I'm trying not to lose it."

"Stop," she begged, even while her eyelids fluttered at the way his erection pushed snugly against her.

"Stop what?" he murmured, rocking gently against her.

"Stop…nothing. Just… Just don't…" He was pressed against the perfect place, his faint movements sending sparks flying through her belly. "Max," she whispered, closing her eyes.

The wind swirled over her skin as his hand bunched her shirt up, exposing her back to the breeze. This was like a movie, the kind she never thought she'd star in. A sexy romance. A dream scene on a beach with a gorgeous man. And he wanted her. Badly. *Her.* Chloe, who'd lived her whole life beneath the radar. Chloe, who'd become an international joke.

Tonight, she was a romantic heroine.

Screw it. She took a deep breath and framed his face with her hands. "Max Sullivan, I want to have sex with you, and if that rocks your celibate world, so be it."

"Jesus, now you've done it," he growled. His hands scooped beneath her, cupping her ass as he stood.

She screamed.

"Let's get this done, Chloe Turner."

"You're going to drop me!" she shouted as he turned and stepped up to the porch.

"Not a chance. If I dropped you, that might postpone the sex for a few minutes."

"I hope we're not skipping the foreplay." She squeezed her eyes shut as he eased her past the doorway.

"For you, no."

"And for you?"

"Is your goal my complete and utter humiliation?"

"Maybe."

"Then by all means, touch me anywhere you want."

Laughing, Chloe forgot her fear of being dropped. And since that fear had overridden her nervousness about the sex…now she felt nothing but giddiness and the tight hold of his hands on her ass.

He walked her all the way to the doorway of one of the bedrooms, then let her slide down his body.

"God, you're soft," he murmured. "And… happy."

That surprised a laugh out of her. "Well, I hope you're happy right now, too."

"You know what I mean."

She did know what he meant. And in that moment she knew she should tell him the truth. That her peace was an illusion. A hastily donned disguise. That she wasn't anything he thought she was.

Yes, she should tell him the truth, but she didn't want to, so Chloe nodded and pulled him down for another kiss.

I am peaceful. I am beautiful. I'm calm and confident and definitely not a Bridezilla hated by the whole world. And I am having a vacation fling with an adorable treasure hunter with control issues.

She laughed, still kissing him, and his fingers tightened on her shoulders. When he slid one hand down to curve around her waist, his touch felt rough and desperate and his breath turned to a growl in his throat.

When he pulled her shirt up, Chloe raised her arms without hesitation. A bra was no different from a bikini top, after all…except that it was made of sheer white lace and her skin had gotten nice and tan in the last few days…

Max dropped her shirt and stared down at her, suddenly still.

"What?" Chloe whispered, aware that his eyes were locked on her chest. She started to raise her arms to cover up.

"Are you on the pill?" Max asked in a low tone.

"Oh. Yes, but…I'd still expect you to…"

His eyes snapped up to meet hers. "Of course! I just like to know I'm being careful."

She smiled nervously. Then grinned. Then began to laugh. "Of course you do."

"Don't laugh." His mouth twisted into a grimace.

"I'm sorry. It's just that…you're so damn adorable."

"I think it's actually called an anxiety problem."

"Shut up," she ordered, reaching for the hem of his shirt to even the score. "You are total hotness, Max."

"Well, if you feel that way about it…" He whipped his shirt off and curved his hands around her naked waist to steer her toward the bed. Not that she needed much steering. He used his foot to slam the door and close out the rest of the world.

Her laughter was still fading, a smile still hovering on her lips, when Chloe found herself caught up in Max's arms and was overwhelmed with the feel of him. As if she'd been standing in a calm sea and was suddenly overtaken by a crashing wave.

His hands slid hot and rough over her back as he dragged his open mouth down her neck. Her belly pressed to his naked skin. He felt like the sun and smelled like it, too. Hot and clean and stunning. Her bra fell away and she gasped loudly at the feel of his skin against her nipples.

Max went to his knees as if the feeling were too much for him, as well.

"Max," she whispered, but her whisper turned to a moan when his mouth touched the underside of her breast.

"My God, you're beautiful." His breath skipped over the curve of her breast.

She could do nothing but breathe, then breathe even harder as his mouth traced a slow path upward. The tanned skin of his face made her skin look like fine white silk. The faint roughness of his chin made her shiver. Nearly dizzy with anticipation, she watched his tongue turn a careful circle around her nipple. She closed her eyes just as his lips closed and heat and suction became her whole world.

She felt everything, the push of his tongue and the sucking and the delicious sharpness when he pressed his teeth into her. She felt it all, and her hands were shaking when she buried them in his hair.

They'd only known each other a few days, and

yet it seemed that every minute, every second, since she'd seen him, Chloe had been waiting to feel his mouth on her. To feel this wildness take over her body.

As he sucked at her and skimmed his hands up her thighs to sneak beneath her skirt, her body tightened to an unbearable knot of need. He was touching the curve of her ass now, slipping beneath the fabric of her panties. His thumbs rested on her hips, but the tips of his fingers were so close to where she needed them.

Her pulse beat there, every push of blood adding pressure to her sex. This was almost painful, and Chloe suddenly understood the desperation of teenage boys who seemed willing to say anything to be touched. She'd say anything right now. Do anything.

A low whimper escaped from her throat. She curled a fist tighter into his hair.

Max kissed his way to the other breast, but more important, his hands edged toward the seam of her body.

She was going to die. Turn in upon herself until there was nothing left. The tension she'd suffered in the past month was nothing compared to this.

But he was so close…. Her breath hitched and then his fingers brushed over wetness.

"Ah," she gasped, body jerking in his hold as

his touch slid over her. Pleasure sprang from his fingertips, jagging through her body on a rough, unsteady course. She felt swollen with lust, breaking open with it.

"Christ," Max cursed. "I can't..."

His hand slipped away, and Chloe gasped in horrified alarm, but then he yanked her underwear down and stripped her bare, thank *God*.

The bed was only a foot behind her, so when he guided her back, Chloe collapsed willingly. Her back had barely touched the mattress when Max pushed her skirt up to expose her completely. Looking at her, he murmured something too low to hear, but Chloe had no time to puzzle it out, because his mouth was on her then. No time to prepare or anticipate. His tongue licked and his thumbs feathered over the sensitive flesh that she'd bared for the sake of her bikini line.

"Max," she whispered. "Oh, Jesus."

Thomas had done this, of course. Who would marry a man who didn't? But he'd never been nearly so thorough.

Max slid his tongue slowly over her, as if listening for every moan or a hitch in her breath. He flicked over her clit, chuckling when she jerked against him, then sucked at the soft skin that framed her sex before circling back to the spot that made her cry out.

"Max," she gasped. "Please."

"Foreplay, Chloe," he whispered. "Remember?"

"I changed my mind!"

"Too late." His tongue traced her again, delving inside for a moment, teasing her, not going nearly as deep as she needed.

"No, please. Just… You've been celibate and I need… Next time. Next time we'll do foreplay."

"Uh-uh." The sound vibrated into her, making her whimper. His tongue flicked against her clit, just enough pressure to torture and not enough to make her come.

"Ohgod-ohgod-ohgod," she chanted, arching her back, trying to open herself wider to him. Her hands clutched the bedspread. They should be clutching his hair, forcing him, but she couldn't relax her muscles enough to let go of the blanket.

Finally, in a small act of mercy, Max pressed a finger slowly inside her, his tongue still torturing her with small, firm licks. But the pressure of his finger was heaven on top of hell, and she moaned his name in relief.

He thrust into her once, twice, and she pushed up to meet him in a desperate attempt to get him deeper.

"Okay," he breathed. "You win. I can't wait."

He deserted her completely, and for a moment, she was lost. Sinking into deep, lonely water, close to weeping with the loss. But she heard the rustle of clothing and a faint rip of a plastic wrapper, and then his strong hands were bracing her hips and inching her farther off the end of the bed…

She curled her fists so tightly that they ached. Lights danced behind her clenched eyelids. And then the head of his cock slid against her sex until it caught snugly just inside her.

"Yes," she prayed aloud.

He pushed slowly, opening her with steady pressure. Chloe tried to breathe and couldn't. Breathing would distract her from the feeling of his wide shaft filling her up.

She didn't need to look to know that he was bigger than Thomas. Her sex squeezed against the welcome invasion.

"Christ," he breathed as his hips settled against her thighs. His fingers spread wide against her stomach as if to hold her steady.

Chloe finally drew a breath, and she opened her eyes.

He looked beautiful above her, face tight with concentration as he stared down at their joined bodies. His shoulders were impossibly wide, his arms corded with tense muscles. Then he raised his gaze to her face, and Chloe gasped. Heat lit his brown eyes so they glinted like copper. He looked wild and tender all at once.

Eyes still locked on hers, Max slid out and thrust hard into her. Oh, boy, he was definitely bigger than Thomas. For a moment, she had to fight the panicked urge to push her toes into the carpet and back away. But then his thumb slid down to brush her clit and the next thrust pushed a pleased cry from her throat.

He wasn't too big at all. He was just *perfect,* and when Chloe arched up to meet him, Max whispered curses under his breath and took her faster. He slid more easily now, as her body finally adjusted to his width, and she could tilt her hips into every thrust, every deep slide of his cock.

She closed her eyes against the brightness of the room, so that all the light gathered into heat inside her. Heat that tightened and circled around every small rub of his thumb.

Oh, God, that was good. So good. And his body was so...*inside* her. More solid than any other part of her, the force coalescing every sensation in her body into that tight center.

Toes pressed hard to the floor, Chloe rose up against his next thrust, and everything inside her squeezed tight around him until the tension set her free. She threw her head back and cried out her shocked pleasure. He grabbed her hips to hold her close against him as the climax shook through her.

Long after she'd stopped jerking against him, his fingers clutched her hips in a hard grip.

Chloe forced her unwilling eyes open to look at him. His gaze was locked on her face, the muscles of his jaw standing out in stark relief. And his hair was a mess. Tousled and slightly damp, as if he were back on the deck of a ship. But she'd done that to him. Made him mad-eyed and wild-haired.

She smiled.

His fierce expression didn't budge. "You have no idea how gorgeous you are when you come."

Though she was limp and boneless, Max lifted her toward him as if she weighed nothing. Still deep inside her, he put his arms around her and kissed her hard.

Chloe curled her legs around his hips as he began to thrust again. He came like that, kissing her, his whole body pressed to hers, their skin slick with sweat.

At that moment, Chloe had the silly and terrifying thought that she could stay wrapped around Max Sullivan forever.

CHAPTER TEN

HER HIP ROSE UP from her waist in an enticing curve, drawing Max's eye every time he tried to form a thought. Not that he was in a thought-conducive position, pressed naked against Chloe's back while she curled into his pillows like a cat. He eased his hand onto her hip and followed the contour up to her ribs. "You are so damn soft."

"I wish you'd stop saying that. You're making me feel fat."

"That's not what I mean," he said. Genevieve had been whip-thin and elegant and well-manicured at all times. Chloe was perfect, with her soft curves and fresh, natural beauty.

"Your skin is soft," he said belatedly, and that was true, too. And she smelled good. And her breasts... and her sex...

Jesus.

Maybe he was just OD'ing on femaleness. Maybe nine months of celibacy had drained his body of any resistance to their delicious charms. Or maybe it was that she was the girl next door he'd always dreamed of.

Max closed his eyes and pressed his mouth to the nape of her neck. Even as he breathed in the scent of her skin, he told himself to cut it out. This was an island fling. She wasn't going to be his girlfriend. She was way too *normal* to be his girlfriend.

But her body fit against his perfectly, melting into him as if she felt the same draw he did.

"So…" she said. "You also have a fear of out-of-wedlock pregnancy?"

The words shocked a cough from his throat. "Good God, can you imagine me with a kid?"

She wiggled onto her back to look up at him. "Aw, I think you'd be an adorably overprotective dad."

Max automatically reached for the headboard to rap it with his knuckles. "Knock on wood when you say shit like that." She laughed, but he wiped a hand over his brow. "I'd be a complete nightmare." But he felt a twist of disappointment in his gut at his own words. He liked kids. But so many bad things could happen to them, and any kid of his would be the one life he actually would be 100 percent responsible for. Max barely bit back a shiver at the thought.

Luckily, he was saved from descent into panicked thoughts by the realization that Chloe's chest was fully visible. "Have I mentioned how gorgeous you are?" He cupped one breast in his hand as a blush crept up her neck.

"Yes. You mentioned it. But I'd like to make clear that I think you're ridiculous."

"I'm not ridiculous." He softly dragged his fingers over her nipple, watching as it pebbled at his touch.

"I'm entirely average."

He noted the faint rasp to her words and smiled as he touched her. "Perhaps you don't understand just how much men like women's bodies. If you mean you have an average dress size…you're naked now, Chloe, and that means you're officially spectacular."

"Really? Is that all it takes?"

"That and your gorgeousness."

"Ha!" She shook her head again, but her smile was more than a little pleased. He pressed a lingering kiss to that grin.

"It's nice," he said. "Being honest with you."

The smile faded. "Lying to everyone can't be fun."

"Oh." Max flushed with shame and dropped to his back. "I prefer to think of it as living in a disguise."

"I'm sorry. I didn't mean—"

"It's fine."

"I just don't know how you have relationships if you never reveal that part of yourself."

He shrugged, aware of the way her hair shifted against his shoulder. "Haven't you ever kept part of yourself hidden from a boyfriend?"

Silence filled the room, and Max was thankful for it. He'd been in several long-term relationships, but he couldn't say any of them had been meaningful, not on his part. He'd spent every month with each of those women watching for a sign that he was free to leave gracefully. Luckily, with women who lived for drama, there was always an obvious ending point. Usually the point at which Max became boring and another man promised scandal and excitement.

He should feel lucky that he'd never been invested enough to have his heart broken, but instead, each breakup had left him emptier. Taking care of a woman wasn't the same thing as loving her. It was draining, and it was a lie.

"Yes," Chloe finally said. "I've hidden things from people before."

Max nodded. "Sometimes you just get caught up in it."

She inhaled so deeply that Max frowned at the ceiling. "Can you really love someone if you keep so many things hidden from them?"

He thought he'd answer no, but something in the tone of her words stopped him. Max didn't think she was talking about him now. "I don't know," he answered carefully. "I keep part of myself separate from my brother, and I obviously love him."

"Yeah," she answered hesitantly.

Max felt fear spiral inside his chest. He liked her, and even though he told himself it didn't matter, he couldn't stand the thought that she might look at him and see an awful, twisted person.

But while he was still deciding what he could say to distract her, Chloe turned toward him and slipped an arm around his chest. "You've got to find a girl who doesn't mind that you're a control freak."

"I'm not a control freak."

"You totally are. Embrace it."

"I just want people to be careful. That's all."

"Uh-huh. Also, you're a control freak."

"I'm n—"

Her hand left trails of shimmery stars against his skin when she edged it beneath the blanket and slid down his stomach. "You're a control freak," she whispered as she wrapped her hand around his half-hard dick. "Admit it."

Max frowned, meaning to deny it as he had his whole life, but she was stroking him, making a faintly sympathetic humming sound in her throat.

"Admit it."

He shook his head, concentrating on the wonderful pressure of her squeezing fingers. "I take care of people," he murmured. "They need me."

But this was a new conversation for him, and his adamance couldn't be sustained, not when Chloe straddled his thighs and continued her persuasive techniques. And she was so damn naked.

"Say it, Max. You'll feel better."

He watched her hand flex and tighten and knew she was right. Look how much better he was already feeling.

"You're right," he admitted. "I am a control freak."

"Good boy. That wasn't so hard, was it?"

No, it hadn't been that hard. On the other hand, as she scooted down and leaned over his dick, Max was pretty sure it had never been so very hard before.

"I really like being honest with you, Chloe Turner."

JENN LEANED OVER to slip her sandal off and shake out yet another rock. "I'm sorry," she murmured to Elliott as she grasped the arm he offered for balance.

Elliott looked down the long, straight stretch of road and frowned. "How about we just take off our shoes and walk on the beach instead? It would be cooler."

She was so aware of the largeness of his forearm

beneath her fingers that it took her far too long to get her sandal back on her foot. By the time she let go of him, she was babbling. "Oh, sure. The beach. And more appropriate on a date, I suppose…even though it's not really a date."

His jaw tensed just as it had when she'd said that over dinner.

"I mean…we both knew that Max and Chloe wanted time alone, so I'm really happy you brought up dinner. It was a good idea."

"Thank you." He looked away from her, eyes sliding over the watery horizon. "I had a nice time."

"So did I!" she said far too loudly. Oh, God, this was impossible, trying to pretend she wasn't having the best time of her life. If she blurted that out, Elliott would likely edge away and ditch her as soon as he had the chance. But she *was* having the time of her life. Whenever she lapsed into anxious silence, Elliott filled the space between them with quiet talk about his work and the places he'd been.

Though he'd occasionally apologize for going on, Jenn had urged him to continue. She liked his voice and his work was fascinating, even when he started talking about viruses that seemed to be made up entirely of numbers and letters.

He was so calm. So steady. He didn't flirt or charm. He didn't make comments with hidden sexual overtures. He just talked.

And he asked questions about her life, too, but Jenn did her best to steer the conversation back to him. When he talked, it soothed her. Elliott didn't seem to want anything from her but company, so her heartbeat was nearly normal during these conversations.

But right now as he stared down at his feet, a frown drawing his brows together, Jenn's heart sped. He was bored or irritated or tired.

"Should we?" she asked, a self-conscious blush heating her face.

Elliott's eyes rose.

"Walk," she stammered. "On the beach?"

"Oh, of course. Jenn, are you okay?"

She knew from the feel of her unbearably hot cheeks that she was blushing like a madwoman. The sun wasn't setting fast enough to cover up that kind of fiery-red. Damn her pale skin. "I'm fine."

"You look—"

"I just get nervous!" She hurried off the shoulder of the narrow road, her feet wobbling a bit on the rocks that marked the line between blacktop and sand.

"Jenn," Elliott said from close behind her.

She wanted to keep going, but when her sandals started filling with sand, she had to stop and kick them off. Elliott caught up and started to reach for her, then shoved his hands in his pockets instead. "I'm sorry. I didn't mean to make you nervous."

"It's not you," she said, hiding her mortification for a few seconds by picking up her sandals and shaking them clean. "It's just talk of being on a date. I get…" Helpless to explain it, she shrugged and forced herself to meet his gaze. Jenn expected to see exasperation. Instead she saw disappointment.

Elliott cleared his throat. "Right. Would you feel more comfortable staying on the road? If you don't want this to be a real date, then—"

"But it's not a real date. Is it?"

"Jenn…I asked you out. You said yes. I thought it was a date, but if this was just about giving Chloe some space, I understand."

"I thought you asked me out for Max's sake."

"Max can take care of himself. I asked you out because I wanted to. But I can imagine I'm not your type."

"You're so smart," she said in a rush, thrown off balance by his admission.

"Yeah…my work…I'm trying to find some hobbies."

She couldn't process that, because her heart was screaming *he likes you, he likes you,* and her mind was starting to panic at the thought. He was too smart, too serious, too good for her. She didn't deserve somebody like him, not with the awful truths she was hiding.

"Elliott, I…"

He smiled, a polite smile that didn't mask the sadness in his eyes when he stepped back to give her some space. "It's no big deal, Jenn, really."

The extra foot of space between them seemed to remove some pressure from her skin. Too much pressure. Yes, her anxiety ratcheted down, but that relief was offset by loneliness. She was no good at relationships, but for the past few months she'd been so profoundly alone, unable to talk to Chloe and afraid to talk to Anna.

Elliott looked like he'd been alone, too. And as anxious as dating made her, she'd had *fun* with him. She'd loved it.

And watching his face shut down into a polite smile dug out a hollow feeling inside her chest.

"I'd like to walk on the beach," she said before she could lose her nerve. "With you."

He kept his hands in his pockets, narrowing his eyes as if he were trying to discern something from her expression.

Jenn raised her chin. "You'd better take off your shoes. It won't be very romantic if you're constantly running away from the waves."

"Yeah…I'm not interested in a pity walk. But thanks."

"Elliott." She laughed, part of her anxiety falling away in the face of his discomfort. Before she could think better of it, Jenn reached out and took his hand. Nervous power zinged through her arm as she tucked her small hand into his large one. She felt his physical hesitation, but she also felt the moment when his fingers curved around hers and cradled her hand in his.

"I want to walk with you," she said again, and when Elliott smiled, her chest exploded in butterfly wings.

They stopped talking, finally, and just walked. Long minutes later, Elliott finally stopped to slip off his shoes, and when he stood again, he turned toward her as if he had something to say.

"I'm divorced."

"Oh." She hadn't been expecting that. "You were married?"

"I was. For a little over a year. But I wasn't a good husband."

The words felt like a knife. "You cheated?"

"No!" He sounded shocked that she'd even suggest it, and her hurt receded to a fading shadow. "God, no. But I work too much. I spend too much time at the office. And even at home, I think about work a lot."

"But you come home every night, right?"

"That's not enough."

No cheating. No traveling for weeks at a time. He hardly sounded like an awful husband, but she obviously had low standards. "Well, I'm sorry you went through that. It must've been hard."

"I just thought I should tell you." His words were somber, as if he were offering something important.

They resumed the walk, though Elliott was quiet this time. The loss of his voice made her feel lonely again, so she reached out to take his hand.

This time, when he stopped, Elliott didn't say a word. Instead, he kissed her.

Jenn inhaled, drawing in the taste of his kiss. His mouth was the barest pressure, only a hint of heat, giving her time to adjust. Five heartbeats passed, then six. Though he'd rested a hand on her upper arm, he didn't pull her closer or tighten his grip, not until she pushed up on her toes and kissed him back.

Her heart beat so hard that it drowned out even the cries of the gulls around them. Elliott had only been waiting for a sign, it seemed, because any sense of innocence in his touch stopped in that moment. His lips brushed hers, parting just enough that she knew he wanted to taste her. When she opened for him, his hand crept up to cradle the nape of her neck. He held her and tasted her, his tongue rubbing slowly over hers as the wind caressed her skin.

Elliott's body was just as solid as she could've imagined. He was a rock, steady and strong, holding all her weight as she sighed and tried to take him deeper. He kissed just as she'd expected, too. Serious and focused, with a sensitivity that matched the sadness in his eyes.

By the time he drew away, she could barely catch her breath.

He brushed his thumb over her cheek, sliding a strand of hair behind her ear. "I'm not the kind of guy you normally date."

She shook her head.

"But this is still a date."

"Okay," she whispered.

He slid his fingers between hers and they walked, and for a moment, Jenn thought that maybe everything would be all right.

CHLOE WATCHED MAX'S ASS as he walked toward the bar. His shorts were baggy and too worn to reveal much, but now that she knew what his butt looked like naked, she only needed the highlights to picture it perfectly. It was taut and muscular and so pale compared to the rest of his skin that the sight of it had made her laugh. Max hadn't even minded; he'd just flashed a smile over his shoulder as if he knew exactly what she found funny about his backside.

God, he was adorable.

Sighing, Chloe watched him lean against the bar with a sort of confidence most people never found. The kind of self-assurance that drew your eye. No wonder he found it so easy to control people. In that moment, she felt she'd do anything for his approval.

As she watched, Max spotted a glass too close to the edge of the bar and edged it toward the middle, his relaxed expression not budging an inch.

Her heart clenched with bittersweet desire. It didn't unclench even a smidgen when a waitress in a very short skirt approached him with a very friendly smile. He smiled back and his eyes swept down her long legs, lingering on the spike heels as he spoke. Then he used his foot to scoot an off-kilter barstool out of her path before she could trip.

In that small moment, Chloe became seriously worried about her heart. It had been broken not a month before—or maybe only bruised?—but now it was swelling with frightening tenderness. The perfect dichotomy of the man fascinated her. His beach bum looks and charming smile gave no hint of the tortured soul beneath.

The waitress brought his beer in record time, and he rewarded her with a wink that, literally, made the woman's eyelashes flutter before she made her way back behind the bar to wait for Chloe's piña colada.

My God, that man worked hard.

"Oh, my word!" a woman's voice crowed from a few feet away. Chloe barely registered it.

"I can't believe it!"

She glanced idly toward her right, then did a double take when she realized that the grandmotherly woman was staring right at her. "Pardon?"

"You're Chloe Turner! Oh, my God, my friends are never going to believe this!"

Chloe had been so removed from the circus that it took a moment for her brain to decipher the words.

She'd forgotten about the life she'd left behind. So when the awful warning behind the words finally sank in, the force of it hit her like a giant fist. "No," she managed.

"Hold on a sec. Let me get a picture for proof."

Pure panic speared down her body like lightning. "No! I'm not that person."

The woman's delighted smile hung on. "You are though, right?"

"No. My name's Jenn. Not…who did you say?"

The smile snapped to a frown as the prospect of a lost story reared its ugly head. "Chloe Turner. The Bridezilla."

Chloe shrugged, trying to keep her eye from twitching.

"The one whose fiancé crashed his plane on purpose!"

"Ooh. Right. No, that's definitely not me. I'm from Florida."

"Florida?" The woman's hand finally emerged from her purse with cell phone in grasp. "Why would someone from Florida come out to a Virginia island?"

"Oh…" Chloe's eyes rolled wildly as she tried to think of a plausible lie. Her gaze landed on Max, propped against the bar, eyes locked on a car race on the television. "You know…an illicit affair."

The woman's eyes slid toward Max and widened. "Oh!"

"Yeah." She cleared her throat and shifted with the need to jump up and sprint from the building.

"Well, you look just like her. Maybe a little thinner."

Nice. Chloe forced a smile as she shrugged and searched out the nearest exit, just in case. But as her gaze shifted, she noted that Max was no longer at his place at the bar and snapped her eyes back to where he'd been. He was halfway back to the table, beer in one hand and piña colada in the other.

Chloe jumped about a foot and spun toward the stranger. "Okay, go on now. This is a secret affair. If he thinks someone knows about it, he'll bolt. Go on!"

The woman's overplucked brown eyebrows fell to

a hard frown, but she headed back toward her table in a huff.

Chloe swung toward Max with a smile that felt as if it might shatter at any moment. "Hey!"

"Hey, yourself. What's wrong?"

"Nothing! Why? What?" She snatched the glass from his hand with a strangled giggle.

His eyes slid to the side. "Who's that woman?"

Perched on the edge of her chair, Chloe swallowed a big gulp of sweet slush. "Who?" she rasped.

"The woman who was over here. The one who's taking your *picture* right now."

Christ on a cracker. Chloe tried not to look in the woman's direction, then realized that would be a singularly strange reaction and snapped around to look.

"Her? Oh, she was asking about my hair. I guess she likes it."

The dilemma Max faced wrote itself in broad strokes across his features as his gaze flicked over her hair. Yes, her hair looked like a twiggy nest that had been ground into his pillow for a good hour. But could he say that to a woman he'd just started sleeping with? No, he could not.

He cleared his throat. "Also, you look upset."

"Nope!"

"Chloe, you're pale as a ghost."

Shit, shit, shit. They should've stayed at his cabin.

They had food and drink there, but he'd looked so boneless and relaxed that she hadn't wanted to subject him to the dangers of the old stove. She'd been the one to suggest that they skip cooking and come to the bar for a burger. What an idiotic idea.

Now she couldn't very well backtrack and ask for the steaks instead, not when he suspected that something strange was going on. "I'm just really hungry all of a sudden. Low blood sugar."

His eyes went round, as if she'd just smacked a sensitive part of his body. "Low blood sugar? Why didn't you say something?" He snatched her drink from her hand and shoved the menu at her. "Let's get you some food. They've got bowls of pretzels at the bar, I'll grab one of those, all right?"

"Sure," she answered his empty chair. Max was back and banging the bowl of pretzels on the table before she could even sneak another sip of her drink.

"What do you want to eat?"

"Guacamole burger," she answered after popping a pretzel obediently into her mouth. "Will that pair well with a piña colada, though?"

"Not funny," he muttered, then took off for the bar at a jog. This anxiety issue of his could really pay off under the right circumstances.

Still pretty damn anxious herself, Chloe stole a glance toward the evil grandmother. She was gone.

The sight of the vacant table should've capped the fear bubbling inside Chloe's chest, but somehow everything just solidified in the space behind her heart.

This wasn't good. It wasn't good at all. This was a small community. The woman would talk to a friend. The friend would call the girl she used to babysit who now just happened to work at the front desk of the resort. The room was registered under Jenn's name, but a quick Internet search would reveal that Jenn Castellan was a name that showed up in interviews about Chloe Turner. Someone would call a gossip rag for the excitement or for the $500 tip-off prize. Either way, this vacation was over. Island Chloe was going home.

CHAPTER ELEVEN

MAX STRETCHED HARD before collapsing back into the pillows. He didn't open his eyes. He couldn't. Whatever time it was, it was way too damn early. Chloe had spent the night, and between talking and making love over and over again, he was so exhausted he felt slightly beat up. In fact, his back still stung faintly with the evidence she'd left with her nails.

Hell, yeah.

That memory perked him up, and Max dared to open his eyes against the glare of sunshine pouring through the white curtains. White curtains. A complete waste of material.

At first he could see nothing but brightness. Then he registered the pillow mounded about two inches from his face. A slight shift of his head revealed the rumpled sheets next to his arm. There was no naked woman curled into them.

Damn.

A few minutes later he summoned the energy to turn his head the other way to check the time. No wonder the sun was so darn bright. It was almost eleven o'clock. He watched the second hand make a few sweeps around the face of the old-fashioned alarm clock and then he pushed up and forced his feet to the floor. He stretched until his spine popped in all the places he was starting to feel his age.

Sure, he was only thirty-five, but he'd spent a lot of those years on the sea lifting heavy tanks and being banged around by storms.

Another reason he needed to get off that damn ship. With a groan, he launched himself from the bed and grabbed a T-shirt and shorts from the floor.

Elliott glanced up from his paper, but wisely only raised an eyebrow in greeting as Max headed for the coffeepot.

"Thank God," Max muttered when he saw the steam rising from the pot. He poured a cup and collapsed into a chair at the table.

Half the cup was empty by the time Elliott folded the paper and cleared his throat. "So, you and Chloe?"

"Yeah?"

Elliott shrugged. "You seem to be hitting it off."

"I guess we are. What about you and Jenn?"

"What about us?"

Max rolled his eyes at the stiffness in his brother's voice. "You seem to like her."

"Of course I like her. She's pretty and sweet. But…she's out of my league. I'm not going to make that mistake again."

Scowling, Max raised his gaze from his coffee to his brother's face. "What the hell are you talking about?" Jenn was nothing like Elliott's ex-wife, as far as Max could tell. She was modest and had a quiet strength about her…along with a lot of nervousness.

"We went out and we had a nice time. That's it. No big deal."

"You gonna ask her out again?"

"I don't think so."

"Why?"

Elliott shook his head. "I don't want to date someone I'll have to worry about. Whether she's happy or bored or needing something better. I need someone who's not so…beautiful."

"She seems really nice."

"She is."

"So you're going to set her aside just because of how she looks?"

His glare was so hot it nearly singed Max's eyebrows. "I don't mean she's good-looking. I mean she's beautiful, and that's too much for me right now."

"All right," Max offered, holding up his hands in appeasement. "I got it. Just don't start crying."

"Jesus." Elliott coughed in a half laugh. "I'll try to hold back."

"Thanks."

"What about you? You think you can talk about Chloe without getting choked up? Because you looked pretty damn starry-eyed last night."

"Ha," he laughed, even as his thoughts turned serious.

"She doesn't seem like the kind of girl you usually date. She's a little…too normal."

"Yes." His heart turned over at the words. "She is. She totally is." Chloe. The thought of her name lodged in his chest and shook there like a crazed bird. She was normal, and she was earthy and sexy and curvy and calm.

And Max was headed back to the damn sea in a few weeks. The sea and people he'd known for years. Friends who had never seen anything past the show he put on for them. Nobody out there on the water was like Chloe.

"I'd better hit the shower," he said, just as a man's shout floated through the front windows. When he glanced over, Max's head swam with discomfort. A few seconds later, he found himself still staring blearily toward the windows. Then a second shout came, this one a different voice.

Suddenly worried about the women, Max stood at the same moment Elliott did, and they rushed for the porch together. The sight that greeted them was…strange. Alarming, yes. But not dangerous.

Two photographers stood on the sand about twenty feet away, their cameras pointed in the direction of the women's cabin. Another man held a professional video camera and panned the beach around them. All of them were weighted down with film and extra equipment. The videographer even had a steady-cam system. These people were a familiar sight to Max. *Paparazzi*.

For a moment, he thought it had something to do with Genevieve. Ridiculous, of course. He hadn't seen her in nine months. And why would she be here, anyway? But Genevieve's insane lifestyle had been his only experience with paparazzi. Luckily, he'd stood on the sidelines for most of that, just as he did now.

"What the hell?" he muttered.

Keeping an eye on the cameramen, Max stepped barefoot onto the sand and stalked toward the other cabin. The cameras began to click when his foot touched Chloe's porch. "What the *hell?*" he repeated with a little more strength as he raised a fist to pound on the door.

It didn't open, so he knocked again. The sun bounced off the closed door and stabbed into his eyes like knives.

Finally, it snapped open. "Max," Chloe said, a tension pulling her voice lower than normal.

"What's going on? Are you okay?"

"Yes," she answered, which would've been ridiculous even if her eyes hadn't been red from crying. There were photographers outside, after all.

"Chloe, there are paparazzi on the sand!"

Her eyes flickered toward them, the intensity in her gaze flat and dark. "I know."

"So what the hell is going on?"

As the clicking grew more frantic behind him, she opened the door wider and pulled him in. The door shut out the cameras with a slam. He swung to face her, holding up his palms and hoping an explanation would fall into them.

But Chloe's jaw was clenched tightly, as if she wouldn't give up the truth for anything. She looked exhausted and sad, but she didn't look shocked. She didn't look like a girl should look when confronted with her first pack of crazed photographers.

"Who are you?" he whispered.

Her gaze met his, hazel eyes unflinching as she stared him down. "You know who I am."

"I don't think I do."

"I'm Chloe Turner. That's all."

He pulled his focus from her eyes and looked at the closed curtains shutting out the sight of the beach.

"That's not all you are, clearly. Can we please not pretend that I'm an idiot? What is all this about?"

A soft scuff distracted him from his growing anger, and Max turned to see Jenn getting up from the couch. Offering him a careful nod, she walked slowly toward her bedroom and closed the door behind her.

Chloe was still standing by the front door of the cabin, as if she were frozen to the floorboards. Her face was nearly as pale as the curtains behind her.

"Maybe you should sit down," he offered, smothering his anger with concern.

She cut a hand through the air, seemingly impatient with his worry. "I didn't do anything wrong," she said. A strange starting point.

He crossed his arms and looked at the floor, because he couldn't watch a woman squirm. He couldn't stare her down and watch panic inch over her face.

"I was engaged." Her voice hitched on the last word.

Max felt his heart hitch, as well. "Engaged?"

"Yes. We'd dated for a couple of years. He asked me to marry him. Then, a month before the wedding, his prop plane crashed into the Great Dismal Swamp."

He jumped as if someone had swiped a knife over his arm. "Oh, God, Chloe. I'm so sorry. I had no idea." He was stepping toward her when her bitter laugh stopped him.

"The plane crashed, but he didn't. Thomas jumped out with a parachute, then caught a bus to a beach resort in Florida. He faked his own death to avoid marrying me."

"What? *When?*"

She bit her lip and twisted her hands together. "A month ago."

He stepped back so quickly that he almost fell over the couch.

"I know," she hurried on. "But it feels like a life-time ago. Honestly—"

"A *month* ago?"

"Yes, but…it's not as bad as it sounds."

"Really? I'm thinking it's worse than it sounds, because none of that explains the photographers out-side." Max was shocked at the fury in his own voice. He had no reason to feel such intense anger, but there was a whole host of emotions brewing inside him, and they all seemed intent on pushing anger to the top of the pile. *Engaged?*

"I…" Chloe's eyelashes fluttered and her hands hovered helplessly in the air, and the gesture stirred up that mass of emotions in Max's chest, revealing sympathy and fear.

"Chloe—"

"When Thomas was caught, he blamed me. That's

why the paparazzi are here. Because he's convinced the world that I'm the worst Bridezilla that ever walked the face of the earth."

Max shook his head in confusion.

"I'm famous for being a crazy bitch, Max. Okay? *That's* who I am."

The more she talked the less sense she made. Chloe wasn't a bitch. And she wasn't crazy.

The sound of the photographers' voices drifted past the closed windows, drawing Max's brow into a scowl.

"I'm sorry," Chloe whispered. "I know I let you think… I just liked being here with you, pretending everything was okay."

"That woman at the bar last night. She knew who you were."

She took a deep breath, and when she exhaled, her body seemed to shrink. "Everyone knows who I am, Max. Everyone who hasn't been living on a boat for the past few months."

"My brother—"

"He doesn't seem like the kind of guy who watches a lot of TV."

Max looked around the room as if there were someone else who could help him debunk this ridiculous story.

Chloe walked past him and dropped heavily onto the couch. "Jenn brought me here to escape. We were hoping it would be isolated enough to give me some peace. And it worked. For a few days."

"This is… So this is the most important thing in your life right now, and you didn't mention a word of it to me?"

She winced. "It's not who I *am*. Or I didn't think it was. For the past few weeks, I've been lost and doubting myself, and here on the island, with you—" she snuck a glance at him "—I could be who I wanted to be. You should be able to understand that."

Well, that was a fucking swipe if he'd ever heard one. "Not even close. I was trying to be myself with you. Big difference."

"You only fessed up when you were caught."

He ground his teeth together, telling himself not to yell. "That was before we had sex, Chloe. Are you seeing the distinction?"

Instead of fighting back, she looked down at her clasped hands. "I'm sorry. I know I should've told you, but I didn't want to."

Max knew his limits. If he stayed, he'd sit next to her on the couch and pull her into his arms and tell her it was all right. He'd find some way to protect her from the tiny but virulent mob outside, and try to figure out a way to make everything better.

He couldn't do it. Not again.

"I've gotta go," he said in such a rush that the words ran together into one desperate gasp.

Chloe's gaze flew to meet his, her face flashing disbelief…as if he'd slapped her. "Oh. Okay."

"I'm sorry." And he was. The muscles of his arms were twitching with the need to pull her close. Walking away didn't feel natural though, and as he turned and stepped away it felt as though he were trying to slip free of a spike impaled through his chest. It hurt. And he knew if he just stopped moving, he'd be able to breathe again.

But Max got his hand on the doorknob and turned it, and he stepped out of Chloe's cabin and left her behind. He had to.

THANK GOD FOR LEAN CUISINE. Chloe didn't have to leave the cabin, didn't have to open the door. She and Jenn were fine for the day, but they couldn't live like this for the rest of the week.

"Maybe the guys will take us fishing," Jenn said as she finished off the last of her chicken alfredo. "We could get out of here and the reporters wouldn't be able to follow."

Chloe slowly shook her head.

"Max was just shocked. He won't stay mad for long."

"He might," Chloe murmured, wallowing in self-pity. "He should be."

"Do you like him?"

She inhaled for a long time, trying to hold off tears, then let her breath out just as slowly. She set her empty Lean Cuisine tray on the coffee table and curled her feet beneath her. "You know I do."

"So give him a couple of hours and then go talk to him."

"What's the point? We're going to have to leave, and he's heading back to the ocean anyway."

"You still shouldn't leave it like this. If you talk it out, you can get in touch again after all this has blown over. Next time he comes back to the States…"

Her heart thumped pitifully at the thought. Maybe Jenn was right. Chloe's life was a disaster right now, but someday it wouldn't be. Maybe someday they could see each other again, casually. Just for a few weeks while he was home.

She didn't blame Max for being mad. She'd pulled him into a maelstrom and he'd been totally blindsided by the storm. He had every right to be furious, but he didn't seem like the type to stay that way for long. "I don't know. We'll see."

Out of the corner of her eye, she saw Jenn tilting her cell phone up to look at the screen. "What's going on?"

"Nothing!"

"I see you reading your e-mail."

"I'm not! I was just checking…something."

Chloe shifted the throw pillow higher on the arm of the couch and laid her head down on it. "Just give it to me straight, Jenn. What are they saying?"

Jenn sighed and waited a few moments, clearly hoping Chloe would change her mind. But Chloe just closed her eyes and waited.

"'Bridezilla on the Beach,'" Jenn said flatly. "'While her fiancé anxiously awaits a hearing that could result in multiple felony charges, Bridezilla Chloe Turner luxuriates at an isolated Virginia island resort—'"

"Luxuriates?" Chloe snorted.

"'—seemingly unconcerned with Thomas De-Lorn's fate or the end of her engagement. This indulgence in the face of tragedy is hardly a surprise, given the stories we've all heard about her selfish nature, but considering that she would've been on her honeymoon this week, you'd think even Chloe Turner would be in a somber mood. Meanwhile…' Is that enough?"

"No, go on."

"Why?"

"Because I want to know."

Jenn let the quiet stretch on for long seconds, and Chloe didn't know if she was resisting or just reading ahead, but she finally picked up the story. "'Police say they are carefully building a case against Mr.

DeLorn, and should have more information to reveal soon. They also say Chloe Turner has cooperated fully in the investigation, which comes as no surprise.' That's it."

"What are you leaving out?"

"Nothing!"

Chloe snuggled deeper into the pillow. Despite the way Max had worked her out the night before, she'd slept fitfully. "Liar. Spill it, Jenn."

Jenn's voice sounded more than hesitant, as if it were being dragged backward through the mud. "It says they have exclusive information about your island partying that they plan to reveal tonight."

Her eyes popped open. "Shit."

"Max would never talk about you!"

"Maybe not. But the hotel clerk will. And the bartender. And everyone else who saw us in that bar together. I'm about to be called heartless and fickle. And worse than that."

"Chloe—"

"We're going to have to leave, Jenn. If they find out about Max, they won't leave him alone. Unless they have to leave to follow me, of course."

Jenn grabbed her arm. "Maybe they won't find out about Max."

"It doesn't matter. The beach is no fun when the water is blocked by those damn buzzards."

"I'm so sorry."

When she heard the roughness of tears in Jenn's voice, Chloe reached to tug her over to lie down, too. She wrapped her arms around Jenn's delicate shoulders and sighed as Jenn settled against the couch. "Thank you so much for this vacation. It's been amazing. Mind-blowing, even."

Jenn huffed out a watery laugh.

"You were right. It was just what I needed."

"This'll be over soon," Jenn whispered. "A few days after the charges are filed, the story will get old."

"Maybe. There are rumors of a federal prosecution, too. Filing a false flight plan. Crashing the plane…"

"Still…it has to get old before then. There'll be another scandal."

"I know. It'll get old. We'll be back to normal. Except we'll all be single again. You and me and Anna. It'll be so much fun."

Jenn didn't answer, but Chloe was too lost in her own twisting thoughts to care. The problem with these damn stories about her was that there was always a grain of truth in them. Some sharp-thorned detail that hooked into her skin and stuck there. In the past, it had been the claims that she'd cared more about the wedding than the groom. At some point, she had obviously gotten too caught up in the wedding plans to notice that her fiancé was willing to do anything to get away. Then she'd been so swept up by the drama that she'd forgotten to be heartbroken over the betrayal.

And now? Now she was very worried they were right about her heartless selfishness. She'd come here to deal with her shock and grief and pain. And yet she'd found herself enjoying hot sex and interesting conversation with a man who was a virtual stranger.

My God, what was wrong with her? Where was her grief and depression and rage and self-examination?

Even now, knowing that the shit was about to hit the fan, knowing Max could be swept up in this, all she could think was that this was going to be her last night on the island, and she wanted to spend it with *him*.

She didn't care that the hearing was coming up, and that she'd learn more awful things about a man she'd supposedly loved. She didn't care that Jenn was obviously whitewashing the gossip she fed her. She didn't even care that Max was rightfully angry. She just wanted to crawl back into his bed and lose herself in the hottest chemistry she'd ever felt.

Tomorrow, Island Chloe would disappear, swallowed up by the inescapable wheels of the twenty-four-hour news cycle. Chloe didn't want to let her go without a fight.

CHAPTER TWELVE

MAX PACED AROUND THE CABIN, crowded by the four walls and hunted by the photographers outside. He edged open the curtain just in time to see the last photographer packing it up as the sky turned from twilight to dusk. Three more of them had arrived on the second ferry, and even though Max hadn't been their primary target, they'd all turned cameras on him whenever he'd opened the door. They didn't know what connection he had to Chloe, but they'd seen him go into her place.

"I knew celibacy was a good idea," he muttered to the windowpane before turning to glare at his brother. "I can't believe you didn't warn me."

"I didn't recognize her!" Elliott protested.

Oh, Elliott had confessed to knowing the whole damn jilted Bridezilla story. But he'd only overheard details in the office and had never connected a name or face to the story. Unfortunately.

"Let me see your phone again."

Elliott groaned. "Why?"

"You know why."

"You've looked at enough of those Web sites."

Max dropped into the recliner he'd pulled in front of the window and let his head fall back against the cushion. He *had* looked at enough of the sites, but his hands itched to scroll through a few more. "None of it makes any sense. She doesn't seem crazy at all."

"So maybe she's not."

"Yeah, well, the next time a woman drives you to fake your own death, I'll be sure to give her the benefit of the doubt."

"Come on," Elliott argued. "The guy is obviously a loser."

Max slumped lower in the chair. "That doesn't exactly recommend her, either, does it?"

A few heartbeats passed in silence before Elliott muttered, "You're being a dick."

He couldn't help but agree. Chloe had shoved him off his axis, and he was happily lashing out. "She lied to me."

"That's true. But you're still acting like a dick."

"Fuck off." He wasn't going to rescue her. He wasn't. Even if the need to rush in and save her was spiraling through his limbs, twisting his muscles into painful knots. Max set his jaw and rubbed hard at his thigh. "It's not my problem. I'm not going to make it my problem."

"Why would you? You're only sleeping with her."

He'd never punched his brother in the face, but

the urge nearly overwhelmed him in that moment. "You don't understand."

"I guess I don't. We're not in the real world on this island. It's a fantasy. Does Chloe know anything more about you than your job?"

Ah, there was the rub. The jagged edge scraping him raw. Chloe knew something important about him. Something no one else knew. And somehow he'd missed everything about her. He'd looked into her eyes and called her peaceful and normal and sweet, and the truth seemed to be the complete opposite of his elaborate delusion.

"What the hell do you want me to do?" he muttered. "Go over and work it all out with a few hours of therapeutic talk? This thing between us was a little vacation fun. That's all. It was going to end in a few days, anyway. And she's got way too much going on to worry about me."

"Huh," Elliott answered "Do you smell frantic justification or is that just me?"

He doesn't understand, Max told himself again. Not getting involved with someone like Chloe Turner…this was the number one mission in Max's life right now. He couldn't give up the ship, he couldn't turn his back on people who depended on him for their safety, but he could at least have some damn peace in his personal life.

Pushing open the window, Max let the humid

sea air wash over him. He breathed deeply, feeling as though he'd been locked in the cabin for weeks. What must it feel like to Chloe, who must be stalked like this in her own home?

Shit.

She had to be freaking out. Crazy or not, nobody could enjoy that.

Then again, Genevieve had loved the attention, frenzied as it was. But that didn't fit Chloe's behavior. Genevieve would've been out on the beach in a big hat and a bikini, pretending to ignore the photographers while giving them her best angle.

Shit.

Elliott made a strangled sound behind him, so Max twisted around to see him staring at his phone. "What is it?"

"The gossip sites are reporting that Chloe Turner's been living it up here on the island. There are several confirmed reports that she came here to be alone with her lover. There's a picture of you coming out of her cabin."

"You're kidding me."

"This is funny. 'A source has confirmed that the boyfriend's name is Elliott Sullivan.'"

"What?" Max sprang up from the chair, alarmed at the bitter jealousy that shot through him at hearing his brother's name. How ridiculous was that?

"I'll bet the source is someone at the hotel. My name is on the room registry."

Max paced the small living room. "I can't believe we've gotten caught up in this."

"I thought you were used to this. Genevieve was on the front page pretty often, wasn't she?"

Max waved a dismissive hand. He'd had nothing to do with that part of Genevieve's life. It hadn't touched him, even when his name had been printed next to hers. So why the hell did the gossip about Chloe feel like torture?

"You think I should go talk to her?"

Elliott snorted in answer.

"I guess talking won't hurt anything."

"Just go. If you don't, you're going to look like an asshole when I go over and ask Jenn if she wants to have a beer on the porch with me."

Well, that left him with no choice, really. Elliott wanted to see Jenn. Max wasn't going to stand in the way of that.

You're pitiful, his inner voice whispered, and Max resolutely ignored it and headed across the sand.

His heart beat like mad as he stepped up to Chloe's porch and raised his hand to knock. This was exactly the kind of behavior he meant to leave behind. This was exactly who he didn't want to be. And still, he set his knuckles hard to the wood, flinching at the crack of sound.

There was no response from within, not even a murmur of voices or a rustle of sound. "It's me," he said, then feebly added, "Max," as an afterthought, wondering if that would help or hurt. Were they not answering because it might be a journalist or because it might be him?

If Chloe didn't answer, it would be a good thing. He would walk away, guilt-free. Well, not guilt-free, really. He never walked away from anything guilt-free. But he could tell himself and Elliott that he'd done what he could. He'd made the attempt.

Just as he was sighing with relief, the scarred wooden door opened so quickly it created a breeze.

"Max," Chloe gasped, and his relief shifted to a sudden, startling pain that stabbed through his heart. Chloe. Eyes swollen and face pale, she shouldn't look beautiful, but she did. She looked...needy. All the cells in Max's body strained forward at the thought.

Christ, he was a mess.

"I wanted to see how you were doing."

She eased her head past the door frame and looked from left to right. "Are they gone?"

"They're gone."

"Are you sure? They could be using night vision."

"Yikes. You don't really think—"

"They've done it before," she snapped, and Max winced in sympathy.

"I'm sorry."

She shook her head, clearing some thought from her mind. "Did you want to come in?"

"Sure, I..." He let the words fade away. He wasn't sure why he was there or why he wanted to come in, but he did.

Luckily, Chloe didn't need an explanation. She just swung the door wide and offered him a tentative smile.

Max walked in, waving to Jenn. She finished rinsing off a dish at the sink, then wiped her hands and headed for the front door.

"Jenn, you don't need to..." He let the halfhearted offer go, both because she obviously wasn't listening and because he was thinking of his brother.

Jenn closed the door behind her, and Max and Chloe were alone.

"So..." Max tucked his hands into his pockets, took a deep breath and asked the question he'd asked so many times before. "Do you want to talk about it?"

"I USED TO BE THAT GIRL," Chloe started. "The one you thought I was. I used to be average and normal and happy. I was calm. My boyfriend was average and normal, too. I even thought he was happy." She flashed a smile at that, though her amusement was admittedly edged with anger. But her anger faded in the face of Max. He looked so sweet, filling up her couch, his ankle propped on one knee, a beer balanced carefully on the other.

Chloe took a deep breath. "He was a good, steady boyfriend. I thought he'd make a good, steady husband. Now I can look back and see that his proposal didn't make me see unicorns or anything."

"Unicorns?" He looked baffled.

"You know, hearts and stars. But I didn't care. We got along well, his mom loved me, and I could picture growing old with him. So I said yes."

"That seems…unromantic."

"In retrospect, yes. I'm an accountant. I'm careful. I'm not the freak show they've made me out to be, Max. I did everything right. And look where that got me."

"But how did this happen?"

"I have no idea. We started planning the wedding. It was a little hectic because his mother kept insisting on how everything should be done. I liked her, but she's got a spine of steel, and I think she supplemented it with Thomas's spine, because his was obviously missing. Oops. Did I say that?"

He gave her a little half smile. "I didn't hear a thing."

"I admit that I wanted the wedding to be perfect.

I wanted everyone to have a great time. Maybe I got carried away with the plans and trying to accommodate Thomas's mom, but I didn't do half the things the gossip sites say I did."

Max glanced down to his beer and the tips of his ears reddened. Clearly, he'd been exploring those Web sites today.

"Yes, I cried at the dressmaker's, but I never, ever yelled at anyone in a store. I don't do that. And my cousin is an attention-seeking brat, so you can toss out every single word she's said about me. The same goes for my freshman roommate."

"Did you really order him to have his tattoo surgically removed before the wedding?"

"Oh my God. Where did you read that? His mother was the one who hated the tattoo. Which was a tiny ankh on the inside of his wrist, by the way. Feel free to call him a pussy. Oh, jeez." Chloe slapped a hand over her mouth and muttered a muffled "Sorry."

"That's fine, but I probably shouldn't mention the little butterfly tat on my ass."

"At least that would be something different."

"For a guy, anyway."

"Seen a lot of butterfly-graced asses, have you?"

Max winked, giving a flash of his carefree-playboy persona.

"Regardless, it wasn't true. Just as it's not true that I bankrupted my parents with the wedding bills, or ordered all my bridesmaids to lose weight, or threw a sample bouquet at the florist's face."

He cocked an eyebrow. "But did you sleep with my brother? Because that's news I could use."

The question made her laugh, even if her laughter was tinged with despair. "I'm so sorry. If I thought there was any chance of dragging you into this... I was stupid. The isolation of this place lulled me into a false sense of security."

He nodded. "Was it the woman at the bar last night?"

"I assume so. She recognized me. It was her or one of her friends or one of their friends. It doesn't matter. That woman can join the long list of people who've ratted me out to the paparazzi. My cousin, my neighbor, my hairstylist, my manicurist, the woman who sold me tennis shoes last week. I guess I should just count myself lucky that my gynecologist isn't a publicity hound."

"Don't worry." He patted her hand. "I'll fill that gap."

"Oh, God," Chloe choked out on a horrified giggle. "That's terrible."

"Oh, you'll get high marks."

She slapped his thigh hard enough to make him yelp, but when she stopped laughing, the horror was still there, bouncing around inside her hollow chest. "You, um… You wouldn't talk to them, though, right?"

Max's normally friendly mouth snapped into a scowl that he aimed at his foot. Though she leaned forward a little, he didn't meet her eyes. "That's awful," he murmured.

"I'm sorry. It has nothing to do with you. But everyone seems to…not that I think you're like everyone else. I honestly don't believe you'd talk to the press, but…"

"I mean, it's awful that you have to think that way, Chloe."

"I guess," she murmured, then decided to jump right into the conversation she wanted to have. "So Jenn and I are leaving tomorrow."

"What?"

"The chaos is only going to get worse. There's no point in staying, and I don't want to drag you any deeper into it. So we're leaving."

"And then what's going to happen?"

She shrugged. "The police are still investigating, but the arraignment is coming up soon. Hopefully, as soon as the charges have been filed, interest will die down. It can't go on much longer. Another scandal will come along. I just have to hold on until all the questions have been answered."

Max's hand touched her thigh, his thumb dragging

back and forth over one small patch of skin. "What kinds of questions?"

"What were his plans? Will he get jail time? Did he have help?"

"Did he?"

"I don't know. I don't know who would've helped him. Then again, he never did anything on his own. He's a total mama's boy. He owns his own home and car and has a good job, but all of that was provided by his mother."

"So maybe he wasn't trying to escape you. Maybe he was escaping his mother."

Hope jumped inside her like an unleashed spring. Maybe it hadn't been her. Maybe she'd just been caught in the crossfire of an Oedipal war. "It's possible."

"Once he was arrested, he couldn't very well point the finger at Mommy, right? She's the one who's going to get him out of this mess."

Chloe was so shocked by the logic of his words that she rocked back in her seat. "Maybe you're right. I never thought of it that way. How did you come up with that so fast?"

"I'm removed from the situation. It's easy for me. Plus I'm something of an expert at crisis management."

"Oh. Right. You take care of people."

"I do." He smiled as if that were a comforting

thought, but Chloe felt a flash of sympathy for all the charity cases that had come before her. Sadly, she was one of them now.

But...beggars couldn't be choosers. "So I'll leave tomorrow, and there'll be an arraignment, and hopefully it will all go away. Maybe in a month or two I'll be able to get my life back together."

He nodded and wrapped his hand around hers, which made her next words easier.

"So I thought... I hoped that even though you're mad and shocked and all that... I hoped maybe you'd stay."

"Stay?"

"Tonight. Just tonight."

His fingers, still laced between hers, twitched. Good twitch or bad twitch?

"I understand if you don't want to."

"Of course I want to."

"But?"

His chest expanded on a silent draw of breath. "But nothing. I'm not going anywhere."

The words loosened some tight coil in her chest, and the relief rose up, up, up until it reached her eyes. Blinking hard, she tried not to let the tears fall. "Okay."

"Okay," he whispered, his gaze on her wet lashes.

Shit. She didn't want to cry. Didn't want to be

another project for him to fix. But in the end, he fixed her problem, too, because when he leaned in to kiss her, crying was the last thing on her mind.

CHAPTER THIRTEEN

JENN WALKED DOWN THE BEACH as fast as she could. The damp sand, packed nearly as hard as cement by the retreating tide, aided her frantic pace.

Everything was falling apart.

She pushed Chloe not to read the news about the case because it wasn't good for her. All the speculation, the vicious rumors… Chloe didn't need to see that. But lately she'd been pushing Chloe away from the Internet for purely selfish reasons: Details of the investigation were starting to come out, and some of them were uncomfortably accurate.

Jenn was getting better at lying, and she hated that. She knew when she'd need to censor the latest stories, so she hesitated over details she didn't mind revealing, just so she could offer those in place of the rumors she didn't want to tell. Rumors that someone had taken pity on the poor, beleaguered bridegroom and agreed to help him escape his wedding. Rumors that this woman had fallen in love with him. Rumors that she'd planned to run away with him.

Jenn was fighting a losing battle, but she couldn't

make her hands loosen their grip. Rumors were just rumors, and there was every chance the police wouldn't discover the truth. Thomas had good reason to keep up his little song and dance. Right now, the press had cast him as a pitiful but sympathetic figure. A hapless, henpecked, harmless chap, just wanting to steal a little joy for his sad life. But if they found out the truth about him, Thomas would be recast as a cheating coward.

Jenn would've preferred that the more truthful version come out, if only it wouldn't hurt Chloe so much. If only it wouldn't ruin ten years of friendship.

Jenn had never had a sister. She had a brother, who was just as arrogant and dismissive as their father. Her mom and dad were both still alive, but Dad had married a young Chinese woman a few years ago and lived in Beijing with his new family. And Jenn's mother... Jenn dutifully went to visit her once a month down in Raleigh, but never for more than a day. Seeing her was like visiting a defeated, pressed-down version of herself. As if she were looking into her future, after the weight of anxiety and self-defeat had squished her into something softer and smaller.

She didn't want to end up the way her mother had. Better never to marry at all than to marry someone who left you mute with the fear of saying something foolish. Something mockable and silly.

Her dad's sharp bark of laughter still made Jenn cringe each time she heard it. Her dad was a bully, and he couldn't bully his clients, so he liked to exercise his pettiness on the women of his family.

With a sigh, Jenn stopped and turned slowly back to face the way she'd come. The sand scraped against the arches of her feet and burrowed up through her toes. None of the cabins were visible from here, not even the main office. It was dark and quiet and should have felt peaceful, but the isolation painted her with loneliness. She was muffled by it, smothered beneath it.

She wanted to be taken care of, but she was desperately afraid of turning into a person who let herself be kept like a pet or a child. She needed to be strong, but she craved the luxury of turning her problems over to someone else. Someone steady. She never let herself lean on anyone.

So Jenn's secrets were her own. Her betrayals could never belong to someone else. With a deep breath, she put one foot in front of the other and started back toward the faint glow that hung in the air above the swaying shadows of the grassy dunes.

"Jenn?"

Slapping a hand to her chest, Jenn gasped so loudly that she scared herself even more.

"I'm sorry…"

She recognized Elliott's voice and the shape of his shoulders as he walked toward her from the dark, but her heart refused to calm. It beat harder against her ribs, crowding out any chance at drawing a deeper breath. "I didn't see you," she managed to say.

"I'm sorry," Elliott repeated. When she said nothing, he cleared his throat. "I, uh, saw you walk away, and… Is everything okay? Do you want to be alone?"

"Yes. I mean, yes, everything's okay. And I don't want to be alone. Or, that is, I don't mind being alone, but I'm happy to be with you, too. Or instead." She was babbling again. The words rose up, unstoppable now. "I guess you heard about Chloe's past. Though it's not really her past, or anything she did. It's someone else's past. Not hers."

"It sounds like it's been tough for her."

"It has been. It's been awful!"

"You've been a good friend, though."

A good friend. The words were too much for her. They wrapped around her throat and wouldn't let her speak, so Jenn shook her head.

"You are," Elliott insisted, because he didn't know the truth.

The truth was that she was a selfish, lying friend. Cowardly, too.

He stepped closer when she shook her head again. "I've read the articles." His hand, warm and wide and tender, cupped her jaw as she swallowed against tears. "You're loyal. And you're there. It seems like every report includes your name because you're there with her wherever she goes. That's sweet."

Well, she wasn't babbling now. Any desire to talk was canceled out by the need to keep his fingers just there beneath her chin, and his thumb, feathering along the angle of her jaw. The tightness in her throat got softer and warmer, until it felt lovely instead of strangling.

"It seems like nothing I do helps," she whispered. "It just keeps getting worse."

"I'm sorry," Elliott murmured, as if she were the one who needed sympathy. He didn't know that she didn't deserve his tenderness, but she wouldn't tell him. She needed this so much. "I'm sorry," he repeated, the words softer in her ear, even though he was leaning closer, his head dipping down toward her.

His mouth brushed hers, asking a question she was only too happy to answer. Yes, she wanted to be kissed. Yes, she needed someone to lean on, just for a moment.

Elliott was no bully, and she knew instinctively

that he would hesitate to take advantage of this moment. He'd think she was too vulnerable, too hurt—and she was. But she needed him to help her, to take over, to make her forget. Jenn opened her mouth and licked at his bottom lip, reveling in the sharpness of his next breath. But that was his only hesitation. He gathered her closer and kissed her back, letting her deeper into him, teasing her into a moan.

Jenn let everything fall away. She let herself fall into Elliott instead, and his arms held her steady and strong as she ran her hands up his back and over his shoulders. He was so much bigger than she was, so much stronger, and that knowledge burrowed deep into her belly until she was rubbing her thigh restlessly against his.

"Jenn," he whispered. When his fingers snuck beneath her shirt and touched the small of her back, she moaned in delight. It had been over two years since a man had touched her like that. Oh, there had been the occasional arm curled around her waist at a bar or the too-friendly hand stroking down her shoulder. But nothing welcome like this. When he spread his fingers and pressed his whole palm to her bare skin, Jenn knew she wanted to make love with Elliott. She wanted it more than she'd wanted anything from her two previous lovers.

Maybe it was him and his careful strength. Or

maybe it was just her loneliness, but Jenn was certain, and that certainty made her bold enough to whisper, "Yes," as she slipped her hands beneath his shirt and framed his waist. She had no idea how many minutes passed before she was flat on her back, but she did know that she'd smiled when he found the front clasp of her bra, and gasped when his hand first caressed her naked breast. Then he'd pushed her shirt up and put his mouth there, and now she was sighing quietly in the night, hoping the rushing waves covered the sound. Or maybe she didn't care about the desperate noise in her throat, because his teeth scraped her nipple as his mouth pulled at her, and Jenn felt greedy with need. Desperate.

She was going to do this, and she was going to love it. And afterward she'd brag and joke and squeal with Chloe about how great it had been. No more talking about fantasies. This time she was going to have memories of Elliott to keep her warm.

My God. This was going to be *so good*.

Clutching his hair, she tugged him back up to her mouth so he'd have to think of another way to make her moan. A way that might involve his hands traveling to impolite places that hadn't been touched in so long.

She whispered his name, as encouraging as she could be without asking for what she wanted. And she couldn't do that. She couldn't ask him to slide his fingers inside her or unbutton his jeans so she could touch him. Shaking now, she spread her knees so he could lie easily between them. That was hint enough, wasn't it? Just in case, she dug her fingers into his ass and pulled him tighter.

Elliott said nothing, but his breath came faster against her neck as he nibbled there. He propped his weight on one elbow so he could shape the curve of her waist and hip with one rough hand.

Touch me, she prayed. Touch me.

Finally, he slid his hand beneath the thin fabric of her shorts and eased them down. They were going to do it. Right here on the beach. The breeze swirled over her, setting little whirlwinds against the skin of her belly. Jenn shivered and kicked her shorts the rest of the way off as Elliott slid to her side.

"Are you cold?" His deep voice made her shiver again.

"No."

"You're shaking."

"I need you." Her face burned as the words left her mouth, but she was glad she'd said them, especially when she saw the tightness of his face in the faint light of the moon.

Time swirled around her then, a storm of seconds and minutes eaten up by his hands as he stripped her bare and touched her where she was hot and desperate. His fingers were wide enough to make her gasp and dig her nails into his shoulders. She barely registered the condom he pulled on. So when he lay between her legs and slid himself into her, Jenn cried out with the shocked joy of it.

He whispered to her as he took her slowly and carefully. He told her she was beautiful and sweet and so hot around him.

He was as intense as she'd thought he would be, and even stronger than she'd imagined. And it was too much. She came quietly, trying to hold back, but as the joy faded away, guilt rushed in to fill the little spaces in her soul. She didn't deserve this. Didn't deserve someone like Elliott.

"Jenn?" he whispered, the words hoarse with need. He was still hard in her, stretching her sex. He hadn't come yet, and she wanted him to.

Nodding, she rubbed her hands up and down his back, unable to talk.

She felt his lips touch her cheek, tentatively.

"Are you crying?"

"No." The denial lost a bit of effectiveness when it emerged as a sob. Oh, no.

"Jenn, what's wrong?"

"Nothing," she croaked, tears choking her.

His arms tightened to steel as he started to rise up, and Jenn grabbed him in a panic. "No. Don't stop. Please." But she was blubbering like an idiot, hot tears spilling down her cheeks and into her hair as he shook his head. "Please keep going. I want you to. I want…"

She sobbed as he slid out of her, leaving her just as alone as she'd been before.

"Don't cry," he kept saying as he zipped his jeans and lifted her onto his lap.

"I'm fine," she repeated again and again as she sobbed into his bare chest, humiliated and exhausted and so, so sorry.

Elliott just pressed kisses to the top of her head and stroked her back until she could finally manage to draw a deep enough breath to calm herself. But calm was hardly a blessing. Now she felt as if she were standing over them both, looking down on the horrifying thing she'd just done. Crying during sex. Like a crazy person. And here she'd been so worried about babbling during their conversations. She should have been worried about having a psychological breakdown during the best sex she'd ever had.

He shook his head. "Did I hurt you? I'm so sorry."

"No, no! It was so nice, and—"

He muttered something under his breath, but she was talking too fast to hear it.

"You were… I loved it. It's just that I've been under a lot of stress, and I'm not a good friend. I'm not sweet. Not at all! I'm a liar and I just… It's too much. I'm so sorry. Let's try again, okay? Can we?

I won't cry this time, I swear." Begging. That was bound to leave a good impression. Shameless begging was totally sexy.

But no, it didn't seem to be working. Elliott cleared his throat and his hands stilled on her back. "That's not necessary."

"I know, but—"

"Here, let me help you find your clothes. I'm sorry if you weren't..."

"I wasn't! I mean... Whatever you were going to say, I wasn't that."

"Okay. Sure." The distance in his voice was a clear desire to be far away from her at that moment. She could understand that. After all, she desperately wished she were still having an out-of-body experience. Anything to distance herself from the situation.

"You're so nice," she whispered in despair.

"Thanks." He shifted her in a way that prompted her to push to her feet, and he was free to stand and dust the sand off his pants, politely handing her the panties he'd pulled off just a few minutes before.

Maybe after the trial, Jenn would consider joining the Catholic church. You probably had to be a member to become a nun. But it would be worth it just to ensure that she'd never find herself in this situation again.

CHAPTER FOURTEEN

NOT ONE HINT OF WHITE capped the dark waves as they cut through the water toward the mainland. It was smooth and safe on the ocean today.

And not one photographer had spotted Jenn and Chloe sneaking out of their cabin that morning. Chloe felt light with relief, and Jenn should be happy, too, so why was she staring out at the water as if they were being chased by ghosts?

Chloe spared a nervous glance at the fluffy white clouds above. Was there an old mariner's rhyme about white clouds? White clouds at night, sailors' delight. White clouds at eight…sailors die a horrible death?

She jogged across the deck to lean against the rail next to Jenn. "What's wrong?"

"Nothing."

"Is it a storm? Are we in trouble?"

Her pale eyebrows drew together and she turned her glare on Chloe. "There is something seriously wrong with you. It's a gorgeous day."

"Yes, it is a gorgeous day, and we escaped the mob, so what the heck is making you so gloomy?"

Jenn's gaze slid to the side and she turned back to the water. "Nothing."

"Spill it."

"I…"

"What?"

When Jenn clenched her eyes tightly shut, Chloe thought she was trying to ignore her, but then she spoke. "I had sex with Elliott."

"Oh my God! Are you kidding me?"

"I wish I was."

"Oh. Ouch. Was it that bad?" Was it possible that one brother could be awesome in bed and the other could be a fumbling troglodyte? Yeah. Bedroom skills probably weren't passed on in the genes.

"No, it wasn't bad. It was good. Really good."

"Omigod!" Chloe squealed, grabbing Jenn's arm to jump up and down. Jenn didn't budge. "You did it! So what's wrong? Are you mad that I wanted to leave the island? I'm so sorry. You could've stayed. You can go back! Just don't get off the ferry."

"The last thing I want to do is go back. I'd rather gouge my eyes out."

Realizing there was something really wrong, Chloe gave up her grip on Jenn's arm and let her smile fall away. "Jenn?"

"It was perfect. He's so sweet. He saw me walking on the beach and came to find me, and then…"

"Then?"

"We did it. Or we started to. And in the middle of it…I started crying."

Chloe's jaw dropped. She wanted to say something supportive, something insightful, but she just found herself staring at Jenn's blushing cheek. "Er…"

"I know."

Okay, maybe it wasn't that bad. "So you got a little choked up?"

"No, I was crying. Sobbing, like I'm sure I got snot all over his chest. He had to stop what he was doing and pat me on the back like a child."

"Oh. Oh, that's…"

"Yeah."

Chloe's own throat grew tight at the image, but not with tears. Don't laugh, she ordered herself. Don't laugh.

"Just laugh already," Jenn said darkly, and Chloe burst into loud guffaws of unladylike, unhelpful laughter. Jenn didn't join her.

"I'm sorry," she gasped. "I'm really sorry. What happened?"

Jenn set her forehead against her arm so that she was staring down at her shoes instead of the water.

"God, I don't know! I, um, climaxed and then I just started crying."

Slapping a hand over her mouth, Chloe tried to control her amusement. It didn't work. "So he was still…active?"

"Yes."

"Christ, Jenn."

Groaning, Jenn shifted on her feet, her back shaking a little. A tiny sob floated up on the wind, and Chloe sobered immediately. "Sweetie? Are you laughing or crying? Jenn?"

"I'm laughing!" she cried, straightening up with a tortured smile on her face. "Why would I be crying? I save all my crying for when I'm having the hottest sex ever with a guy I really like!"

Cringing, Chloe half groaned and half laughed

"It was so bad After I stopped crying, I begged him to put it back in."

"You did *not!*"

"Okay, I didn't say it exactly like that, but I asked if we could try again, as if he were ever going to get another hard-on within twenty feet of me."

"That might be the worst story I've ever heard."

Jenn raised an eyebrow. "Really? Worse than…"

"Oh, Thomas faking his death. Touché. Worst *sex* story I've ever heard, then. But," she said as Jenn's face crumpled, "I'm sure it wasn't as bad as you think."

She nodded. "He probably thought it was cute that he gave me an orgasm and then, instead of getting his *own* orgasm, he got to comfort a hysterically crying naked girl."

"Better than a hysterically crying girl who's fully dressed."

"Yeah, I guess that's true." A deep breath expanded her slender chest. "But I never want to talk about this again, all right? Ever."

"All right."

"Thank you."

"Mmm-hmm." Chloe managed to hold her tongue for a full thirty seconds. She tried to distract herself by watching the approaching coastline as it got larger on the horizon. A heron burst from the water ahead of them, white feathers flashing like angel wings. "So… Anyway… Do big penises run in families? Because…"

The genuine laugh that burst from Jenn's mouth made Chloe grin. The strain had vanished from her voice, thank God. "I think they do." She giggled. "It was dark, but it certainly felt… I can't believe I'm talking about this!"

"Aw, welcome to the twenty-first century, sweetheart. I think it's cute that before you knew the boys, you were talking about a threesome, and now you can't even mention the word *penis* without turning bright red."

Jenn swung her hip into Chloe's, knocking her off balance. "Shut up."

Once she'd found her sea legs again, Chloe slung her arm around Jenn's shoulders and they faced the dock together. "So what's wrong? Why were you crying?"

"I don't know. I've been feeling stressed and I'm having trouble sleeping. And I hadn't been with a man in a long time. I don't know. It was all too much."

Chloe gave her shoulders a squeeze. Like Jenn, she had no idea what she was feeling.

She'd stepped onto the ferry feeling equal parts relief, dread and heartache. And still, the heartache had nothing to do with Thomas. Her heart ached for Max, a man she'd known only a few days.

They'd said their goodbyes that morning. He'd held her tight, and kissed her hard, but in the end, Max had let her go. Of course he had. He had no obligation to her and no say over what she did. It had been a quick fling, nothing more.

Yet her heart hurt around the edges every time it beat.

He'd let her go. Or she'd run away.

Still, she could've sworn she'd seen weary relief in his eyes. But how could she begrudge him that?

Given even the briefest opportunity, Chloe would happily wave goodbye to the mess of her life. Heck, she was relieved just to get away from the photographers on the island for a few hours. They'd be back soon enough.

Maybe sooner than she'd expected. As the ferry drew closer to the dock, Jenn stiffened beside her at the exact moment that Chloe spotted the four men standing on the dock sporting cameras and bored expressions. "Oh, shit."

"The guys on the island must have put out the word you'd gotten away."

"Damn it." Her throat burned with hot tears of frustration and fear.

"Come stay with me," Jenn urged, glaring toward the men as they perked up and walked farther out onto the dock.

"No, they'll just follow me there and ruin your life, too."

"I don't care."

The ferry engine roared as it slowed, easing up against the bumpers. "Come on," Chloe said softly. "Let's get this over with."

Walking through a crowd of paparazzi—and Chloe would argue that even four photographers was a crowd—was a strange experience. She'd been raised in Virginia, where men opened doors for you and carried your bags, even if you told them you didn't need help. But the paparazzi were like a scrum of hungry animals. They didn't want to ease her way. They didn't want to step aside or open doors or take her bags. They wanted to hold her back so they could get a few more pictures. They wanted to block doors so she couldn't escape. And if they pushed her into losing her temper, all the better.

Cruel bastards.

Chloe carried her bags and kept her head down as she stepped off the ramp.

"Chloe!" they shouted, their voices climbing over one another, trying to get her attention. "Chloe, over here!"

She pushed on, ignoring the jostling of their bodies against hers. Her skin crawled with the need to run, to flee the danger of men crowding around her, shouting, bumping into her. It was worse at the DA's office, when there were dozens of them. It was suffocation and horror. But this was enough.

"Chloe! Chloe! Tell us about your new boyfriend!"

"Chloe, does Mr. Sullivan know what you are?"

She frowned at her feet and pushed on.

"How long have you been sleeping with him? Did you know him before the plane crash?"

"Is it true that you hate your cousin?"

"Chloe, why wouldn't you let her be in the wedding?"

She was almost to the car. Almost there. During the occasional silence between camera clicks, she could hear the wheels of Jenn's rolling bag just behind her.

"Chloe, who's Thomas's other woman?"

What? She almost paused. Almost stopped and turned around, but she managed to override that impulse and rush the last few yards to Jenn's car.

The sharp clang of car keys hitting the ground made her groan, but then she heard Jenn scoop them up and the car beeped a friendly welcome. Chloe reached for the trunk Jenn had popped open, threw her bags inside and leaped into the passenger's seat just as another question hit her ears. "Is it true that he was cheating? Were you both cheating?"

Jenn slammed her door and started the car with what would've been a roar if not for the tiny four-cylinder engine.

"What was that about?" Chloe asked.

Her friend shrugged.

"Are there rumors that Thomas was cheating?"

"You know the cops are trying to figure out if someone helped him pull it off. That's all."

"Yeah…"

"It's that same old story. They assume there must have been a woman."

"Maybe there was." It made sense. Max had theorized that Thomas wasn't running away from Chloe, he was running from his mother. But maybe he was running *to* someone instead. Her heart beat harder. "You know what? I think they're right. I think he was cheating."

"You can't listen to them. Think of all the ridiculous things they've said about you."

"But it doesn't make sense otherwise. I wasn't really that bad. I wasn't! So if he wasn't running *from* me, he must've been running *to* something. Someone."

Jenn's hands clutched the steering wheel so tightly that her knuckles showed like bones with no skin drawn over them.

"Is this what you didn't want to tell me?"

Jenn's head jerked up half an inch, but she didn't look at Chloe. "What?"

"That there are rumors he was cheating?"

"These people will say anything, print anything!"

Chloe crossed her arms and slipped down in her seat to spoil any photographs the paparazzi would try to take from behind. "It feels right, though. I wonder how long he was cheating. That fucking asshole."

"Chloe, don't. The simplest explanation is usually the truth, right? Thomas spent his whole life under his mother's thumb. He started dating you because he liked you, but then I think he took you to meet his mother and it exploded in his face. You said you were the first girlfriend of his that she ever liked, right?"

"Yeah."

"Well, he was stuck then, wasn't he? She liked you. She wanted him to marry you. Hell, I'll bet she even helped him pick out the ring."

Chloe squirmed. "She may have mentioned something about that."

"Thomas got swept up. Maybe he kind of wanted to marry you, but he felt like he was being pushed along by an unstoppable force."

That hurt a little, but hadn't she felt that herself? Not so much because of his mother, though her enthusiastic approval of the match had been a kind of pressure. Mostly Chloe had felt swept along by her own plans for life. She'd wanted to get married and have kids. She'd wanted to get away from her cramped, quiet apartment and move into a nice house with a nice man. Thomas had seemed good enough. So she'd moved in with him, and then it had been time to get married, hadn't it?

Jesus. She'd thought he was *good enough*. What kind of love was that?

"Thomas panicked," Jenn said. "He freaked out and did something stupid."

"How could I have been so blind? It couldn't have been spur of the moment. It took some planning. Our life was a lie. Did I ever know anything about him? Was he even a decent guy?"

Jenn sighed, her shoulders slumping a bit. "He was funny. And thoughtful. He wasn't a monster and you weren't blind."

"I was a little blind."

"Okay, a little. But he didn't kill anyone."

"Wow," Chloe huffed. "Your standards for my love life are pretty low, Jenn."

"I just mean… He was desperate to get away, but all the flight experts agree that he deliberately crashed the plane into a completely unpopulated area. He didn't want to hurt anyone. Not even you, really. He just wanted to disappear."

Chloe nodded. There were holes in that theory, but it felt true. He'd thought he was sparing her some sort of shame. Boy, had that backfired.

Jenn flashed an anxious look in the rearview mirror. No doubt they were leading a caravan down the narrow road that led out of the swampy coast and into the heart of Virginia Beach.

Chloe watched a beautiful old mansion slide by her window. Dark brown waterways cut the estate into a green island of manicured lawn. A sign ahead said "No Fishing from the Bridge," but three men stood next to it, poles cutting lazy lines through the air.

"It's weird. When Mrs. DeLorn called and left messages, I thought she was going to apologize for her son. I thought she and I were close. I mean, if what we're saying is true, she may have been the whole reason for the marriage in the first place.

"At first I expected her to try to patch things up, try to explain, maybe even try to get us back together. But she was calling to remind me of all the times she'd helped Thomas financially. I didn't know what she was talking about. What the hell does that have to do with anything?"

"That is weird. Maybe she feels guilty and she had no idea what to say."

"Oh, Jesus, it doesn't matter. Whatever the hell is going on, he was right. We shouldn't have been getting married."

In her peripheral vision, she saw the flash of Jenn's blond hair as Jenn snapped her head around to look at Chloe. "You think that's true?"

"Yeah. Look at me. I don't even miss him, do I? I miss the house, and I miss my old, normal life. But I just had a fling with a big, hot treasure hunter, and damned if I didn't love it."

"Well, sure, but—"

"If I'd really loved Thomas, wouldn't I be a little more devastated?"

"You're still in shock."

"I don't feel like I'm in shock. I feel like I'm

alive." Her cell phone rang, cutting through her introspective mood. Chloe dug it out of her purse and looked at the display. "Reporter. Shit, I guess I've got more than one bar again." A push of a button silenced the ringer, and she flipped idly through the missed calls. There were a lot of them. "Anna called last week."

Jenn coughed loudly, then patted herself on the chest to clear her throat. "She was probably calling to check on you."

"I'll call her soon. Let's do something fun when this is over. We'll all go out to dinner and flirt with guys."

"Oh, yeah. But I don't know. She's been so busy..."

"Then we'll go to D.C. and stay at her hotel! She offered to get us a day at the spa one time, right? Let's plan it. I'll call her and set it up for two weeks from now. It'll be just what we all need."

"No! I mean... I'll call her. Don't worry about it."

"I'm not going to let you pay for anything else."

"Okay, I'll just... Damn it, Chloe. You've got enough on your hands. Don't call Anna. I'll talk to her, all right?"

Chloe looked over at Jenn's white knuckles and nodded. "Okay, okay. Calm down. You're such a mother hen sometimes."

Jenn's laugh held as much tension as her hands, so Chloe dropped the subject and huddled down in her seat. It was going to be a long drive.

THE AFTERNOON FISHING TRIP had been a complete disaster. Oh, he and Elliott had caught lots of fish. Apparently, depressed silence was an excellent tool in luring fish close to a boat. And the weather had been great. Sunny and still. Perfect for women who liked to lounge in the sun in bikinis.

Max looked up as Elliott walked out of his room, toweling off his wet hair. No bikinis here, just a couple of moping, pitiful men.

"You think I should've gone with her," Max grumbled.

"What?" Elliott asked, slinging the towel over the shoulder of his gray T-shirt, about as depressing a color as you could wear.

"You think I should've tried to help instead of letting her go."

"Who, Chloe?"

"Yes, Chloe!"

Elliott shrugged and fell onto the couch, propping his feet up on the arm as he lay down. "I have no idea."

"So why are you avoiding me?"

"I'm not avoiding you. We've been on a boat together all day."

Max stalked to the fridge and popped the top off a Corona. "You know what I mean. What the fuck's wrong with you if you aren't pissed at me?"

Silence.

He glared at the back of the couch. "Elliott."

"I don't want to talk about it."

Standing a little straighter, Max narrowed his eyes at the brown tweed. "Wait a minute, does this have something to do with Jenn?"

"Crap," his brother muttered.

Max settled into a chair at the kitchen table, the weight of his guilt easing off a bit as he turned his mind to something else. "What happened? A fight?"

"No. No fight. Kind of the opposite."

"Oh? Oh! I see. What the hell are you so depressed about then?"

"I told you I don't want to talk about it."

Since his brother couldn't see him, Max didn't bother hiding his sudden grin. "Don't worry, man. I hear it happens to every guy at some point."

"Fuck off. That was definitely not the problem. Again, just the opposite."

Well, that was interesting, if a bit disturbing. "Did you take a Viagra or something?" A mud-colored pillow came sailing over the couch and hit Max square in the face. "Good aim. Now what happened?"

"Jesus Christ." Elliott's dark voice indicated he wasn't going to tell the story, but then the words came, as rough as if they were being forcibly dragged from his throat. "Everything was going great until she started crying."

He set the beer down with a clunk. "Crying?"

"Yes. Sobbing."

"Er. Some women do that when they come. Did she come?"

Elliott gave a muffled-sounding growl. Max could hear the scraping sound of hands rubbing over an unshaven jaw. "I don't know. She was pretty quiet about it all. Then she said it was 'nice.'"

"Oh. I see." He cringed in sympathetic embarrassment. "So…"

"Yeah. *So.*"

"Well, welcome to my world of dating crazy women. How do you like it? Pretty interesting, huh?"

"I don't think this is the kind of crazy you normally date."

"Oh, you're wrong about that. You think none of my girlfriends have ever cried during sex? Instability isn't always the best bed partner. Speaking of which… On the off chance that Jenn is off her rocker, did you use protection?"

Elliott's feet disappeared and he sat up to glare at Max. "You're kidding, right?"

"Why?" Max's blood pressure leaped to a frantic

pace at the thought that his brother had done something stupid. "You didn't?"

"You started stuffing condoms into my wallet the day I turned fourteen."

He cleared his throat, worried that Elliott was finally going to figure out that Max had a little problem with anxiety.

"Every single time you put a rubber in there, I took it out and threw it away, and the next morning, there'd be a new one. Then you started buying me a fresh box of condoms every month. Remember? Apparently, you thought I was using them all."

"Er…"

"I was too damn embarrassed to tell you that your expectations were a little premature. I wasn't quite the ladies' man you were. But you did start a good habit for me. I never leave home without one, so I guess I should thank you for that psychosis."

Max inhaled, the air cool and delicious when combined with the relief rising up in his chest. Elliott thought Max's motivation had been sexual precociousness. "Good," he said with a forcibly arrogant smile. "Glad to know I passed something useful on to my little brother."

Elliott lay back down without a word.

"So. Do you think I should've tried to help Chloe out?"

"What, exactly, could you do for her?"

Well, that was a stupid question. He could be there to stop her from doing something foolish. Anything foolish. Like getting engaged to a mama's boy who was too much of a pussy to break up with his fiancée in a normal way. Okay, the danger may have already passed on that one, but she clearly wasn't a genius at making life decisions. "I don't know. Anything."

"I think you should get back to being your normal self. Worrying doesn't suit you. You're not even being logical about it. I don't know why Chloe's got you so tied up in knots, but she's gone now. Let it go."

"I could say the same thing to you," Max snapped.

"When the hell was I ever carefree?" his brother shot back, and then they were at an impasse, because Max refused to reveal the truth.

I've never been carefree, either.

In the end, talking to Elliot was only making him feel worse. He hunched over his beer, miserable.

Still, he couldn't help sneaking a few looks toward his bedroom as he finished his beer. He'd given Chloe his number before she'd left. Working on the ship, he wasn't in the habit of keeping his phone close by. Satellite phones weren't exactly cheap, so he had to keep it clear of the water. But now he was wondering where a guy could get one of those dorky phone clips to keep it on his person at all times. He wandered casually into his bedroom to pick it up.

The voice-mail icon on the display may as well have been made of pure, uncontained electricity, because it sent a painful shock through his body. Had something happened? Did she need him? Shit, he should never have let her sail away without him.

He fumbled with the buttons, briefly forgetting his password even though it was his birth date.

Finally, he pressed the phone to his ear and held his breath…then let it out on a great rush of disappointment when he heard his captain's voice.

"Hey, Max!" he said in his thick Greek accent. "Listen, you know how much I respect you, and I know how you feel about Randy Martin."

"Aw, shit," Max muttered.

"I don't know what went down between you two, and I don't need to know. You wanted him off the ship and so he went. But he called me up. Wants to come back. He promises not to cause trouble this time, and he's a great diver, Max. One of the best young guys out there right now. Think about it, okay?"

"Shit," he said more loudly. The message clicked off.

"Everything all right?" Elliott called.

"Yeah, yeah." Randy Martin, that fucking bastard. He'd shown up for the new season two years before, a hot-shot young diver with a huge chip on his shoulder. He hadn't had any use for a safety-conscious dive supervisor and he'd made that clear. But Max's word was law on that ship; he could even override the captain when they were at a dive site. Randy had tested Max one too many times, staying down for forty minutes on a strict thirty-minute dive. He'd smirked at Max when he'd finally emerged from the water. The same smirk he offered every time he put a foot over the line. After two weeks, they'd stopped to restock in Tangier, and Randy had found himself waving goodbye to his new friends.

But the entire crew, the captain included, had bought into Max's subtle hints that it had been more than his recklessness that had triggered Max's temper. There may not have been a fight over a girl during that first night onshore, but no one needed to know that except Max.

And now Randy wanted back onboard. What a prick.

Max's first instinct was to call the captain back with a drop-dead refusal. He'd never even come close to losing a diver on a job and he wasn't going to let this bastard ruin his reputation. Or his sanity. Even if he hated the guy, Max wouldn't be able to live with that on his conscience. That was the entirety of his job: keeping people alive while they did something immeasurably dangerous.

And how in the hell had he ended up with the worst job in the whole damn world? He supervised a dozen people who threw themselves into harm's way every damn day. People who whined and argued when he set time limits based on visibility and dive depth. People who refused to rest when he ordered a day off. People who thanked him for keeping them safe, even as they cursed him for treating them like children.

He couldn't count the number of times he'd had to bite back a shout of "I won't treat you like a child if you stop acting like one!" That didn't fit with his image, after all, so Max had perfected peaceful smiles and friendly winks. And really, they weren't all bad. Most divers were educated and well aware of the dangers and respected his efforts. But there was one on every goddamn trip. And none had been as bad as Randy.

Max pulled up the captain's number, pretending for a moment that he was calling to quit. He didn't need a job. He'd received a full share of the profits made on every single dive for the past twelve years, and it wasn't easy to spend money when you spent three-quarters of your life at sea.

So he could quit. But he wouldn't. After a dozen years of being tempted by this very thing, he knew he wasn't going to walk away. These people's lives were in his hands.

"Sullivan?" the captain's deep voice said over the tinny line.

"Hey, Cap. How's Greece?"

"Lovely. I'd invite you to come for the rest of the month, but I have my daughters to think of. They are beautiful, and you are not the marrying kind."

Max smiled. "No, I'm not."

"Dare I ask if you're using your time off wisely?"

"Now, that would be a ridiculous question, wouldn't it?"

"Ha. You're just like I was in my youth. You'll settle down someday."

Yeah, Max was a real party animal.

"So," the captain said tentatively, "you got my message about Randy? Think you can set aside your differences for a few months?"

"I don't think so, Cap."

"Perhaps if you just avoid him in port? There are plenty of women to go around."

Max considered a few lines. Some harmless falsehoods that would cover the truth. But then he thought of how free he'd felt speaking the truth to Chloe. The captain didn't need to be manipulated in this case. Max didn't have to smile and lie. He took a deep breath. "He's reckless and he disobeyed my direct orders on several occasions. He's a danger to himself and everyone on the team. I won't work with him again."

Silence hissed through the phone.

"Captain?"

"I've never heard you speak a cross word about anyone, Sullivan. Consider him banned from the ship."

His shoulders slumped in relief. "Good. Thank you."

"Is everything all right, Max? You sound a bit grim."

"I'm good," he lied, purposefully adding some reckless good humor to his tone. "Just overdoing it, I'm sure."

"Okay, then. I'll see you in a few weeks. Let's see if we can get that site finished up. My researchers have turned up some great leads on that Macedonian wreck I was telling you about."

Max hung up and leaned against the wall, letting his eyes close and his head fall back. Maybe this island trip hadn't been a complete disaster. If he could learn to throw a little truth around with his bullshit, maybe his life would be easier. But the idea didn't stop the hot pressure that settled on his chest when he thought of returning to the ship. He didn't want to go back. He never did. But he'd known some of those divers for more than ten years and their lives were his responsibility. How was he ever supposed to set himself free of that?

In the end, it would probably make no difference. He picked up lead weights of responsibility everywhere he went, even when he made every effort to keep a distance.

Chloe Turner was just one stop in a long line of trouble, and Max could see the endless string of his life stretching on forever, punctuated in even intervals by anchors. He wouldn't be able to move past this one without adding it to his load.

Damn.

Pushing off the wall, he walked to the doorway to find Elliott still sprawled out on the couch, his forearm covering his eyes.

Max set his shoulders. Going after Chloe would be a huge mistake, the kind he'd determined not to keep making in his life. He couldn't keep picking up burdens, but the problem was he'd already walked right up to hers. Now it was sitting in his path, blocking his way at every turn.

Max raised his chin and pasted a smile on his face. "Hey, Elliott, what do you say we go get drunk?"

"I say yes."

"Then let's get to it."

CHAPTER FIFTEEN

TWO NIGHTS LATER, Max couldn't deny that they'd successfully carried out their plan for drunkenness. In fact, he'd been nursing a hangover for twenty-four hours straight, but he couldn't talk himself out of bellying up to the bar again, regardless. So here they sat, morose and silent and staring at the largest television in the bar.

The place was packed now, loud with the chatter of locals excited about their brush with fame. Max and Elliott had managed to maintain their anonymity for the most part, but occasionally, someone put two and two together, and figured one of these guys from the resort must be the man sleeping with the infamous Bridezilla.

Like tonight's bartender, for example. "So," he said with a suspiciously casual air. "Which one of you is Elliott?"

Max and Elliott exchanged a glance of tired impatience. "Who wants to know?" Max asked.

"Just curious," the guy said.

"Right."

"That Chloe girl…I heard she's totally nuts. Is that true?"

Max picked up his glass of Scotch and knocked back the contents like a college guy doing shots.

The bartender leaned closer. "I've heard those psycho girls are real awesome in the sack. If—"

Max dropped the tumbler to the bar and grabbed the front of the guy's shirt. "Shut. The. Fuck. Up."

Too late, he registered the flash of a camera out of the corner of his eye. He whipped his head around and found a smug-faced man lowering a very expensive-looking camera. The entire herd of paparazzi had followed Chloe back to Richmond, but apparently this guy had wised up and come back to the island to follow up on the "Bridezilla's lover" angle.

Max shoved the bartender back with a muttered warning, then tacked on an order for another Scotch. But fuck if he was going to leave a tip. Resolutely ignoring the reporter, he tipped his face back up to watch the coverage of Chloe. It was the same video that had been playing all day. First, her holding up a hand as she got into the passenger seat of a car and sped away from the docking area of the ferry. Then a shot of the back of that car, driven by Jenn. Then pictures of her ex-fiancé heading into a courthouse. Charges Expected To Be Filed Against Runaway Groom On Monday, the crawl said.

Fascinated and furious at the same time, Max squinted at the shaky video of the guy. He looked…normal, Max supposed. Objectively decent-looking. But surely the thin line of his mouth hinted at smarminess. Surely his jaw was a little weak. And Max knew full well that the guy's healthy tan was a result of the week he'd spent on the beach in hiding, but it was unseemly for him to look like he'd just gotten back from vacation.

"Dickhead," Max bit out as he grabbed the new glass of Scotch and made himself sip slowly.

The last video clip was a new one. Chloe, head down, the hood of a sweatshirt pulled over her hair, walked through a parking lot somewhere. Something caught her attention and she glanced toward the camera for a split second. Max's heart lurched, throwing itself against his ribs. Her sweet hazel eyes didn't look warm anymore. They were sad and… wild. As if she were about to curl into a ball and scream.

Pulse thumping hard through his entire body, Max stared at the television long after the anchor had moved on to another story, as if Chloe were trapped in that rectangle on the wall.

"She looks okay," Elliott said, the tone more a question than a statement.

"No, she doesn't."

His brother cleared his throat. "I guess. Whatever

these bastards are saying, she didn't seem crazy to me."

She hadn't seemed crazy to Max, either, not until the paparazzi had shown up. Guilt gnawed at him like a Rottweiler with a bone.

Max nudged him with his elbow. "Ready to go?"

He was probably asking about tonight, about the bar, but Max's muscles tightened with the need to leave, to get to Chloe and protect her from the hordes of paparazzi.

He knew it was ridiculous to want to save her. What the hell was he supposed to do? Magically make it all disappear? The hearing was coming up on Monday, for God's sake.

He couldn't do it. Getting involved with Chloe was exactly the kind of entanglement he could no longer handle.

Celibacy. He should've stuck with the celibacy.

"Yeah," he finally answered, pushing up from the bar stool.

"You must be Elliott," a man said from behind him. Max swung around to find the photographer holding out a hand.

"What the fuck do you want?"

"I just wanted to introduce myself. I'm Chaz Sorenson."

"Chaz, huh?" Max sneered. "Well, have a nice night, Chaz."

"I wondered if you'd be interested in answering a few questions."

"No." He pushed past him and followed Elliott toward the door.

"Did you know she was engaged when you slept with her?"

"She's not engaged."

"So you did sleep with her?"

Max's feet froze to the ground as his hands folded into fists. The faint white light above the door turned a hazy red in his vision.

"Sullivan," his brother said carefully. "Nobody needs that kind of trouble."

True. Breaking this guy's nose would do nothing to help Chloe, and it probably wouldn't be great for Max, either. Plus there was always the danger that the guy would fall over and crack his head open on a table. Not worth the risk of manslaughter charges. Max managed to move one foot closer to the door, and then the other.

"Let me give you my card," the guy was saying, but Elliott opened the door and Max forced himself to walk through it.

When he glanced back at the closing door, Max caught another glimpse of Chloe's face glowing from one of the television sets. Another channel. Another gossip reporter with a gleeful smile. He stepped out of the bar and rolled his shoulders, trying to pull in a tight breath of salty air. Not that salty air ever did anything good for his nerves. "You sure you don't mind your name mixed up in all this?"

Elliott huffed a laugh. "Nah. It'll do wonders for my reputation. And they don't deserve the truth."

Once they were a dozen feet out on the sand, Max looked back at the bar. For once, the parking lot was full of cars. "Listen. How would you feel about ditching this place tomorrow?"

"Sure. I've got all the boating skills down now, thanks to you. Let's get the hell out of Dodge. It's lost its charm anyway."

"By charm, I assume you mean Jenn?"

"Whatever." Elliott threw a glance in Max's direction. "Are you coming back to my place in D.C.?"

It suddenly felt like the inside of Max's skull was lined with sandpaper. His brain hurt. He couldn't think. Chloe's wild eyes kept interfering with his vision. Monday was going to be an awful day for her, especially if the rumors about her ex-fiancé were true.

Max steeled himself. It wasn't his concern. He wasn't responsible for Chloe. She'd told him so herself. She had her family. She had Jenn.

Don't. Do. It.

But if she had her friends and family, that meant

she didn't really *need* Max. That meant he could offer moral support the way any normal person would do. She didn't need rescuing, she just needed a friend. The justification proved irresistible.

Max tried to lock his jaw, but the words pushed themselves out like gleeful ghosts. "You know what? Why don't you drop me in Richmond."

He couldn't help but think that anxiety had a way of making everything sound like a bad omen. Surely this would turn out fine.

CHAPTER SIXTEEN

CHLOE'S APARTMENT WAS STIFLING. Sweat tickled her hairline and made her scalp itch. She tossed an evil glare toward the window air conditioner. Oh, it was pretending to do a good job, blasting cool air out in gales, but the room stayed thick with heat. Or was it just her?

Pacing, she swiped a shaky hand over her forehead. She couldn't breathe. The air pressed in on her, squeezing her throat like two strong hands. "Oh, God."

She tried to make herself breathe, but there was something wrong. She needed to get out of her tiny place. Rushing for the window, she edged up one blind and pressed her nose close to the pane, hoping some miracle had scattered the group of paparazzi like a flock of startled birds. But no, they were still there. If only an unwed actress would get knocked up. If only some starlet would lock herself in her house and start smashing windows. Then they'd all go away, lured by bloodier meat.

Her heart twisted and pounded in her chest.

"It's a panic attack," she told herself. "You're not dying." It had only happened once before, and it hadn't been so bad. She'd hyperventilated until she'd passed out, and then everything had been fine when she'd finally woken up.

Chloe sprinted to the door and opened it, ducking down as soon as she did. The cameras could see her from one little corner, but the solid wood railing protected her if she crouched down. Chloe edged out and sat down on the first step. The sun made it hotter here, but there was a breeze and her throat opened enough to calm her down.

She'd managed to get through this month with anger and denial, but both of those emotions were starting to peel away. There was something worse ahead; she could feel it coming like a bad storm. And since she'd lived with the fake death of her fiancé, followed by his brutally public betrayal, something worse had to be pretty bad. And Chloe was very, very afraid it had something to do with Jenn.

Her best friend's behavior had grown increasingly erratic since they'd left the island. Jenn had become more than stressed...she'd become furtive. Secretive. Jumpy.

Chloe slipped her cell phone out of her pocket. It had quieted down since she'd started blocking all the unfamiliar numbers that popped up. Jenn had stopped calling, too. She'd only sent a few text messages about how slammed she was at work. Chloe had called her twice, but Jenn hadn't called her back.

Even as she told herself to let it go, she pressed in the first few numbers of Anna's cell. A pause and a few deep breaths later, she hit the last number and held her breath. If Chloe didn't know what was going on with Jenn, maybe Anna did.

"Chloe!" Anna's voice sounded low and rushed.

"Hey, what's wrong?"

"Nothing. I've been trying to call you for a couple of days."

"Really?" She pressed the phone closer to her ear as if it could solve the mystery. "I didn't notice any recent calls from you. Were you using your cell phone?"

"Yes! Listen, I…" A murmur of distant voices floated in the background and Anna's words got softer. "This isn't a good time. Can I call you back?"

"Yeah, I just wanted to catch up. And I wanted to know if you think—"

"I've got to go!"

Anna hung up without saying goodbye, but not before a man's unfriendly voice came through loud and clear. "All right, Ms. Fenton," he said, just before the sound of a heavy door clapping shut was cut off by the line going dead.

It probably had something to do with work. Of course it did. So why did that voice send shivery fingers of dread down Chloe's spine?

All right, Ms. Fenton. Chloe stared at the dead face of the phone. Hadn't she heard that voice just a week before? *You're free to go, Ms. Turner.*

The man's name was Detective Jackson. He was the lead investigator in the case against Thomas. He'd questioned all of them. Chloe and Jenn and even Chloe's mom and dad.

Why was Anna there now? She must know something. Something about Thomas or Chloe. Or Jenn. What could she possibly know?

Chloe knew the answer was just below the surface, waiting to be teased out, but she kept her fingers tightly curled. She'd find out on Monday. Monday would be soon enough.

Monday would be the day her life would start over. Or at least that was what she kept telling herself at night when she couldn't sleep.

When her stomach growled, Chloe realized that the panic had passed for the moment. She could sneak back into her house and stick a frozen meal in the microwave and get a little work done.

Her boss was letting her work from home for a while, mostly because he'd been supremely irritated by the photographers outside the front door of the office. After this all died down, Chloe was pretty sure she'd be let go. Her work had gotten sloppy. Her boss was an old-school, no-nonsense accountant. He didn't find this little media frenzy at all exciting.

Chloe crawled back through her door and slammed it behind her. For one heartbeat, she thought she'd broken the pane of glass in the door, but the sharp, musical sound went on too long and she realized that her phone was ringing. It was the landline, which hadn't been tracked down by the press yet, because it was under her landlady's name. Only a few people had that number...

She raced for the receiver and answered with a breathless hello.

"May I please speak with Chloe?"

Max's phone voice was a little different from his regular voice, softened with a touch more Virginia twang.

"It's me. Hi, Max."

"Hey, there, Chloe. How are you doing?"

"Great," she answered, only a little irony peeking through.

"I don't want to be weird..."

"Okay." A smile tugging at her face, she raised a curious eyebrow.

"I was worried about you."

"That's okay, too."

"So I thought I'd come by and see how you're doing. But maybe this is a bad time?"

A bad time? Her pulse surged into overdrive, heart beating so hard it should've hurt. But it didn't hurt at all. "Right now?"

"I just checked into a hotel downtown. Is that near you?"

"It's not far. But it's hard for me to get away before dark. The, uh, cameras…" Wow, could she be a worse date?

"Would it be better if I came over there?"

She glanced at the clock. It was only three, and she didn't want to wait, but she had more worries than the paparazzi. Her place was a mess and her legs needed shaving in a very bad way. Bouncing on her toes with anticipation, Chloe squeezed her eyes shut and shook her head. He wanted normal, and she'd do her best to give it to him. She wasn't a panic-attacked sideshow freak. She was cool as a cucumber. "If you're willing to bring dinner, I could fit you in around eight."

There was a soft sound on the other side of the line. It sounded very much like a relieved sigh. "Is Chinese okay?"

In answer, she gave him the address, her voice steady and cheerful and normal as hell. Then she hung up and threw the phone hard at her couch before dancing around her small room. Oh, yes, she could make it until Monday. She could make it real good.

MAX WAS NERVOUS. Like, going-out-on-a-first-date nervous. It made no sense, of course. He and Chloe had already gone out several times, not to mention all that mind-blowing sex they'd had. Funny that you could lose count of that sort of thing when it was spread out over only three days, but several of those encounters had run together into one long night.

He rubbed his palms against his jeans and craned his neck to see where the taxi driver was taking him.

Her address was 410½, so he'd envisioned her living in one of the refurbished town houses that made up the residential area west of downtown Richmond. They were charming and beautiful and quirky, all jammed in together on tree-lined streets. She probably lived on the top floor, and he could see her curled up in a little window seat, reading in the shade of an ancient oak.

She and Jenn would walk to dinner on their girls' nights out. On Sundays, Chloe probably went to her parents' house for a barbecue. Yeah, there was nothing insane or alarming about these little streets.

But the cab rolled past that neighborhood and entered an area of well-kept antebellum mansions. Every house was large and stately, though each stood out as different from its neighbor. Some were white stone with pillars, hemmed in by rock walls. Some were aging brick, the darkness relieved by white-washed balustrades and balconies.

Max frowned at them all, confused by the transition.

The cab slowed with an ear-piercing squeal of worn brakes. "Here's 410. The ½ must be in the back. Want me to try to find an alley?"

Max cast a doubtful eye around. The house was only one lot from the corner. If there were an alley, Max could find it. The lampposts along the street were lit and the sun hadn't quite finished setting. He paid the driver, grabbed the bag of Chinese food and found himself standing in front of a mansion that had seen better days. In fact, those better days may have been in the mid-nineteenth century.

This house was… Max squinted through the overgrown vegetation—red brick. Or maybe it was brownstone. He couldn't see much past the ivy and moss. The front yard had reverted to old Richmond. Really old Richmond. Like back when only native Americans had lived on this land.

Was this some ancestral family home? Max looked up the street, then down. He found no clue waiting for him, but he didn't see any photographers, either.

He took a few wary steps toward the wrought-iron gate. Unlike most of the fences on this block, this one rose high. Eight feet high. He reached gingerly for the handle of the gate, but it didn't respond to his first careful nudge. After trying to no avail, Max shrugged and threw his whole weight into it. The latch finally snapped up and the gate slipped open a foot, screaming against the scarred cement beneath.

"Christ," he muttered, wondering if you could get tetanus if you didn't actually have a cut. He wiped a few of the rust flakes off his hand and stepped back, giving up. He clearly needed to go around to the back. Nobody had used this entrance in years. Just as he reached out to tug the gate back into place, a very distinctive clack broke through the silence. Someone had just dropped a chamber into a shotgun. And that someone was very close.

Max's blood froze in his veins and he was stuck like that, two fingers on the gate and eyes wide as saucers.

"You'd better get the hell out of here if you know what's good for you."

"Um." His eyes rolled, but he couldn't see anything past the overgrown bushes.

"Damn patterazzi."

Paparazzi. Someone thought he was a reporter. "I'm not—" A deep, dark growl interrupted him, and Max looked down to see a vicious black dog only inches from his legs. A dark rumble of warning bubbled up from its throat while its jowls quivered. "Oh, fuck." Max dropped the sack of food and slowly raised both his hands as he eased backward. "Ma'am, I'm sorry. I don't know who you are, but I'm here to see Chloe Turner."

"I'll bet you are!"

"She invited me over, ma'am. I apologize about the mixup. If you can just tell me how to get to 410½, I'll be on my—"

"Mrs. Schlessing!" Chloe shouted from somewhere within the thicket. "Mrs. Schlessing, that's Max! He's my guest."

A head of gray, curly hair poked out from the bush on the left. "You sure?"

"Yes, ma'am." Chloe suddenly jogged into view, her cheeks flushed and her hair bouncing from the run. "Brutus," she ordered in a low voice. "Heel." The dog spun, its growl morphing into a happy yelp as he trotted back to the old woman.

"I'm sorry," Chloe panted, tucking a strand of hair behind her ear. "I should have told you to come through the back." She cringed deliberately and tilted her head in Mrs. Schlessing's direction. The woman, apparently satisfied with her work, had already headed back into the jungle, a flash of pink housedress his last glimpse of her.

Chloe slipped through the gate and tugged it shut

behind her. "Come on. I'll show you the way." She picked up the bag before heading off.

Max took a few steps with her, then stopped and turned to face her. "What the hell was that?"

"That was Mrs. Schlessing. I rent the apartment from her."

"Okay, but…what the hell *was that?*"

"Oh." She looked over her shoulder toward the gate, and her face grew even brighter red. "Sorry. It's just that we've had a lot of trouble with people trying to sneak in. She wouldn't have shot you, really."

This wasn't the reunion he'd been expecting. Not at all. This was…crazy. But then, he'd known he was fooling himself, hadn't he? Oh, he hadn't expected shotgun and mad-dog kind of insanity, but he hadn't truly believed he'd find her snuggled into a cozy window seat, waiting for a homemade apple pie to finish cooling.

He'd warned himself not to come, but here he was. Max faced forward and resumed their walk, taking the food from her like the gentleman his mother had raised him to be.

"So I see you live in a haunted house."

This time she smiled, and the tightness inside Max loosened by a few degrees. God, she was pretty. And soft. None of that had been affected by her crazy life. "I don't live in the haunted part of it. I have the carriage house."

"What a relief."

"Max…thank you for coming." Chloe took his hand, waking up nerves in it he hadn't ever been aware of before. Like the nerves where her fingers slid in between his, setting off a shivery pleasure. Apparently, that part of his skin was incredibly sensitive. How could he never have noticed?

She smiled up at him again as they ducked around the corner. And God, she looked so happy that even with the dog and the shotgun and the crazy old lady, Max couldn't believe he'd come close to telling his brother to forget the detour and drive straight to D.C. Chloe's happy eyes were everything in that moment, and Max followed her into the dark alley without a whisper of hesitation.

She hurried him toward a wooden gate just as tall as the wrought-iron one, and Max braced himself for thorns and grasping vines. He was more than a little surprised when they emerged into a very normal backyard, lit by harmless porch lights. No giant spiderwebs. No creeping zombies. "Nobody uses the front," she explained needlessly. "It's just Mrs. Schlessing in the house now, and she doesn't like people much."

"You don't say."

"It's private here," she said, gesturing toward the backyard before she led him up a set of rickety wooden stairs. "This is my place. The paparazzi are gone for the night. Nothing ever happens here after dark. Not till now anyway. Er, not that I think we're going to… Hey, here we are."

She opened a huge wooden door. The window in it was shielded by a blue curtain.

Once he stepped inside, Max was surprised again. He'd still been expecting quaint, but he had no idea why. Chloe was living in an overstuffed dorm room. Moving boxes were piled along one wall, leaking the occasional extension cord or shoelace between the seams. The coffee table was made of wooden crates. Literally.

"Oh. It's nice."

She stiffened and slid her hand out of his. "I lived in a house before. A nice house. But I had to move out with no notice."

"Sure, I understand."

"I couldn't move into my parents' place. The photographers… It wouldn't be right."

"Come on. It's great." He gestured as if it were a grand loft and not a tiny 300-square-foot room. "Reminds me of living on the ship."

"Right."

"Are you hungry?" He held up the bag and gestured toward the little round table that marked the boundary between the kitchen half of the room and the living-room half. "You know, if you add some raised edges to the cabinets, your plates won't slide off when the sea gets rough."

"Oh, that's funny."

She smiled, but he'd hurt her feelings. He could tell by the tight distance in that grin. Regret hit Max hard. Yes, her life was a mess, but she was living the immediate aftermath of a personal disaster. He put the bag onto the table and turned to her.

"I'm sorry. You've got all this going on. I probably shouldn't have come."

The hurt deepened on her face, turning her mouth down.

Max shook his head. Where the hell was all his charm? He'd lost it somewhere back on that island. "But…I just wanted to see you."

"Why?"

Why? Why, indeed? Some of it was out of a sense of responsibility. Some of it stemmed from worry. And some of it was just the truth. So Max chose to give her the truth, even though it felt as frightening as each time he set foot back on the ship. "Because," he said. "I missed you."

THE WORDS DIDN'T SLAM through her. They didn't stop her breath and send her heart racing into overdrive. Instead, Max's words slid over her skin like a question. A tentative touch. She waited to see what she would feel.

"I'm sorry," he said. "Was that weird?"

Chloe cocked her head, waiting... Finally, her skin grew warm in answer. Her nerves thrilled gently. She felt suffused with a quiet happiness. "No," she finally answered. "No, it wasn't weird. I missed you, too."

She didn't realize how tense Max's smile had become until it relaxed. "Really?"

"I did," she answered. As if to prove it, her body swayed toward him of its own volition. Max met her in the middle, his mouth taking hers in a kiss that started soft and escalated to deep and hot within a few seconds.

And from then on, none of it mattered. Not her worries over her life or Max's reaction to it. Because he was here, and she wasn't alone.

She held tightly to his body, wishing she could simply melt into him and stay warm and safe inside him. But the second-best option was to have him warm and safe inside her, so Chloe tugged him toward the bedroom. He hesitated for a moment, to edge her to the side and reach around to lock the apartment door.

His paranoia made her smile as she nibbled at his bottom lip. She gave up his mouth to tug his shirt up and off, then reached for the button of his jeans. When her hand brushed his stomach, the muscles jumped, reminding her that she didn't know much about him. Was he ticklish? Where did he like to be kissed and stroked?

She pulled him to her bed and pushed him down on his back, determined to find out.

Max raised an eyebrow. "Am I being taken advantage of?"

"Strange city. No car. A vicious dog between you and freedom. You're mine now and there's nothing you can do about it."

Eyes narrowing, he swept his gaze down her body as she started unbuttoning her sleeveless shirt. "What are you planning to do with me?"

Chloe let the shirt slide off her arms and stood straight to maintain the illusion of rock-hard abs as she unzipped her jeans. "I'm going to find out how much you missed me."

If she was going to be cast as the wild girl, she'd damn well play the part, so Chloe put her hands on either side of Max's knees and crawled up the bed to have a comfortable seat on his lap. When she settled herself against his erection, she took his wrists in her hands and pressed them into the bed.

"Ooh. Seems like you missed me a little bit." She wriggled her hips against his.

"A *little?*"

"Mmm." Leaning slowly over, she opened her mouth on his chin and pressed her teeth into his flesh. He inhaled sharply, hips tilting up to hers.

Power zinged through her, flashing into her like water over parched earth. She'd hardly touched him and already, her body was going tight with lust.

She nibbled her way along his jawline, pressing his hands down hard. "You don't feel like a man left in desperate straits."

"Liar," he muttered, thrusting hard against her.

"Mmm. Maybe you missed me a...*medium* amount."

"Shit," he muttered as she sucked at a tender spot on his neck. "You're cruel."

When she pressed her naked stomach against his, they both sighed. The sensation was so sweet that Chloe simply laid her body against his for a long moment, feeling their hearts beating against each other.

"Chloe," Max said, twisting his arms to loosen her grip.

"No, not yet." If he wrapped himself around her and held her close...she'd be lost. She felt too much for him already. So Chloe lifted herself an inch off him and kissed her way down his chest. Curious, she ran her tongue around his nipple and watched goose bumps spring up around it. "Does that tickle?"

"Yes!"

"And this?" She sucked gently and scraped her teeth against him.

"Ah! Yes. No."

"Hmm." Taking her time with the exploration, she brushed her lips over the crisp brown hair of his chest, then tested for ticklish spots with her tongue and teeth, all the while pressing herself rhythmically against his erection. "I'm still not convinced that you truly missed me."

"Slide your mouth a little lower, and you'll know for sure."

"Really?" Chloe rose up and rested her ass against his thighs as she released his wrists. "All right then. Show me."

Surprise flared in his eyes, but it was quickly swallowed up by heat. Max reached for his zipper and Chloe tried to hide the way her breath quickened. But when he pulled his cock free, a sigh slipped from her lips. His hand circled the shaft and he gave himself one slow stroke while she watched. Her sex squeezed in sympathetic response. This felt dirtier than anything she'd ever done. And when Max reached for her hand and wrapped it around that hot flesh, her whole body shuddered. He was unbelievable heavy in her palm, and when Chloe tightened her fingers, there wasn't even a hint of yielding flesh.

She snuck a glance past her lashes and found Max's gaze locked on her grip, his lips slightly parted, eyes lit with hard need.

"This much, hmm?"

"Yes," he answered gruffly.

"Oh, my." Chloe scooted backward, sliding her hand all the way down to the thick base of his shaft. Watching his face the entire time, Chloe lowered her head and touched the tip of her tongue to his flesh. He grabbed a handful of the blanket as she slipped her tongue over him, pressing it to the underside of the head. When she closed her lips around him and sucked gently, he let loose the breath he'd been holding.

She teased him for a long time before she slid deeper in tiny increments. She loved the taste of him, the scent of his body, the smoothness of him against her mouth. And she loved the way his stomach tightened with every curl of her tongue. He was sensitive to every increase in pressure and pace. With Max, a blow job seemed designed for her pleasure, not his. With a moan of need, she took him as deep as she could, swallowing against the weight of his cock.

Chloe squirmed as she pleasured him, wiggling against the building need between her legs. She wanted to have sex with him right now, but that need was overridden by the desire to make him come like this. To hear his shout of need and feel his whole body spasm as he came.

When his hand touched her, it was trembling. "Wait, Chloe. Jesus." He urged her up.

Chloe licked her lips and tried to bend back to her task.

Though he groaned with the struggle, Max shook his head and pulled her up to straddle him. Instead of taking her, though, he tugged her down so that her stomach pressed into his wet shaft. "God, I missed you."

He kissed her then, and slid both his hands beneath her underwear to pull her tighter against his body. A moment later, the room shifted, and she was on her back on the mattress, and Max had her panties halfway down her legs. "My turn."

She wasn't in the mood to demur. In fact, Chloe helpfully kicked off her underwear and waited impatiently as he knelt between her legs with an evil smile. "How much have you missed me?"

"Well… It's only been a few days."

"Oh, sure," he agreed, dragging one finger down her belly with deliberate slowness. He traced the very edge of her hair, then followed the line down to the sensitive skin just above the hollow of her thigh. She jumped.

"Ticklish?" he murmured.

"Horny!"

"But it's only been a few days." His fingers traced the plump lips of her sex, offering nothing more.

"Okay, I take that back! I missed you like crazy. Come on now, you said it was your turn!"

"So I did." But instead of giving her what she needed, Max propped himself up on his elbows and feathered both thumbs over her, teasing her into a frustrated groan.

"I'm still not convinced you really missed me," he said, his mouth drawing closer, the words touching her with torturous faintness. "Maybe you'd better show me."

His tongue touched her with almost the same ghostlike whisper as his words. She whimpered, any attitude lost now in the darkness of her closed eyes. The world shrank down to that place between her legs where Max's mouth hovered.

His tongue ran lightly down her sex, then slowly up. Chloe held her breath and silently prayed for mercy. Max finally granted it, flicking his tongue over the spot where she most needed it.

"Oh, God," she moaned, hips twitching at the electric shock of pleasure.

"You did miss me."

"I did, I did." She let her knees fall farther open, trying to offer encouragement. It worked. Max finally put some effort into his work, and Chloe's thighs were trembling in an embarrassingly short amount of time. She already felt that rise of tension, heavy enough to feel that she was sinking into the bed, but strangely buoyant, too, raising her up, up.

And then he stopped.

"What are you—?"

"Shh. Slow down."

"No!"

"Yes." He nibbled at the top of her thigh, but before she could complain, Max slid two fingers inside her and sent her arching off the bed. In response, he wrapped his other arm around her thigh and held her still.

Chloe felt primal, fighting against his hold, trying to get closer to his hand. She needed him deeper, harder, needed him to push every anxious second she'd suffered out of her body.

"Please," she breathed. "Oh, please."

He made a thoughtful little purr in his throat, then pushed up on his knees while Chloe gasped at his abrupt withdrawal. He tugged a condom from his pocket, and his hands shook as he unwrapped it and slid it on. Not as much as Chloe's hands were shaking, though. She was right on the edge, in pain and empty.

This time he didn't make her wait. Max entered her in one hard, ruthless thrust. Her muscles froze with the shock of it, but her heart tripped over itself with greedy joy.

"Chloe," Max murmured as he began to thrust. Oh, God, it felt so good. So good.

She dug her nails into his ass to pull him tighter. Max kissed her hard, devouring her mouth as he shifted higher on her body. And, sweet Lord, that was just what she needed.

Chloe dug her nails in harder and he growled in response. Good. She felt like an animal and she wanted him to be a beast, too. He braced his hands against the bed and raised his chest, giving him more leverage. Arching her neck hard to the side, she closed her eyes and concentrated on the feel of him fucking her. Hard. And suddenly she was caught up in a wave of brutal pleasure. She cried out, screaming as her body jerked against his, squeezing his cock even tighter.

By the time Max came, she was almost done shaking, but she couldn't stop whispering, "Oh, God," under her breath. Max was still above her, weight resting on his hands, head hanging down as he panted. She slid a hand into his messy hair and pulled him down to lie on her.

"Good Lord, Max."

He made a sound like a mix between a groan and a purr. Chloe's heartbeat slowed, but she felt a little twitch of pain at the end of every beat. She was so happy in that moment that it hurt. If she could stay just like this forever, body melting, sex still stretched tight by his body, she would.

"I think you've ruined me for other men," she whispered.

"I was going to say the same thing about you."

She opened her eyes and smiled at the ceiling.

"But with women, I mean."

"Uh-huh."

He grinned, and she could feel the curve of it against her neck. The pain in her heart burned brighter. It was too soon for this. Too soon because she barely knew him, and too soon because she was surely on the rebound. Max was nothing like Thomas, so she found herself falling for him. Simple as that.

Except that it wasn't that simple. Max was nothing like anyone she'd ever known. Charming and grumpy at the same time. Laid-back and constantly worried. He was complicated, and the layers fascinated her.

"You smell so good," Max whispered against her neck.

"I could put on some sunscreen for old times' sake."

He shook his head, edging off her to get rid of the condom. "Why don't girls wear that nice coconut oil anymore?"

"Because it was meant to increase UV exposure? Those girls who used to smell like coconut? They *look* like coconuts now."

When he lay back down and tucked her into his shoulder, Chloe snuggled in with a happy sigh.

"So how did you find this place if that crazy woman doesn't like people?"

"My dad was her mailman for twenty years. He said that every single day he'd find her standing next to her mailbox, waiting for the mail. Not anything specific, just waiting for the chance to glare at him if he was late. Then one day she wasn't there. He thought it was a little odd, but the next day she wasn't there, either, and she hadn't picked up the mail from the day before. He got worried. He braved the forest in the front yard and knocked on her door and heard the dog barking, so he called the police. She'd had a stroke and hit her head on a table, and she would've died if he hadn't noticed."

"Wow."

"Now that he's retired, he stops by once a week to see her. She's still ornery, but now she serves him cookies in her kitchen and complains bitterly about the new mail carrier. When my dad mentioned my search for an apartment, she offered me this."

"I like it."

"Liar."

He let that go, and so did Chloe. It wasn't important. This place was only temporary and it reflected nothing about her but her misery.

She decided to change the subject. "How long before you have to go back to your job?"

Max sighed so hard that her head sank two inches before he inhaled. "Three weeks."

"I'll bet you can't wait. Especially after a vacation like this."

"Mmm."

She could picture him out there on the open ocean, sun-bleached hair whipping in the wind, smile on his face as he took control of every situation. "God, you must love it out there. No stray people wandering in with their strange problems."

He took another deep breath, the air in his lungs whooshing under her ear.

"It's just you and your friends. How many people are on the ship?"

"Between eighteen and twenty. Most are divers."

"Wow."

"And I'm responsible for every single one."

Chloe's eyes popped open and she frowned at the little bookshelf against the far wall. Her gaze caught on *Moby-Dick*. Uh-oh. "What do you mean?"

"I'm the dive supervisor. I'm responsible for every person who touches the water."

"That sounds perfect for you."

"Sure." Such a simple word, but Chloe heard years of stress inside that one, small syllable.

She pushed up on her hands so that she could see his face. "Max?"

"Yeah?" He didn't open his eyes.

"Do you like your job?"

He shrugged as if the answer were inconsequential, but he still wouldn't open his eyes.

"Max?"

"I hate it," he said flatly. He finally looked at her and his eyes were dark with misery. "It's ridiculous. Who wouldn't want to live on a boat in the middle of the Mediterranean Sea and hunt for treasure? It's a dream job. That's what got me interested. I had an ulcer my sophomore year of college—"

"Max!"

"It was a stressful year. I was trying to help Elliott decide on a school. I didn't want him to make any mistakes—"

"Everybody makes mistakes."

"Okay, I didn't want him to make any really bad mistakes. And I had a girlfriend who…" He waved a dismissive hand. "Anyway, with school on top of everything else, I was a little stressed out. I saw a diving show on TV, and it looked so…quiet. And the first time I tried diving, I fell in love. The technical aspects of it were a little scary, but once I was in the water, it was just me. I'd never felt peaceful before. Ever. And in that moment, on my first dive, I was at peace."

She thought of the dive on the wreck and nodded. "I can see that."

"I thought I'd found the solution to my insane life. Living out on a boat, isolated, a limited number of people to think about." He shook his head. "I don't know. It was a mistake."

"Do you hate it that much?"

"Yes. At first, when I was just a diver, it was okay. But on my second ship, I didn't trust the supervisor. He was lax. So I started rechecking everything and…it became my job, and I hate it."

"So quit! There must be something else you can do."

His muscles had slowly hardened to steel beneath her. "I can't quit."

"You're under contract or something?"

"No. But I can't leave. What if I leave and something happens to one of the divers?"

"Wouldn't they have a new dive supervisor?"

"No one's as good as I am." The words didn't sound boastful or arrogant. They sounded resigned.

Poor Max. She could argue with him, try to convince him that he was being ridiculous. But she must have spent too much time pressed against him, absorbing his thoughts, because she could see the logic of his argument.

But how long did his responsibility extend? How many years did the obligation remain? Five years after he left? Ten? He wouldn't be able to tell her, so she didn't ask. She laid her head back down.

"Okay, so what would you do if you could do anything? If there were no repercussions to leaving the ship, what would you do?"

He was quiet for a long moment, and Chloe used the time to spread her fingers wide over his heart. His skin looked so brown against her pale hand.

"It's boring," he finally said.

"That sounds perfect for you. What is it?"

"I want to be a carpenter. Maybe a cabinetmaker."

"Really?"

"Then I'd never have to see the ocean again. Or a boat. Or divers."

"Are you good at that kind of stuff?"

"I worked for a carpenter in high school and college. I liked the precision of it. You were careful and you measured and, in the end, everything fit together perfectly. I was good at it. Before I gave it up for diving, I worked for a guy who designed custom furniture. The last time I was on leave I made a whole wall of built-in bookshelves for Elliott. It was so relaxing."

"Could you make a living doing that?"

"It might take a while to be profitable, but I'm lucky enough not to have to worry about that."

"Are you saying you've been hoarding treasure for all these years?"

His chuckle rumbled through her. "Exactly."

"Wow. A carpenter."

"Yeah, what do you think of the smell of sawdust?"

"Hot. Much hotter than old seaweed. You should... You really feel that you can't leave the ship?"

He put his hand over hers and dragged his fingertips lightly over her knuckles. "No one in the industry has a better record than I do. How do I get past that? My shipmates are like family. How can I turn them over to someone I know isn't as careful as I am?"

She didn't know the answer to that. It wasn't his responsibility to take care of these people for the rest of his life, except that for him, it was. The weight of it pulled his voice down when he spoke about the ship. It pulled *him* down.

She didn't have an answer, so she just wrapped her arms around him and held him until they both fell asleep.

CHAPTER SEVENTEEN

MAX WAS IN HEAVEN. He woke slowly, aware that he was in a dark, unfamiliar room. No water sounds drifted to his ears. No crashing waves or lapping ocean. In fact, the only thing he could hear was an air conditioner whirring away somewhere to his left, keeping the room cold while a pile of covers kept his body warm. The round ass pressed against his dick was helping keep his body temperature up, too.

Chloe.

He stretched slowly, careful not to wake her. She stirred enough to make him gasp, then settled back into sleep. This was what he'd been missing in his life. A sweet, soft woman and not one other person to think about.

Hard as he was, he didn't do anything more than sneak an arm around her waist. She murmured something too soft to hear and curled her fingers over his to hold him tightly. Max closed his eyes and wondered what it would be like to live like this. On land, in a tiny apartment, with Chloe.

He had no right to think such things, of course.

His job would take him away soon, and Chloe wasn't in a place that invited long-term commitment, but inside his own head, Max could think whatever he wanted to. Then again, he couldn't think of much of anything when Chloe nudged her ass even tighter against him with a sleepy little sigh.

Nice.

Fingers still covered by hers, he slid his hand up to cup her breast. Her hand tightened against his, pressing him into her. She was awake, and she wanted him.

Max made love to her more slowly than he'd ever made love to anyone. It seemed as if a whole hour had passed before he collapsed on his back, as exhausted as if he'd never even slept. But Chloe was wide-awake. She bounced up to her knees, making for a very nice, if sadly unlit view.

"It's only six-thirty," she said.

"Mmm. More sleep."

"Okay, but…the paparazzi will be here in an hour, and unless you want to have Ramen noodles for breakfast, we should sneak out now."

The bed was so soft. He curled a hand around the silk skin of her thigh and closed his eyes. "Ramen is great."

When she slapped his arm, Max's eyes popped wide-open. "Get up. I used up a lot of calories last night. *And* this morning. I want blueberry pan-cakes."

His stomach growled in response, and Max aimed a glare at his traitorous belly.

"Come on. Shower with me?"

Well, then. "Is your shower big enough for two?"

"Nah. I was just trying to trick you into getting up."

"Heartless witch." But heartless or not, Max decided he'd do anything to make her happy, even stumble out of bed before dawn. They showered and dressed, then Max stopped to lecture her about not having a smoke detector in her bedroom before they tiptoed down the stairs and opened the ancient wooden garage door. It was Sunday morning, and not another soul seemed to be awake. Relieved, Max started to open the passenger-side door, but Chloe shook her head.

"Wrong side. You sit over here."

He walked around the white SUV. "You want me to drive?"

"Nope," she said as she slid into her seat and slammed the door.

Max opened his door with a frown. "If you... What the hell?" There was no steering wheel, no gas pedal.

"My dad got it at auction from the post office for a steal."

"A steal? The steering wheel's on the wrong side!"

"It's a mail carrier truck. On rural routes, the driver can stick mail in the boxes without having to get out of the truck."

"But…" Max registered some vague memory of seeing an arm reach out of a truck to stick a stack of envelopes in a mailbox. "But it's on the wrong side."

"Come on. I'm hungry."

Frowning, he sat down and buckled his seat belt, his head buzzing with the wrongness of the layout. He kept frowning even when Chloe leaned in to kiss him on the cheek.

She backed out of the garage, then hopped out to lower the door, the rising sun sneaking through the houses to light her face in a rosy glow. But Max barely noticed this; he was too busy feeling nervous.

He was okay when she eased the truck down the narrow alley and onto the tree-shaded side street, but before he could prepare himself, Chloe turned onto the wider street that fronted the house, and soon they were driving way too fast for Max's taste. He clutched the handle of the door, totally disoriented by the vehicle's mixed-up layout. His foot pressed against a phantom brake pedal, toes straining so hard that they hurt. He was in the position of responsibility, the driver's seat, and there was nothing he could do to control the truck.

"How far is the restaurant?" he managed to ask past his clenched jaw.

"About five minutes. Why?"

"I don't like this."

"We'll sneak back into my place from the front."

"No, I mean, I don't like *this*."

Chloe finally seemed to register that he was digging his nails into the upholstery. "What's wrong?"

"This truck is wrong!"

"Whoa. Are you freaking out?"

Max gripped the door handle tighter as Chloe passed a slow-moving sedan. "I'm not freaking out. You can't tell me that anyone likes riding in this truck."

"Er...actually, no one seems to care much. They think it's funny."

"Funny?" She was driving way too close to the center line. How could she not see that? Another car approached, its headlights aglow in the pinkish light, and Max squeezed his eyes shut. "Would you mind easing over to the right a little? I think your perspective is off."

"You're not having a panic attack, are you?"

"No."

"Are you sure? You look pale."

He forced a smile and ignored the bead of sweat sliding down his hairline. "Hey, I've got a better idea for breakfast. Why don't we just go back to your place? If you've got a can of whipped cream, all I need is you and a kitchen table."

"Seriously, Max? Even you aren't pulling that off."

"Oh, Jesus," he prayed as Chloe sped up to make a quick turn past a yellow light.

She patted his hand. "We're almost there now. No point in turning back."

He pressed his foot harder to the floorboard, his toes numb from the pressure, and clenched his jaw to keep from shouting something ridiculous. Like *Please stop the car and let me out here before I throw up!*

The car bumped over something, but he kept his eyes closed until it rolled to a gentle stop. He cracked one eyelid open and saw a sidewalk and a fence. Forcing the other eye open, he made out the rest of the parking lot and popped open the handle of the door. When he set his foot to the asphalt, Max felt like an astronaut stepping out of a space shuttle after a safe landing back on earth. He just managed not to fall to his knees and kiss the wonderfully solid ground.

"Maybe you should ride in the backseat on the way home."

"Maybe I should."

Chloe cleared her throat while he rolled his shoulders and stretched his tight neck. "So…no control issues, huh?"

"None at all."

"So you're ready to eat?"

His stomach turned, but he managed to hold out an arm and tilt his head charmingly toward the restaurant. "I'm starving. After you, madam." But when he considered the ride home, Max found himself ordering toast and coffee, and he willfully ignored every raised eyebrow Chloe aimed in his direction. He wanted this weekend to be totally normal, and so it would be, despite the complete, chaotic mess that seemed to dominate Chloe's everyday life.

She's normal, he repeated to himself over and over again. *Everything is totally normal.*

But it was just the start of the day, after all.

"So what does your dad do now?" Max asked.

Chloe glanced at the rearview mirror. He did look slightly less crazed in the backseat, but she noticed that he kept his eyes closed. "Now he gardens. And does something like Meals on Wheels.

Mom is trying to get him to take up golf to get him out of the house more, but he says he enjoys their time together too much for that."

"And your mom disagrees?"

"She's used to having the house to herself." She caught him smiling in the mirror, and she smiled back, even though he couldn't see her. "See? I told you I was normal. Perfectly average and normal. I even had a dog named Lassie when I was growing up."

"You did not."

"Did, too. So what was your family like? Obviously I know your brother, but what about your parents?"

The smile faded and he let his head fall back onto the headrest. "Papa was a rolling stone. He'd show up out of the blue and hang around for a few months, then be on his way again. He liked the idea of having two big, strong sons, but he wasn't interested in taking care of a family."

"Ooh." When she looked again, Max met her eyes in the mirror.

"Yeah, it's so transparent it's kind of embarrassing. I've been the man of the house since I was seven years old. But a seven-year-old can't tell his mother what to do, and little brothers are kind of resistant to that sort of thing, too. I imagine that's when I started developing creative ways to take charge."

"You mean 'maintain complete control over everyone around you'?"

"I just like things to be safe and sound, that's all."

Chloe let it go. She didn't even start humming "Queen of Denial." He knew what he was. There was no need to force him to say it, unless, of course, she had him naked and at her mercy.

She turned onto her street and heard Max breathe a sigh of relief as she pulled up to the curb in front of Mrs. Schlessing's house. "I'll move the truck back to the garage tonight after dark. Let's try to get up the stairs quickly. Sometimes they won't notice if they're on the phone."

"Got it."

But something was a little off today. Before they reached the wrought-iron gate, a man appeared on the corner, camera pointed in their direction. As Max pushed the screeching gate open, the man started jogging toward them. "Max!" he yelled. "Max Sullivan!"

Chloe stumbled as she squeezed through the narrow opening. "They found out your real name."

"Damn it." He forced himself through, though the metal must have scraped his back, then he slammed the gate shut and started up the overgrown path after Chloe. A huge mass of fur and muscle came barreling past them, fangs bared in a vicious growl. Max yelped and pressed into one of the bushes, but the dog aimed straight for the gate, slamming into the metal and pushing his muzzle through the bars to snap at the photographer. That distracted the guy enough for Chloe and Max to disappear into the vines.

"I'm sorry," Chloe offered feebly, mortified that he had to suffer the experience of crazed photographers screaming out his name. "I'm really sorry."

He said, "No big deal," but his voice had that pulled-down sound again.

The path drew close to the main house, and Mrs. Schlessing appeared on the porch in housecoat and slippers, her shotgun cradled in her arms.

"It's okay, Mrs. Schlessing. It's just the press again. I parked in front to try to avoid them."

"Damn pushy vultures."

"The gate's shut and Brutus has it covered. You can put the gun away."

She was still muttering when they turned to follow the path around to the side of the house.

"Is that thing really loaded?" Max whispered.

"I'm pretty sure it is." Smiling over her shoulder, Chloe didn't register the voices at first. Not until she saw Max's eyes widen, his gaze focused somewhere ahead.

Chloe whipped around to make sure the carriage house wasn't on fire. It wasn't, but from the sound of it, a whole brigade of people seemed ready to capture every lick of flame on film if it was. Up to this point, she'd been mildly hounded. At most, three or four photographers had staked out the alleyway, trying to capture a moment of her life that would earn them a paycheck. But now… She couldn't see them past the fence, but she could see the three video cameras that had been erected on top of a van parked in the alley. Every lens was focused straight on her. And Max. "Oh, God. What's going on?" This didn't make sense. It was Sunday. Surely the DA hadn't made any announcements. She stopped in her tracks, wondering what she should do. Go forward or go back? But when Max bumped her heel from behind, she started walking again. Fast. Then faster, until she was jogging toward the stairs. "Come on," she urged Max, waving for him to hurry.

"Max!" Someone else shouted, and Chloe cringed.

"Max! How did you end up with the Bridezilla?"

"Is she a friend of Genevieve Bianca?"

Chloe was halfway up the stairs. She heard the still cameras clicking and whirring. The video cameras were menacing in their silence, as always. Something about their blank, impassive lenses creeped her out. Too many bad science fiction movies, maybe.

"Chloe! How long have you been sleeping with Max Sullivan?"

She couldn't find her keys. She'd just had them. Where could they possibly—she patted her right pocket and snatched them out in triumph, keeping her face tilted down toward the doorknob.

"Max! What does Genevieve think of your dating Chloe Turner?"

"Where did you meet?"

She turned the key so hard that her wrist yelped with pain, but that little twinge didn't bother her, because she was finally through the door and co-cooned in darkness. The first thing she'd done when she'd moved in was buy light-blocking shades. If she couldn't see out, they couldn't see in.

Max slipped inside and shut the door behind him.

"Oh, my God, Max. What's wrong with them?"

He shook his head and collapsed slowly back against the door.

"It's never..." Though she tried hard to draw a breath, her throat had squeezed itself shut "...been like...this."

"Chloe?"

He took a step forward, and she held up a shaking hand. "I'm...fine." Her heart beat so hard it felt like every thump set off a violent shaking inside the chambers. "Just..." The voices rose to shouts outside.

She couldn't make out more than Max's name, but it was enough to keep her pulse going.

Max lurched forward and grabbed her arms before she realized that the floor was getting wavy beneath her feet. When she leaned straight into him, he shifted and tucked his hands beneath her knees to pick her up. "Breathe, Chloe. Jesus, I'm calling an ambulance."

"No! Panic attack." She managed to draw a deeper breath and the scent of his shirt wound through her like opium. "I'm fine."

He laid her down on her bed, and began touching her. Her forehead, her cheek, the pulse beneath her jaw. Then he set his ear to her chest. She couldn't believe his head didn't bounce right off with the force of her heartbeat. But he kept stroking her shoulder and making soft shussing sounds, and eventually Chloe could breathe without strangling on her own adrenaline. "I'm sorry," she whispered, horrified.

"Are you okay? You scared me half to death."

"I'm sorry." Regret swelled up in her, pushing tears to her eyes. She didn't want to be this person. A person people screamed at and chased. A person who had panic attacks and lived like a hermit. A freak in a traveling sideshow with circus cars that seemed to follow her everywhere. "I'm sorry. You can leave if you want to."

"I'll get you a glass of water."

Chloe lay in the dark, staring up at a water stain on the ceiling, and she told herself it was going to be okay. Max would come back and he'd make a joke, and he wouldn't care about having his name on television. He'd stay with her tonight, and tomorrow he'd hold her hand and watch the press conference. He'd be there for her when the final shoe dropped.

She knew the fact that she was telling herself this meant that it wasn't going to happen. If it were going to happen, she wouldn't be holding so hard to the fantasy.

And when Max returned with a glass, even in the dim light, she could see the way his eyes shifted nervously to the window. The way he stuck his hands in his pockets as she sipped. He looked at the door, then down at his watch. Finally, he sat heavily on the bed and held his head in his hands.

While her apartment had felt secret and cozy with Max in her bed, it wasn't. It was a cave. A box. A trap she couldn't escape. And Max looked far too big within its confines.

"Chloe." He lifted his head. "I'm making this worse."

"It's my fault. It's only been a month—"

"But part of it's me."

"Why?"

He ran a hand through his hair, setting it into crazy lines. "Genevieve Bianca."

"Yeah." Chloe laughed. "What the heck was that about?"

"She, um… The truth is…I dated her."

"Genevieve Bianca? The heiress?"

"Yes."

"Are you serious? That's crazy. When did you date Genevieve Bianca?"

His eyes slid to meet hers before darting away. "We broke it off about nine months ago."

Nine months ago. "Oh," she breathed. "I see." Genevieve Bianca. Good Lord. That woman was thin and fashionable and so rich she was famous just for that. And everyone agreed that she was remarkably nice for an heiress, if a bit of a magnet for users and troubled playboys.

Max wasn't either of those things. Chloe curled her hands to fists. "She was one of those women."

He didn't answer.

"She was one of those women you stayed with just so you could help her." And that was when it hit her. Chloe drew in a ragged breath and sat up so quickly that the room spun. "Oh, my God. *I'm* one of those women!"

Despite her shock, she half expected him to protest, to offer at least a token denial, but he didn't. He just sat there, staring at her lap.

"I'm one of them."

Finally, Max shook his head. "No, not at all."

She didn't want to hear him lie, so Chloe frantically changed the subject. "Genevieve Bianca? How long were you with her?"

"We were dating on and off for a few months. I wouldn't say I was 'with' her."

"Max."

His big shoulders curved down in defeat. "I don't really know what happened. We finished a site early. The captain had some connection to her uncle. They wanted to see a real treasure wreck. He invited them out for a postseason dive, and I was the one in charge of instructing and outfitting them." He raised a heavy hand, as if he was too tired to complete a gesture. "The dives were done for the season, and…we hung out."

"And?"

"And she seemed like she needed someone around her who wasn't looking for a handout. I don't know."

"She needed help."

"Yes."

"So you stuck around?"

"I suppose I did. When I wasn't working."

Chloe felt suddenly drained, as if she were a puppet whose strings had just been cut. She wished she hadn't bothered sitting up. Now flinging herself back down would just look melodramatic, and she wanted to hold herself still. Genevieve had needed help and Max hadn't been working. That sounded awfully familiar.

"So," he said, "that's why the press is so crazed today. They finally figured out who I was. I wasn't really part of her red carpet entourage. I only occasionally shared a picture with Genevieve, but that was enough, I suppose."

She nodded as if she understood, but it was just starting to hit her. All her imaginings of Max were constructed around the isolation of his job. A romantic fantasy world, where Max sailed over turquoise seas by day and lounged in his solitary cabin at night. She'd forgotten that he sometimes got off the boat and wandered free and handsome through the world. With someone willowy and vulnerable.

This was awful.

"I'm sorry," Max murmured. "I should have told you. I should have *warned* you. But it never occurred to me that they'd make the connection."

"Unfortunately, they're pretty damn good at what they do."

He took her hand and cradled it carefully in his own. "I'm really, really sorry, Chloe."

She didn't want to be another one of those girls. Actually, she did. She wanted to be coddled and stroked and taken care of, but…in a different way. She didn't want to be coddled and stroked and taken care of because she needed him. She wanted all that because he needed *her*.

But that wouldn't be good for Max. Not with his history.

Chloe took a deep breath. "Maybe you should go."

The edges of his eyes tightened. He squeezed her hand. "Maybe I should."

Oh, no. She hadn't meant for him to agree. Not so quickly. Not so easily.

"You should go stay with your parents. It's only going to be a few more days, and you need to be with someone."

Her head felt strangely light when she shook it. "I don't."

"You do. Maybe Jenn could come stay with you."

Now she felt panicked again. Why had she suggested he leave? "No. Jenn and I... I don't know what's wrong with her. She's been acting strange. We haven't talked since Thursday night. I called her, but she hasn't called back."

He ran his free hand through his hair with a sigh. "I'll only draw more attention to you if I stay."

"Just for a little while then. Just until tomorrow?"

He met her gaze, his eyes fathomless brown. A burst of laughter leaked from the window that faced the alley, and he looked toward it. She saw defeat flash over his face like a wince. "If you need me to stay, then I'll—"

"Never mind." The words didn't want to leave her mouth, but she pushed them out. "You're right. You should go. I'll call you a cab and have it pick you up in front."

"Wait, Chloe. I can stay until—"

"I know what you're doing, and I don't need that. I need to work this out on my own."

His gaze dropped, as if he could hide his intentions.

"I'm fine, Max. I've been living like this for weeks now. It's no big deal. My parents will be relieved if I come stay with them. That's a good idea. They've been worried."

"Damn it, Chloe, I want to stay. I swear I want to stay. But that's the problem. I have this *need* to help, and I promised myself I wouldn't do this anymore. It's why I stopped dating. Why I stopped even looking at women. Living like this, it's killing me."

Like this, he said. Not like that. Like *this*.

She didn't try to defend herself. How could she? She wanted him around for the same reasons those other women had. She was using him for his sweetness and his body and his beautiful way of worrying about her. Just like the others.

But unlike the others, Max had been honest with

her. And she owed him something more than falling at his feet and begging him to stay. Her panicked mind formed the argument: *You just got here. You came to* me. *Please stay.*

And he would.

Chloe pushed past him to start picking up the remnants of their night together. The clothes he'd stripped from her body. The wineglasses empty next to the bed. The high school yearbook he'd spotted in one of the boxes and insisted on paging through. "You have to stop somewhere, Max. As you said, you can't keep living like this. Now is as good a time as any."

She grabbed her phone and asked the Directory Assistance operator for the phone number of a local cab company, the whole time praying that Max would grab the phone from her hand because he couldn't bear to leave. But he didn't touch her.

Chloe ordered the cab, then turned slowly to face him. "Believe me, I'd get out if I could. I understand."

"I want to stay," he said softly. "You know that."

She didn't know what to say, didn't know how to separate his attraction to her from his need to rescue damsels in distress. Maybe he did like her, but he had to hate her a little, too. Just as she found herself hating him a little. He'd taken care of all those other women, so why the hell did he have to take a stand with her? Why couldn't he just offer his support?

She set the phone carefully on the table, afraid if she moved too quickly she'd fall apart. "Dispatch said it would only be three minutes. There's a driver nearby."

"Chloe…"

"Just go, Max. Wait inside the gate. They won't be able to bother you there."

He pulled her into his arms, but she stayed stiff. If she put her hands on him, if she tilted her head up for a kiss, she'd start crying. She'd weep and wail and beg him not to go. Max would stay if she asked him to, but that would be like asking someone to love you. A cheap and petty ruse that left you lonelier than you were before. And if you asked someone to love you, wasn't that a guarantee he never would?

His arms fell slowly, as if he were still waiting for her to change her mind. "I'm going to stay here in Richmond, okay? In case you need me."

"Need you," she repeated dully. Hurt hardened into convenient fury. "In case I *need* you? Thanks, but no thanks."

"Regardless—"

"I'm not some wilting flower looking for a protector, Max. I've done this on my own. I got through my fiancé dying. Then I got through the suspicions that he wasn't dead at all. And the humiliation and betrayal of being exposed to *everyone*. And now... whatever the news is on Monday, I'll get through that, too. What's the alternative? Should I scream at the world to stop and let me off?"

"I didn't mean—"

"I know what you meant, you arrogant asshole. Yeah, I wanted you here. I admit it. But I didn't want a big strong daddy to take care of me. I wanted you here as an equal, but I guess you're not up for that." She knew her anger didn't match what he'd done. He owed her nothing, not time or caring or even respect. But she had to put space between them or he'd stay and she'd call him.

And she had more than enough anger inside her to muster up.

"I'm sorry," he repeated, looking a little lost in the face of her bitterness.

"Yeah," she agreed. "You are. And you really should go now, because I don't like you looking at my life as if it's a fucking mess when you've been living a lie for thirty years."

"Hey. My life has nothing to with this."

"Not true. If you hadn't been screwed up for so long, would you be running away right now?"

All traces of regret disappeared from his face. Now he looked furious. "I'm not running away. This isn't my responsibility, goddamn it. You're the one who told me I didn't have to take care of every person I met."

"Oh, sure, start with *me*. I guess I don't mean as much to you as those other women you couldn't bear to leave."

"That's not it at all," he shouted. "You mean more to me."

She couldn't take this anymore. *I care about you. That's why I'm throwing you to the wolves.* "Get out. And don't bother hanging around Richmond. I don't need you and I won't call you."

His jaw hard as the blade of a knife, Max glared at her. He shook his head, then looked down at the floor.

Despite her crazy tirade, despite his anger, he didn't seem inclined to move, so Chloe stalked to the door and shoved it open. Flashbulbs crackled like an electrical storm, lighting up the trees in eerie bursts of colorless light. "Goodbye, Max."

He stayed in her bedroom for a moment, glaring at his shoes, but what choice did he have? She'd opened the cage and he wanted out. Chloe didn't even hear the questions shouted from the alley. The voices sounded like screaming ghosts as she stared at Max's profile, memorizing the sad curve of his neck and the flexing muscles of his arms. Her body was winding up inside, like a clockwork toy about to snap.

"Get out!" she managed to choke out. Too loudly, she supposed. There was an almost indiscernible lull in the questions outside, before they began shouting anew.

Max rolled his shoulders and walked toward her. "Just…take care of yourself," he said as he stopped in front of her. When she didn't respond, he stepped out the door and started down the stairs. Unwilling to watch him leave, Chloe slammed the door shut with so much force that a picture fell off her wall, the glass cracking into a dozen shards. She felt the echo of the same sound inside her as she slid down to crouch on the floor, her face resting against the door.

Stupid. He was a stranger. He didn't matter.

But that gear was turning inside her, and her nerves began to shred. She drew a deep breath, but with the windows all tightly closed, it was stale and humid in here, and the vague scent of leftover Chinese food left her nauseated.

Pressing a hand to her stomach, Chloe pushed herself to her feet and went to open the window that faced the backyard. It didn't help. Unless she opened a window facing the alley, no breeze would travel through. The smell of the food was stronger here.

Desperate, Chloe grabbed a trash bag and yanked open the fridge, but before she'd finished dropping the five containers into the bag, she realized her mistake. She couldn't throw it away. The garbage cans were downstairs, tucked against the side of the carriage house. Chloe narrowed her eyes. The roar outside had died down. Probably half the cameramen had followed Max around to the front. She could either take the food to the trash now, or live with the pervasive smell until dark. But she felt about half a minute away from throwing up at this point, and the smell was much stronger now.

Dropping the last container in the bag, Chloe headed for the door. She eased it open, noticing no change in the chatter below. Every beat of her heart seemed to knock against her roiling stomach, so Chloe took a deep breath and pushed the door wide enough to block them out. But this time it didn't work. The neighbor on the far corner of the alley had apparently given in to bribery. Someone shouted her name, and she looked up to find two photographers and a video technician perched on the flat roof, their cameras aimed right at her. It wasn't a perfect view. A huge tree cut through their line of vision, but it was enough. She stood there gawking at them for a good five seconds.

"Hey, Chloe," someone yelled from below. "Are you going to marry Max Sullivan?"

"Chloe, why'd he leave so soon? Did you turn psycho on him?"

"Were you cheating on Thomas with Max?"

"Chloe, did you show Max your wedding dress?"

Her jaw trembled. Every nerve in her body seemed to shake. She just wanted to be able to take the trash out. Just wanted to date a nice man and go out to breakfast and not skulk around as if she were going to get caught doing something wrong.

"Is it true that Max wants you to lose weight to look more like Genevieve?"

Chloe thought of Max sleeping with that fashionable stick figure. She thought of him comparing her body to Chloe's. She knew what was coming. Sites that put their pictures side by side. Sites that polled their readers as to who was sexier.

"Chloe, who are you wearing today?" one of the men yelled. The rest of them laughed as Chloe glanced down at her favorite T-shirt. It was a worn green shirt with the Lucky Charms leprechaun on the front. She'd worn it for Max and joked about having a little Irish in her thanks to him. He'd growled and kissed her.

Now these people who'd driven him away were laughing at her secret joke. Tomorrow, even if the truth was painful, even if her worst fears about Jenn came true, they'd laugh again.

"Bastards," she growled, her hand reaching for the edge of the door. Instead of ducking back inside, she closed the door behind her and stepped up to the railing to glare down at the dozen people below.

"Stop it!" she yelled, watching their eyes light with glee. Cameras whirred and snapped in a frantic cacophony. She wanted to hit them, to hurt them as much as they'd hurt her.

Eyeing one wolflike grin, she recognized one of the first guys who'd started following her. Chloe reached into the trash bag and grabbed one of the flimsy boxes of food. "Stop it!" she screamed…then she threw the box as hard as she could.

Her aim wasn't perfect, but the box caught his elbow and exploded noodles all over him. Triumph surged up to replace the fear that fueled her rage, but the triumph proved an even hotter fuel. While the other photographers laughed and hooted at their stunned friend, Chloe reached into the bag again. She aimed this box into the thicket of video cameras, and this time her aim was true. The biggest, baddest camera disappeared behind an explosion of brown goo. The laughter stopped, and the men gasped as if she had just tossed garbage on a child.

"Hey!" somebody yelled. There were curses and shouts, but the cameras kept clicking, and Chloe kept throwing. By the time she was done, half the mob below was covered in rice or noodles or sauce, and Chloe was panting as if she'd just run a hundred-meter sprint.

"Psycho-bitch!" one of the videographers screamed.

Chloe gave him the finger and flounced back inside with a sneer, her nausea just a memory. But as she washed her hands, her sneer faded. The reality of what she'd just done began to sink in.

"It was worth it," she whispered, knowing full well that it hadn't been. She snapped off the kitchen light and retreated to the bedroom to sit on her rumpled bed. She thought of calling Jenn. Or Anna. But she felt cut off from them, too. Adrift.

Chloe took off her shoes and her leprechaun T-shirt and her jeans. She curled up beneath the sheets she'd shared with Max Sullivan for just one night. And she cried harder than she ever had for Thomas.

CHAPTER EIGHTEEN

TWO HOURS WITH HIS HANDS on a steering wheel
went a long way toward grounding Max's soul. He
was back in the driver's seat, in complete control of
the rented Ford Explorer, dictating speed, accelera-
tion and position on the freeway. In fact, it was so
soothing that by the time he pulled onto his brother's
Alexandria street, Max was confident he'd done the
right thing in leaving Chloe. Yes, he'd wanted to see
her, but he should never have gone there with the
trial still pending.

Chloe was right. He had no business trying to help
other people when his own life was so screwed up.
She was right, and that's why he'd been so furious.

When he found his gaze straying to his cell, Max
jerked his eyes back to the street with a curse. The
phone hadn't rung, so obviously there was no message from Chloe. She'd made it clear that she wasn't
going to call.

He regretted hurting her, but she'd been okay
when he'd left. Pissed, but pissed was better than
sad. Anger gave you energy and arrogance and

righteousness. Anger would get her through until tomorrow.

And whatever she'd said to him in the heat of the moment, he'd call her tomorrow and make sure she was okay. And he'd call her again after that. And maybe...maybe after his next stint on the water, he'd get in touch and see where they were. There was something good between them, and Max wasn't ready to let her go for good.

Max parked the truck in front of his brother's high-rise condo and jogged up to the fourth floor. His phone began to ring the moment Max's knuckles hit the door.

He dropped his bag to the floor and fumbled for the phone, but just when he got it out of his pocket, the door opened and he found himself facing Elliott with a phone pressed to his ear.

Max looked at his phone with disappointment.

"I was just calling you," Elliott said.

"Right. What's up?"

"What the hell's going on?"

He shrugged, trying to think how he'd explain why he was back. He hadn't called Elliott on the drive for this very reason.

"Mom called a few minutes ago. Have you seen the video?"

"No, I haven't. But I know the press found out

who I was. That's why I left. Chloe doesn't need more attention."

"Um… Right. I think you'd better see this."

Max's heart dropped. For a moment, he had the horrible fear that they'd left the shades open last night in Chloe's bedroom. "Come on, Elliott. What is it?"

Elliott tilted his head toward his office, and Max followed him in, waiting impatiently as Elliott pulled up one of the more popular gossip sites. "Mom called to say she was seeing all kinds of stuff about you dating some crazy woman…"

The site finally loaded and the headline was hardly subtle. BRIDEZILLA BAD BEHAVIOR FINALLY CAUGHT ON TAPE!

Max lowered himself slowly to the chair and scrolled down. The freeze-frame of the video showed Chloe's carriage house, the camera zeroed in on a blurry image of Chloe at the top of the stairs. His chest tightened at the sight of her, exactly as he'd left her. Her cute shirt glowing green and her hair pulled back in a clip.

After hesitating for a few seconds, he called up his courage and hit Play, expecting to see him and Chloe racing up the stairs. But the bad behavior wasn't about their affair at all.

He watched as Chloe slammed the door shut and glared down at the alley below her. Her face was tight with rage, teeth bared in fury. Max winced. "Stop it!" she yelled. And that was when she began her attack.

"Holy shit," Max breathed as Chloe rained vengeance down on her foes. A few pieces of rice splattered the screen, but they failed to block the sight of her rampage. The last few seconds of the video zoomed in on Chloe's flushed face, then pulled back to show her giving the finger to the world. "Oh, no."

"Did something happen?" Elliott asked.

"I don't know. This must have been after I left."

"And she was fine when you left?"

Max almost managed to bite back his moan, but Elliott must have caught the start of it.

"Don't tell me Max Sullivan has finally lost his touch?"

"What the hell does that mean?"

"It means that you've left a trail of beautiful, wild women behind you, and all of them still love you. That's not normal, man. My ex-wife hates my guts, and *she* left *me*."

Max stared at the freeze-frame of Chloe, the hair on his arms rising as if he were seeing a ghost. "Your wife left because she was missing something," he murmured. "I give women something they need. Then they're done with me."

"What?"

"Nothing." Max read the accompanying story, then cruised around to a few more sites. They were all the same. Him. The video of Chloe. The video of him and Chloe scrambling up the stairs. Pictures of him with Genevieve. Pictures of Chloe when she was engaged. And lots and lots of editorials sympathizing with poor Thomas DeLorn, engaged to a psycho control-freak like crazy Chloe Turner.

His hands shook as he rubbed them over his face. "We got into a fight," he said, the words echoing off his palms and back into his head.

"About what?"

"Oh, Christ, Elliott. It was my fault. I've been…"

He hesitated, half hoping that Elliott would give him some space and walk away, but Elliott took the opposite approach and sat down on the desk to face him.

Okay. This was it, then. "I'm trying to change my life. I can't maintain these crazed relationships anymore. I can't keep dating women because they *need* someone."

Elliott's brow creased with obvious confusion. "But you date wild women. Party girls. Popular girls."

"Yeah." Max sighed. He dug his fingertips into his forehead. "Yeah. I have an image…" An image that attracted fun, glamorous women, and a personality that left him holding on to the damaged ones. "It's complicated."

"How?"

"I'm not as laid-back as you think."

Elliott's mouth flattened with skepticism.

"I tend to get involved with women out of a misguided desire to help them."

"Help them do what?"

He shrugged. "I don't know. Get their lives together. Learn to protect themselves. Whatever it is, it's dishonest and it's not right. I'm trying to change it."

"You're saying that's why you like Chloe? Because she's vulnerable?"

Max winced. "You make it sound like I'm preying on weak women or something. And Chloe isn't... She's not like that, or I didn't know she was. I like her because she sees the truth in me. No one else ever has."

"What truth?"

Max stared at Elliott, telling himself that his little brother wasn't a kid anymore. They could talk as adults. They could be honest. "I... I have some, uh, control issues."

"Well, I know you like to take charge, but—"

"No, it's kind of a problem. I worry. A lot. I need to take care of people."

"Like who?"

"Like everyone." His brother's frown was creasing deeper into his forehead, and Max had had enough honesty for now, so he changed the subject. "Anyway, I liked Chloe because I thought she was calm and normal, so this is all freaking me out. We argued because I thought I should leave. And then I left. She seemed okay."

His brother glanced toward the computer.

"Obviously, I was wrong." Max reached for the phone and dialed Chloe's number. It went immediately to a message that said her voice-mail folder was full. "Her phone's off." He tried the landline and found it busy.

"I could try Jenn," Elliott offered.

Max cleared his throat, wondering what he should say about Jenn. "There's a little strain between them right now. Jenn's been acting odd."

"Odd how?"

Crying during sex, for instance, Max wanted to say. "She's been distant." He gave his brother a significant look. "And stressed."

Elliott merely looked concerned. He didn't seem to associate Jenn's stress with her bizarre behavior that last night on the island. "I hope she's okay."

"Did Jenn say anything to you about what's been bothering her? Anything about Chloe? Or Thomas?"

Elliott's face finally registered the implication

of Max's tone. His cheeks reddened. "I know what those gossip sites are saying, and you're way off base."

"I'm just asking, Elliott."

"It's offensive."

"So she didn't say anything to you?"

His brother pushed off the desk and walked out, giving Max his answer. Shit. Could it be that Thomas DeLorn had been cheating with Jenn? He couldn't imagine Jenn doing such a thing, but you never really knew people. His own life was a testament to that.

He paged through a few days' worth of gossip, not finding anything that made him feel better about himself or Jenn. The police had been hinting for a while now that Thomas had been helped by someone. According to anonymous sources who claimed to work at the Florida resort where he'd hidden out, Thomas DeLorn had clearly been waiting for someone.

Could it have been Jenn? Max stared at the bookshelves he'd built for his brother, trying to think, but he couldn't come up with a plausible alternative explanation for Jenn's withdrawal.

He went to look for his brother. Elliott was on the balcony, clutching a beer. He didn't look up when Max joined him.

"I'm sorry," Max said. "I like Jenn. But even Chloe is suspicious and she loves Jenn like a sister."

"She said she was an awful friend," Elliott muttered.

"Who? Chloe said that?"

"No. Jenn said that. When she started crying that night, Jenn said she'd been a liar and an awful friend to Chloe."

All the air left his lungs. "Are you sure?"

"I don't think she meant that, though. I can't imagine her going behind Chloe's back like that. She's so protective of her."

"That could just be guilt."

Elliott's head drooped. "I suppose."

Max raised his phone just as Elliott turned toward him.

"It was a private conversation. You can't tell Chloe about that."

"What the fuck are you talking about? She needs to know."

"If it's true, she'll find out soon enough," Elliott said, leaving Max out on the balcony and sending an unsubtle message with the slam of his office door.

"Goddamn it." Even in the short time he'd known them, Max could see that Chloe and Jenn were as close as sisters. They were totally at ease with each other, protective and affectionate. If those rumors about infidelity were grounded on truth, and if the truth involved Jenn, surely that would be an even deeper blow than the one her fiancé had dealt. The kind of blow that just might break her in two.

If Max passed on the details of his brother's conversation with Jenn, would it help her brace for the pain? He supposed it didn't matter. Even if he could convince himself that Elliott would get over it, Max didn't have a way of getting in touch with her. After that little public breakdown, he imagined that Chloe wasn't going to be answering her phone for a while.

There was nothing to be done.

From the fourth floor, the neighborhood was a sea of treetops, rippling in the breeze. He tried to let the sight bring him a little peace. At least he wasn't out on the ocean. Then again, maybe the ocean would be more peaceful than this. Boy, he'd reached a sorry point in his life when he was wishing for the sea.

When his phone rang, Max was still staring out at the green waves. The chime was so muffled by his tense grip that it took him a moment to place the sound, and when he finally flipped it open, he answered with a desperate "Hello?"

"Max Sullivan?" an unfamiliar male voice responded.

"Yes."

"This is John Johnson with Daily Net—"

"No comment," Max snapped.

"Wait! A source is reporting that Chloe Turner

didn't confess her true identity to you until your affair became public. Is that true?"

"Jesus, she didn't 'confess' anything."

"So she never told you who she was?"

"That's not what—"

"Genevieve Bianca has said publicly that she feels your friendship helped her overcome some big issues in her personal life. Do you think you can help Chloe Turner?"

"That's ridiculous. Chloe's fine the way she is. She's great. I couldn't help her if I wanted to. And I don't want to."

"So—"

Max hung up, then tried Chloe one more time just in case. No answer. It didn't occur to him until the next morning that he'd royally screwed up.

CHAPTER NINETEEN

AT SEVEN MONDAY MORNING, the sunlight was still weak and pretty, and not quite warm enough to suffocate. Jenn sat in her car at the courthouse, waiting for the day to start and swallow her up. She hadn't been able to sleep, so she'd gotten up early and driven to Chloe's place, determined to tell her the truth. No one had opened the door. The one photographer on the scene had snapped a few pictures of her, then told her that Chloe wasn't there and Max was gone. Maybe they were holed up in a secret hotel room somewhere, or that was what Jenn kept telling herself, anyway.

Though the phone felt too heavy to lift in Jenn's weary hand, she raised it to her ear and pressed Play for the tenth time that night.

"Jenn? Hi, it's Elliott. Sullivan. I've been thinking about what you said the other night. And I've seen the news… If you… It's none of my business, of course, but I just wanted to tell you that I don't care what you've done. Maybe you haven't done anything at all. And it's not that I don't care. I'm saying that if you need someone to talk to, call me. Maybe I'm not the most comforting guy in the world, but... Anyway. I hope you're doing okay. Bye."

The obvious worry in his voice brought tears to her eyes, just as it had the first time she'd heard it six hours earlier.

She'd let this go on too long. She'd wanted to shield Chloe, not give her awful suspicions. And if even Elliott Sullivan suspected that Thomas had been sleeping around and Jenn had something to do with that... Crap. What a terrible mess.

Of course, now that she was ready to tell the truth, Chloe was nowhere to be found.

Jenn started the car, thinking she should drive out to Chloe's parents' house and see if she was there, but there were already two satellite television trucks parked in a corner of the courthouse lot, and a third was pulling in from the street. If Jenn left now, she might miss Chloe altogether. What if they were on their way early? She couldn't risk it.

So Jenn was waiting, feeling distinctly like a prisoner counting down the minutes to her execution. She had no control. Her only hope lay in the hands of Anna, and a last-minute phone call promising a pardon seemed highly unlikely. Anna was determined to resolve everyone's guilt by exposing the entire sordid affair to the unflinching rays of the sun. Jenn was beginning to hate her.

No, she already hated her.

The sky started its turn from gray to blue, already going bright white at the edges, and Jenn took a deep breath, ignoring the one tear that plopped onto her chest. This was the day she'd lose both of her best friends.

CHLOE SAT AT HER PARENTS' kitchen table, a mug of coffee cooling in her hand. Her stomach already burned with acid, but she kept sipping anyway, comforted by the normalcy of the act. She was dressed just as she should be, in a somber dove-gray shirt and black skirt, but she couldn't help thinking that she wanted to change. She should wear magenta or electric blue, as a slap in the face to Thomas and the press. *I'm not brought low by this; I'm still standing.*

But the magenta blouse had emphasized the redness of her eyes, and the blue had given her pale face a green tinge. The gray did nothing to flatter her, either, but at least it fit her mood.

A new morning talk show blasted its theme music through the kitchen, and Chloe's mom glared at the remote control tucked safely in Chloe's grip.

"You don't need to see this."

Chloe shrugged. "I've already seen it."

"So once is enough."

"I disagree." The host of the show offered a

thorough recap of the month's worth of Runaway Husband/Chloe the Bridezilla stories. It was thorough but brief—nothing she hadn't heard before. Then he got to the more current news. "New revelations are expected today, as the Commonwealth of Virginia has announced that additional charges will be filed in the case. There are hints that the charges involve a mystery woman, perhaps even the Bridezilla herself, and will address the questions surrounding the financial aspects of this case. Where did Thomas DeLorn get the money to help him escape his fiancée's prison of obsessive love?"

"Nice one," she said. Now that she'd had some time to think it over, she wished she had kept Thomas chained in a dungeon somewhere. It would've served him right.

"Isn't Jenn going to come with us?" her mom asked, interrupting the morning show's replay of Chloe's video tirade.

"No. But I have a feeling we'll see her there." Her calm today wasn't the same calm she'd felt over Thomas's betrayal. This was more like the pregnant stillness of the sky before a really awful storm swept through. Whether she'd loved Thomas or not, she had no doubt that she loved Jenn Castellan a lot more.

A pixilated rectangle on the television covered the video of Chloe's middle finger without obscuring any sign of what she'd meant, and Chloe winced at the sight of it. A moment's pleasure for a lifetime of pain. Well, at least the rest of the world felt good about it. She'd confirmed every suspicion they'd had about her. It was so obvious now that she *had* thrown that bouquet in the florist's face. Look at the viciousness of her throwing arm! And she was clearly petty enough to keep her cousin out of the wedding for being too short. Look at that bitchy smirk!

"Oh, sweetie." Her mom sighed, just as she'd done the other three times they'd watched it.

"Yeah, I know, Mom." Catching a glimpse of the sorrow on her mother's face, Chloe relented and aimed the remote at the television, but her finger hadn't yet hit the power button when Max appeared on the screen. At first, it was just a picture of him in shades and a T-shirt against a backdrop of sand. A picture someone had snapped on the island, probably. She turned up the volume a little, hating the way her stomach dropped as the voice-over woman described his relationship with Genevieve Bianca. After only twenty-four hours of exposure, Chloe already hated the one picture of Genevieve and Max that everyone seemed to have purchased the rights to. Genevieve looked gorgeous and delicate as she always did, her smile slightly sad, her eyes big and guileless. And Max... Max was shockingly gorgeous in a black tux, his sun-streaked hair adding an endearing touch of messiness to his look.

She hated that skinny bitch, especially because there didn't seem to be anything bitchy about her.

"And this morning we've got an exclusive comment from Max Sullivan. His first words about his relationship with Chloe Turner!"

The coffee mug dropped to the table with a sickening thud.

"A source is reporting that Chloe Turner didn't confess her true identity to you until your affair became public. Is that true?"

"She didn't confess anything."

"So she never told you who she was? Interesting. Now, Genevieve Bianca has said publicly that she feels your friendship helped her overcome some big issues in her personal life. Do you think you can help Chloe Turner?"

"That's ridiculous. I couldn't help her if I wanted to. And I don't want to."

Her mother gasped. "How could he say that about you?"

Chloe had been trying not to wrinkle her clothes, but she gave up the fight and slumped against her chair as her lungs deflated. *Oh, God.*

"Oh, sweetheart, I'm so sorry."

Her mom's hand touched her shoulder, and Chloe shook her head. "It's okay." She wanted it to be okay, but how could it be? Max had left in anger, and someone had obviously caught him before he'd had time to cool down. She knew he'd never have said anything like that under normal circumstances. But she'd thrown his past in his face.

Yes, he'd spoken in anger, but even in the midst of their argument, he must have known that bad-mouthing her to the press would be the one blow she couldn't forgive.

If she was a martyr, this would be the perfect opportunity to wallow in self-pity.

Chloe swallowed back her tears and turned off the TV. She didn't have time to stop and let her heart break. Today's emotional schedule was already full. Still, the pain managed to shoulder its way past her defenses. All Chloe could do was keep moving.

She was rinsing out her coffee cup when her dad walked into the kitchen. His thick brown eyebrows met in a frown over his eyes. "Are you still determined to do this?"

"I'm going to the courthouse, yes, but I don't want to drag you with me. Bad enough that they followed me here." She jerked her head in the direction of the street, where the press hovered like a pack of hungry dogs. There'd been no avoiding them. After her food-throwing temper tantrum, they weren't going to give up their hunt just because of a little darkness.

Her dad grunted his disgust. "I don't think

you need to do this, but I'm not going to let you face those vultures alone. And I'd like to look Mr. Thomas DeLorn in the eye and see what he has to say for himself."

"I'm sure his lawyers have advised him not to say anything at all."

"Beth," he said to her mom, "you should stay home. It's going to be a real mess outside the courthouse."

Her mom crossed her arms. "Don't talk to me like I'm some helpless old biddy. I'm sixty years old, and everyone knows that sixty is the new fifty. I think you should be the one to stay home. Your blood pressure is going to go through the roof."

"Dad, did you take your pills?"

Even as he muttered about being coddled like a baby, he went to the cabinet for his blood pressure medicine and took one before grabbing his car keys. "Fine. Everyone in the car."

Two blocks from the courthouse, the street was packed with traffic. The hearing was set to start in thirty minutes, so her dad grabbed a spot at a meter and parked there. By the time they got to the parking lot of the courthouse itself, reporters were starting to crowd around them. They shouted questions about Thomas, and his alleged lover, and Chloe's frightening temper. They flung zingers about Max and even managed to work Genevieve Bianca into the mix, because—why not? Genevieve sold papers.

Chloe put her head down and soldiered on, both arms looped around her parents' elbows. For once, she was happy for the panic that threw her heart into overdrive. She could hardly hear their rude questions past the thumping in her ears.

Her mom kept her head down, too, and Chloe was glad about that, but her dad's face was turning red. She tugged on his arm and winked when he looked at her. He didn't smile, but he took a deep breath.

Over the awful din, she thought she heard a familiar voice call her name. It sounded like Jenn, but Chloe could see nothing past the flashing cameras and boom microphones.

In reality, she knew there were no more than twenty people surrounding her, but it felt like an army of madmen, and she couldn't imagine living like this for the rest of her life. For a brief moment, a spark of sympathy blazed for Genevieve Bianca and people like her, but that was the extent of her kindness toward the woman. Petty or not, Chloe was painfully jealous that she'd had Max for months. Chloe had only gotten a few days.

A moment later, she was relieved that Max had only been connected to her for a few days, because she registered the surreal fact that there were people in the crowd wearing T-shirts that read Team Chloe

and Team Thomas. If there had been Team Genevieve T-shirts, Chloe's self-esteem couldn't have
borne it.

A lifetime later, they were finally through the
metal detectors and cleared to go into the courtroom. Chloe looked back and caught sight of Jenn's
wavy blond hair. It *had* been her, shouting Chloe's
name over the crowd. The big sound guy blocking
Jenn's face shifted for a moment, and Chloe met her
friend's gaze. "I'm sorry," Jenn mouthed.

As if she'd just jumped off a high dive, Chloe's
stomach floated weightless for a moment before set-
tling into her gut with a sickening thud. It seemed in-
evitable now, what she would hear in the courtroom,
and Chloe almost decided to flee. "Never mind,"
hovered on her lips, and she only managed to hold
it in when she looked back at the gauntlet behind
them.

There was no turning back now. The truth was
aimed straight for her anyway. May as well pretend
to be brave in the face of it.

Ironically, the courtroom was a peaceful oasis.
Every head in the room turned toward them when
they entered, but the talk was kept to low whispers.
Even Thomas turned around, and for the first time
since his death and resurrection, Chloe found herself
looking at the man she'd planned to marry.

It wasn't hard to meet his gaze. The hard part

was acknowledging that nervous tension was her only response to the sight of Thomas. Well, tension and a bit of bitter gloating when his eyes dropped to the floor. He actually started to rise, and when his attorney glanced back and saw Chloe, he put a hand on Thomas's shoulder and pushed him back down. Thomas obeyed easily, and he didn't look at her again.

He was too weak for me, she realized with a certainty she hadn't felt about much in the past month. *I am strong.* She'd never said those words to herself, but they were true. She didn't need Max or even Jenn. Oh, she wanted them both at her side with a desperation that made her chest ache, but she didn't *need* them.

One way or another, she'd get through this.

Space was made for her and her parents in one of the middle rows, and almost immediately after they sat, the bailiff quieted the court and the hearing began.

She'd expected something dramatic, but the lawyers got into the mechanics of the case in calm, deliberate voices. While they droned on, Chloe stared at the back of Thomas's head. She knew that hairline. The closely cropped dark blond hair. The shaved nape that got prickly when he needed a trim. He'd loved it when Chloe would pet him there, or he'd pretended to, anyway. Her memories were no longer trustworthy. They were more like Russian dolls, the real meanings nested beneath layers of interior shells.

He might have really loved her at some point. Or perhaps he was gay and she'd been a beard. Or maybe he'd wanted her for her awesomely cool postal delivery truck.

A woman leaned forward to whisper in Thomas's ear. His mother.

Maybe his mother had been behind the whole thing. She'd desperately wanted grandchildren. What if she'd only wanted Chloe for her womb, and once she'd had her grandchild, Mrs. DeLorn had planned to chop Chloe up and raise the child as her own? Thomas's flight may have been an idiotic attempt to save Chloe's life.

But probably not.

While Chloe glared at the back of Mrs. DeLorn's head, the woman glanced back as if she could feel the heat. Her gaze was distant and worried, though, and didn't pick Chloe out of the crowd. She whispered again to Thomas, and he shook his head.

Even if Mrs. DeLorn hadn't planned to murder Chloe and steal her own grandchild, the woman was up to something. What the hell could it be?

The lawyers all approached the judge's bench for

a hushed conversation. Finally, the D.A. was invited to declare the charges.

The quiet room slipped into complete silence. And then the D.A. dropped his bomb.

CHAPTER TWENTY

MAX HAD ARRIVED TOO LATE. He hadn't decided to return to Richmond until the morning. D.C. traffic had been hell, and now he was late and Chloe was in there alone. Well, not alone exactly.

He'd heard from the news reports being filed around him that Chloe Turner had entered the courtroom at 8:45 a.m., flanked by her parents. Max had arrived at 8:59 a.m. and hadn't been allowed access to the courthouse at all. Now he stood with the rest of the crowd, neck craned and eyes fixed on the front doors, waiting for any hint of what was going on inside. There were no cameras allowed in the hearing. Justice was blind and so was the press for now.

Shifting from foot to foot, Max waited impatiently for the news. He'd been an ass, and Chloe might never forgive him, but he wanted to be here to offer support, even if she didn't accept it. When he shifted restlessly, Max caught sight of wavy blond hair caught back in a headband, and tilted his head a little farther to the left. When the woman raised her thumb to her mouth to chew the nail, Max recognized the gesture. That was Jenn on the top steps of the courthouse.

He didn't know whether to feel relief or anger or sympathy for her, but then there was no time to think of Jenn at all. Figures shifted behind the glass, and then a man came running out, holding a notebook high. "I've got it!"

The crowd shushed itself, and everyone held their breath.

Two counts of fraud.

Three counts of forgery.

And...seven counts of felony embezzlement.

Embezzlement?

There was no reverent pause. The crowd didn't draw in a collective breath. The man's notebook tilted and he looked up as if he were done, and that was the signal for a frantic explosion of sound and movement. Little teams moved into blank corners of the sidewalk to fire up the cameras and read the indictment again. Others rushed up the stairs, eager to make contact with someone who could explain this strange turn of events.

Max just stood there, dumbfounded. Embezzlement. And Jenn was an accountant. Had she helped him with that? He looked for her again, but everyone had shifted and he couldn't pick her out.

He paced forward and back, waiting. A woman

spoke to his right, a camera held close to her mouth as she tried to calmly recite the exciting news. Max recognized her. She'd introduced Chloe's infamous video this morning, then reported the things Max had said to that reporter, all of them twisted so that they became a more delicious treat for the masses.

Rage surged through him, as strong as the horror he'd felt when he'd read the first "details" of his conversation with the reporter. How the hell did he end up hurting Chloe when he was trying to help? If this was what it was like to live as a nonneurotic person, maybe he wasn't cut out for it. It was dangerous, and people got hurt. *Chloe* got hurt.

A man rushed past him, signaling to the woman that he had more news, and then all four doors at the top of the stairs flew open and people began to come down.

The reporters cut their feed off just that quickly and a tide of bodies pushed forward to meet the wave of people coming down. Max braced himself, trying to spot Chloe. If he looked away, she might be swallowed up and swept away from him.

Hints of gossip drifted past him. Embezzlement. Fifty thousand dollars. There was a woman. A federal grand jury was being convened. But he couldn't follow any of the hints to their conclusion, because his only goal was reaching Chloe.

A podium appeared and the lawyers descended

like royalty. And there, in the midst of them, was the guy Max recognized from the gossip sites. Thomas DeLorn. The man who'd betrayed Chloe in the worst way possible. Max watched him for a moment as the press screamed around him. What kind of a stupid asshole would've tried to escape from Chloe Turner?

Max blinked. What kind of a stupid asshole was *Max?*

Finally, he spotted her, too pale but still pretty enough to make his heart lurch. She paused at the top step, a frown creasing her brow as she hesitated, clearly confused by something. An older couple stood behind her, obviously her parents, and they looked confused, as well. As the trio bypassed the crowd in the middle of the stairs and sneaked down at the very edge, Max realized what had struck them as odd. No one was following them. The press didn't turn their way. The laser-sharp paparazzi beam was aimed squarely at Thomas DeLorn now. Chloe's part in the media-stoked drama was done.

Max rushed across the sidewalk to the side of the stairs where Chloe would end up, but then he saw that she had been stopped after all. Not by a reporter, but by Jenn.

Everything inside him was urging him to get to her now. To pull her into his arms and apologize and kiss her senseless. But that wasn't what was going to happen. Not in front of her parents, certainly. And probably not even if they were all alone.

He'd left when he should've stayed. In the frantic pressure of that moment, he'd made the wrong choice. Or maybe this was just what it felt like to make a tough decision. To walk away from a responsibility that wasn't really his.

Max made his feet stay still instead of racing up to her. He'd come to warn her about Jenn, but it was way too late for that. He'd walked away and he could never take that back.

CHLOE MOVED STIFFLY DOWN the steps, uncomfortably aware of Jenn at her back. Jenn wanted to talk, so she was going to drive Chloe home, as if she needed the support now.

But she was ready for the truth, and when her foot hit the sidewalk, she walked briskly toward the parking lot. Only to be stopped dead in her tracks by the sight of *him*. *Max*. Turning away from her as if he were about to leave.

When he glanced back and spotted her, he stood straight in surprise, lips parting as if he were about to speak.

His eyes slid to a spot over her shoulder, then back to her, a question etched over his brow. Chloe glanced back and saw her parents waiting behind her. Her dad was frowning at Jenn, but her mom aimed her glare straight at Max.

Well, this was going to be awkward. Then again, her mind was spinning too fast to worry about awkwardness, so perhaps this was a good time. She tipped her chin in a nod, and Max closed the distance between them.

"Leaving again?" she asked, realizing it was a bitchy thing to say, even as the words left her lips.

He flushed, but met her gaze straight on. "Yes."

"All right then."

"But I need to apologize. About the reporter."

"Hey, I'm used to it."

"No, listen. Please. That wasn't what I said. I mean it. I'd never, ever do that to you. They took my words out of context."

Hope bloomed in her chest, and she moved quickly to smother it. "You said you couldn't help me if you wanted to."

"I said you were great. I said you were fine the way you were. *That's* why I couldn't help you. They left that part out, Chloe, I swear."

She looked at him, standing there a few inches from her personal space, hands open at his sides, as if he didn't know whether to touch her or not. The hope refused to be smothered. It could be true. How many times had the press twisted her words? How many times had they made up outright lies?

"Max…"

He stepped closer, his voice dropping. "I would never, ever do that to you, Chloe. I swear, I'd never hurt you on purpose. You have to believe that."

Did she? Looking up into his pained eyes, she did believe him. Yes, she'd hurt him the day before, but he'd been trying to do the right thing. Max would always try to do the right thing.

"I believe you," she whispered, and his face showed the same lurch from agony to hope that she felt inside her chest.

Behind her, her mom cleared her throat, and Max's gaze flickered in that direction. He looked back at her with a question in his eyes. A horrible time to introduce the parents, but her life was one big jumble of weirdness at the moment. He could deal with it or leave.

"Max, these are my parents, Beth Turner and Jimmy Turner. Mom and Dad, this is Max Sullivan."

Max took the hand her father offered. "Mr. and Mrs. Turner," he said like a nice Southern boy.

When her mom folded her hands together, clearly not offering one to Max, he looked down at the ground. "I apologize for anything you might have seen about me on the news. I swear I only want good things for Chloe. My words were twisted around."

Her mom acknowledged the apology with only

a raised eyebrow before she turned to Chloe. "All right, sweetie. You give us a call later. I'm going to get your dad out into his garden before he has a stroke."

A muttered argument about who was in better shape trailed behind them as they walked away. Chloe accidentally met Jenn's red-rimmed eyes and spun back toward Max in response.

"I told you not to hang around."

"I didn't. I went back to D.C."

Ouch. That hurt.

His eyes focused on Jenn for a split second. "I was worried, but I know you can take care of yourself. I know that, Chloe. I didn't mean to imply… But then this morning, when I heard the interview, I had to come. I couldn't let you think I would say that."

"Okay."

"Look…" He finally touched her, his fingers sending shivers from her elbow all the way to her knees. "Can we talk somewhere?"

She wanted to say yes. Wanted to tuck her hand around his arm and walk away from Jenn and her tortured eyes. If Max was back to take care of her, in that split second of vulnerability, she wanted him to whisk her away.

But she was strong. She was.

"Come by my place in a little while?"

His whole body softened and his mouth curved

into a brief, brilliant smile before he pressed it back into seriousness.

"Yes. Absolutely. Half an hour?"

She now had the perfect excuse to keep her conversation with Jenn to a minimum. "Yes. Perfect."

Max kissed her cheek, the scent of him hurting her heart, and then she was alone with Jenn Castellan, the friend she'd loved more than any boy. More than even a sister.

Jenn led her to her car, and before she could start the engine, Chloe said, "Tell me."

Jenn's hands closed over the steering wheel. "I'm so sorry."

"Just tell me."

"I know what you think, but it wasn't me. I'd never do that to you. Never."

That snapped her out of her bitter fugue. "Then who?" she asked even as she realized that she knew.

"Anna," Jenn said.

"Oh, my God."

"I'm sorry."

"But…they hardly know each other. They've only met a few times. And you've been acting so weird. Why have you been acting so weird?"

Jenn took a shuddering breath and wiped her eyes. "I knew about it, and I didn't tell you. And then

I knew if you ever found out, you'd hate me, too. Maybe even more."

"Anna told you?"

"No," Jenn whispered.

"Then how could you know?"

"I saw them together. At Anna's apartment. I went by to bring her a few books she wanted to read and she was walking him out."

"Wait a minute, you're talking about *after* the plane crash, right?"

Even before Jenn shook her head, Chloe finally understood why her friend had been so upset for all these weeks. "How long?" she managed to get out past her tight throat. "How long have you known that one of my friends was sleeping with my fiancé?"

"I saw them together three months ago. I'm so sorry, Chloe. I didn't know what to do, but Anna promised me it had only happened that one time and she'd cut it off right away. I thought she had, I swear."

"And you thought that was okay? As long as it didn't happen again?"

"No, but I thought hurting you wouldn't serve any purpose!"

"Jenn. Jesus Christ, would you just listen to yourself? I was going to *marry* him. You were going to let me marry him."

"My mom was always—"

"Damn it, it's time for you to grow up. You're not your mom, and I'm *definitely* not your mom. Oh, and—news flash, Jenn—not every man is like your dad, either, so get over it."

Jenn smothered a sob, and Chloe closed her eyes against the guilt. "I'm sorry," she whispered.

"No, you're right. I'm a coward. I was afraid to hurt you, so I lied. And then it got worse and worse."

"The crash."

"I swear I thought it was over between them, Chloe!"

All the tension she'd felt over the past week seemed to coalesce in her shoulders at that moment. She tried twisting her neck, but nothing popped. "Maybe you'd better start driving. I have to be back at my place to meet Max."

Jenn didn't try to protest or defend herself, but Chloe didn't feel any satisfaction. She could be mean to Jenn for that very reason. It was safe to be mean to someone who wouldn't fight back. But she was so angry, bubbling over with it, and she had to get it out.

"I gather it wasn't over?" she snapped as they pulled out of the lot and headed away from the courthouse. Not one reporter even looked in their direction. It felt strange, like stepping out of a dark theater in the middle of the day. Disorienting to be set free into the bright, beautiful sunlight.

"When the plane crashed," Jenn said, her voice raspy with tears, "I was so glad I hadn't told you. I thought 'It's over. She never needs to know.'"

"You're saying you were relieved. That he was dead."

"No! Or maybe I was! I didn't want you to marry him anymore, obviously, but I didn't know how to stop the wedding without hurting you."

"That's so fucking stupid, Jenn! You were going to sentence me to a lifetime with a man who was lying and cheating before we even got married."

"I know. As soon as they found Thomas in Florida, Anna called me. She was completely freaked out and panicking. I told her not to tell anyone. Not you, not the police."

Chloe's jaw felt too tight to move, but she managed to whisper, "Tell them what?"

For a long moment, Jenn didn't speak. Her careful breathing betrayed an attempt to control tears. Finally, she nodded to herself and took one last breath. "She said they both felt trapped in their lives. Anna in her family's business and Thomas in his. They talked about running away, but Anna said that was just part of a fantasy. She didn't really think he'd put it in motion."

"So they were in love."

"I guess they thought they were. But Anna said she realized how sick it was, and she sent him a letter. She told Thomas it was wrong and she didn't want to live like that. She said they could either build a life together or he could marry you, but he couldn't have you both."

"Wow. She was...she was going to steal him from me."

"She thought he'd stay with you. She was trying to end it."

"Well, that certainly didn't work out very well!"

"I guess he thought she was telling him she was ready to run away. When he called her...she couldn't believe it."

Chloe stared out the windshield, stunned by the story. If this were a soap opera, she'd be the villain, the cold fiancée keeping Thomas from his true love.

"Chloe." Jenn reached for her hand, but when Chloe instinctively drew away, Jenn put her hand back on the steering wheel. Beautiful houses slipped past the windows, white paint glowing in the cheerful morning light. Meanwhile, Chloe was driving through her own personal hurricane.

"He fell in love with someone else and I didn't even notice."

"Anna thinks it was more about running away from his mother than it was about her."

"Well, I'm happy Anna has such great insight into *my* fiancé. Did she help him embezzle money? Did she steal money from her father?"

"I don't know. She's cooperating with the district attorney. We didn't talk about that."

Chloe swallowed hard. She stared ahead, not seeing the road. Instead, she saw the DeLorn Limited phone numbers flashing to life on her phone. "His mother," she breathed.

"What?"

"He stole that money from his mother. That's what the embezzlement charges are."

"They haven't said what—"

"That phone call from his mom. *That's* what it was about. She's trying to convince the D.A. that she gave Thomas money, so they wouldn't charge him for stealing from the company."

Jenn looked shocked, but Chloe was nodding to herself. "She wants to pay off the bills from the wedding. I'll bet she'll try to convince me to testify on his behalf. Jesus, she must be delusional."

"I'm sorry," Jenn said, though it wasn't clear who she was apologizing for. Chloe didn't respond, and for the last five minutes of their drive, neither said a word. But as the car bumped over the curb on the turn into Chloe's alley, words were jolted from her mouth.

"I can't believe you didn't tell me."

"I'm sorry. I'm so sorry. I just… I never wanted to see that look on your face. The look on your face right now… I'm sorry." She was sobbing openly now. "I'm so sorry."

Infuriated by the urge to wrap her arms around her friend, Chloe got out of the car and slammed the door behind her. If Anna was there, Chloe would slap her face, but slamming the car door was the best she could do in Anna's absence.

Her conscience tried to tug her back to her weeping friend, but she pushed herself up the stairs and into her sad little apartment.

Her defiance was cheap and easy now that the paparazzi had lost interest, but she still felt a surge of power when she raised the shade on the largest window facing the alley. Dust motes swirled crazily in the light. She hadn't opened this shade once in the month she'd lived here. Bracing herself, she pushed hard on the window and managed to raise the swollen sash about four inches. That was enough to satisfy her, and she crossed to the facing window and opened that one, as well. A breeze chased over her skin, and Chloe dropped into a chair at the small table and rested her head in her hands.

They'd all betrayed her. Everyone she'd loved most.

And yet the only thing that mattered to her at that moment was the breeze sliding over her skin and the room brightening with the smell of fresh-cut grass. She was too tired to care about anything else, frankly, and she knew she'd feel bad about that later.

But for now she just sat there and breathed and felt comfortable in her apartment for the first time.

When the knock came, Chloe didn't jump or even open her eyes. "Who is it?"

"It's Max."

"Come in."

The door opened, setting a wave of air curling over her. Nice.

"Chloe? Are you okay?"

"I don't know." She raised her head to see him watching her with his hands in his pockets. And she decided she was ready for more truth. "Why did you leave yesterday?"

He tipped his head back and looked at the ceiling. "Chloe...I don't know how to handle this. You *told* me to go. You told me you needed to work it out on your own."

Even though he couldn't see her, she nodded. She *had* told him to go, so she couldn't figure out why she was so damn mad at him. "I didn't need you," she conceded. "And I know I told you to leave, but…"

He shook his head and ran a hand through his hair before looking at her again. "But what? Chloe, I swear, this is new territory for me. I'm lost. I can't take care of you, and you don't want to be taken care of! So what was I supposed to do?"

"You're supposed to…" It was impossible to explain. The words tumbled in her mind, still full of hurt and anger. "You're supposed to *stay*, Max. You stay because I don't need you. You stay because when someone tells you they're strong and they don't need help, you stand there and offer it anyway!"

"I don't—"

She was sobbing now, and she didn't care. "You stay because I *am* strong and I'm not a crazy bitch, and I deserve to have someone at my side, just because he c-cares about me!"

"Oh, Jesus, Chloe. I'm so sorry." He crouched down to hold her, but she held up a hand to stop him. After a few ragged sobs, she took a deep breath and managed to get the crying under control.

"I'm okay. I'm fine."

He watched her with tortured eyes, his hands still open as if he needed to touch her.

"Max…there's a difference between offering support and taking care of someone like a child. You're going to have to figure that out."

"You're right. I know you're right."

"You can't run away when there's a problem."

"I'm sorry," he whispered. "I've never done this before."

"Done what?" She sniffed hard.

He was quiet for a moment. "Had a real, normal relationship."

Suddenly, Chloe wasn't mad anymore. She wasn't even hurt. She held herself very still. "Is that what this is?"

"Well, it's real. And strangely enough, it feels surprisingly normal. But… Christ, Chloe, I'm going back to sea in a few weeks, so what the hell am I supposed to do about that?"

It felt real and normal? With her? On a day like this, that was all she needed to hear. Nothing more, nothing less. "Max, I hear what you're saying. I know our next conversation is going to get complicated. I know my life is a mess and so is yours. But just for today… Just for today, let's pretend it's all really simple."

He stood and shook his head. "We already tried that. It didn't work out so well."

Chloe watched his strong chest rise and fall. A few stray dust motes danced past his neck. She stood and went to him, pressing her hands to the tight muscles beneath his shirt. "Please? I can't figure anything else out today."

"All right," he murmured. "Not today." His hands settled on her shoulders, thumbs feathering up her neck. "But you're totally taking advantage of my guilt."

A grin stole her worry away. "I can accept that."

"You don't want to tell me what happened with Jenn?"

"It wasn't her. That's all I want to say. Today, I'm too fragile to talk about any of that."

"Fragile, huh?"

"Yes. And needy."

"Chloe, you're full of shit."

"Shh. Just pretend." They were both smiling when their lips touched. It made no sense. She'd just had one of the worst days of her life, and she was dragging Max and all his issues down into it. But in the end, they both went willingly.

JENN RODE HOME WITH the windows down, and by the time she reached her apartment in the suburbs of Richmond, she was pretty sure all her tears were dried. All of them. She felt as if she'd been crying nonstop for the past month, feeling sorry for herself even more than she'd felt bad for Chloe.

But now it was done. She'd confessed. And she'd heard a hard truth about herself. She was living her life afraid of becoming her mother. Hell, she'd known that before, but it sounded so much more pitiful coming from someone else's mouth.

Chloe was right. Jenn had been raised to believe that all men were cheaters. How many times had her dad said that? "Men aren't wired to eat the same meal every day for the rest of their lives. They like variety." Her mother had accepted that, and so had Jenn. Her mission hadn't been to save Chloe from being cheated on. It had been to keep the truth from being thrown in her face.

All men cheated, but the good ones kept it quiet. That was all Jenn had expected for herself or her friends. Utterly pitiful.

Jenn trudged up the stairs to her place, thinking she'd take a long bath and then sleep the day away. She'd called in sick to work and didn't feel the least bit guilty about that. She *was* sick.

But her plans for sleeping away her pain were over as soon as she opened the door and saw someone jumping up from the couch. Anna's familiar curly black hair was pulled back into a severe braid, and her makeup was smudged. She was the shortest of the three friends, only five-foot-one, but she'd always seemed taller—her energy pulsed from her wherever she went. But not today.

Jenn dropped her purse on the ground and held out her hand. "Give me the key."

Anna clutched the key in her hand and didn't budge.

"I told her everything," Jenn said. "She'll probably never talk to either of us again. So give me my goddamn key."

Anna's eyes widened with shock. "If you'd let me tell her a month ago—"

"I should've told her *three* months ago, but I'm not going to let my stupidity take the blame for your betrayal. Now give me my key and get out. And don't ever come here again."

"I'm sorry. I've ruined my life, too, you know. My dad is ashamed of me. Thomas won't return my calls. You're my best friend. I need you."

In the past, Jenn would've relented at the sight of Anna's brown eyes brimming with tears. She couldn't stand to see people in pain, but right now her own pain was filling her up and there was no room for empathy, so she held her hand higher and watched as Anna skirted the couch.

The key was hot from Anna's grip when she pressed it into Jenn's palm.

"Wait," Jenn said, and hope flashed over Anna's face. "Tell me about the embezzlement."

"I can't. The D.A...."

"Did you help him?"

"No! I didn't know anything about it. He... We talked about living on an island in the Caribbean.

He'd fly one of those little tourist planes and I'd be a chef. We fantasized about how much money we'd need to get by for a little while, but I had no idea he'd— I thought we were just pretending. Jenn, please. I know what I did was—"

"Goodbye, Anna. And don't you dare call Chloe and try to explain your actions away. It's bad enough I've had to listen to it."

Anna's shoulders slumped and she walked to the dining-room table to grab her purse. Even on this awful day, her purse matched her heels. Anna had been the fashion advisor for all of them, and if Jenn and Chloe were still friends after this, there'd be no more daylong shopping trips. It would just be the two of them, wearing out-of-season clothes at restaurants that hadn't been hot for years. Anna wouldn't be there to get them the best table or offer the latest Virginia gossip. It would never be the same again.

But Jenn would take that new form of their friendship and hold on with both hands if Chloe gave her the chance.

"I'll call you in a few weeks," Anna said on her way out, but Jenn just closed the door. She toed off her shoes and walked carefully to her couch before lowering herself down. The soft leather swallowed her up, muffling the world, still warm from Anna's body.

Jenn had almost let her best friend marry a man

who'd cheated on her. She'd done it because, in the deepest, darkest recesses of her brain, she believed that even if you loved a man and gave him everything, he was going to betray you. Because even the best woman couldn't be good enough to satisfy a man.

If she didn't get past that, she'd live her whole life waiting to be betrayed. Waiting to have her heart broken. Like her mom, she'd never demand anything better for herself.

Key still clutched in her hand, Jenn tugged her phone from the pocket of her jeans and called up Elliott's message. She knew it by heart, of course, but she still listened to every syllable of his awkward words. He wasn't smooth. He wasn't charming. He was perfect.

Jenn pushed the call-back button and took a deep, terrified breath.

"Dr. Sullivan," he snapped. The background of his life was filled with ringing phones and people talking over each other. Before Jenn could speak, he said, "Hold on a second," and his voice turned away to ask someone to bring a copy of a revised report to his office before three. "Okay," he said into the phone.

She started to say his name, then changed her mind, intimidated by the official sound of his title. "Um…this is Jenn Castellan." A statement of fact that sounded so much like a question that she winced.

He didn't say a word, and she was about to repeat herself when Elliott murmured, "Just a moment." The sounds around him changed as he moved through his world. Then a door closed and everything went quiet.

"Jenn? Are you okay?"

Oh, God, this was the voice she remembered. Steady and focused and comforting in a way she couldn't explain. She refused to let herself cry, clearing her throat against the urge. "I'm good," she said.

"Are you sure? Because things seem to have come to a head."

"Yes. I'm not sure what's going to happen between Chloe and me, but I just… You said I could call if I wanted to talk, but I'm sure you're busy."

"No, I'm supposed to be at lunch, so talk as long as you want."

"It wasn't me." She waited a few breaths, then made herself continue. "I don't want you to think I'm that kind of woman. It wasn't me sleeping with him, it was our friend, Anna. But I knew about it and didn't say anything, so maybe that's just as bad."

"No," he said immediately.

"Anna told me it was over, and I thought that

should be the end of it, and that's awful. But I didn't want you to think it was me."

"Even if it had been... I could tell it was killing you."

She felt the ghosts of his hands on her back, holding her while she cried. "Elliott?"

"Yes?"

"You live in D.C., so we never have to see each other again. And you probably shouldn't see me again if your brother is involved with Chloe because she might hate me forever. But I'm not sure I'll have the courage to say this any other time—"

"Jenn—"

"No, don't. I'm being honest today, so let me say this."

He stayed silent in answer, and Jenn nodded, squeezing the key so hard that it hurt. "I like you. That may sound weird considering what a complete disaster I've been. I'm not good with men. They make me nervous. But I like you a lot, and I know I started crying when we were... I know you're probably relieved to be rid of me, but...I like you. And I'd love to see you again." When she paused, she realized she was breathing into the phone, probably sounding as close to a crazy stalker girl as she possibly could. She squeezed her eyes shut and tipped the phone away from her face.

"You're serious?"

Oh, God. He lives two hours away, she told herself. If he says no, you can pretend this never happened. "Yes."

"But, the crying? I was under the impression that things didn't, uh, go well."

"Oh, Elliott. I know they didn't go well with you, but with me… It was just too much to handle. You felt so good, and I was in such a bad place, and… maybe we could just take this more slowly?"

"Yes," he said, such a simple answer that she didn't understand it.

"What?"

"Yes. I'm good with taking it slow. I've been divorced less than a year, and you're the first woman I've dated since then."

She swiped a tear off her cheek. "Really?"

"Really."

"What about Chloe and Max?"

"She'll forgive you, Jenn. You're a beautiful person and she loves you."

Apparently, her tears weren't dried up at all, because they began to fall in earnest at his words. She made herself speak past them, even though her throat screamed with pain. "Maybe I could call you tomorrow?"

"Yes. But I'll call you tonight to see how you're doing."

Jenn said goodbye before she could say anything

embarrassing. She was now officially dating a man
who intimidated her. A doctor. A man who treated
her like an equal even when she acted like a lost
child. And she wasn't going to let her fear screw up
the best thing she'd done in years.

CHAPTER TWENTY-ONE

THEY MADE LOVE. And took a nap. They played three games of Yahtzee as if they didn't have a worry in the world. Then, because Chloe could now come and go as she pleased, Max took her to the movies.

After only a few hours, she felt as refreshed as if she'd been on vacation for a month. And when she suggested a restaurant in the heart of Shockoe Slip, the trendiest area in Richmond, Max took her there, too. People stared at them, but Chloe didn't care in the least. She held Max's hand and sipped the last of her wine and she felt…happy.

"I went online while you were in the shower," Max said, signaling that make-believe time was over.

She sighed a little at the loss of it, but didn't really mourn. "Yeah, maybe my next place will have a shower big enough for two."

"Promises, promises." But his smile faded quickly. "Are you saying you might be willing to give me another shot? In a few weeks I'll be back at work. I won't be able to see you for two months."

It seemed crazy even to consider it. Despite having steady jobs and adult responsibilities, each of them was at an utterly unstable point in their lives. "We just started dating. You might go over there and fall in love with the new cook on your boat."

"No, I never sleep with crew members. It causes too much distraction when I need to be focused on my job."

"Jeez, Max. No declaration of ever-faithful love?"

He offered an easy grin. "Oh, I'll be faithful. You can't trust condoms in a shipboard environment. Too much heat and humidity."

"Wow, that's like poetry. Maybe you should write a book."

"Oh, yeah? What about you? You'll be the one hanging out on land with unlimited access to the whole male population of Virginia."

"And climate-controlled drugstores."

He tilted his beer in her direction. "Exactly."

"I'll wait for you. If you want me to."

He opened his hand to look down at her fingers, touching each knuckle with his thumb as if he were biding his time. "You can forgive me? For walking away when you needed me?"

She cocked her head and studied him. His tan face and the laugh lines around his eyes, which might be from smiling or from worrying too much. "That did hurt."

"I know. I swear I'll learn. If we decide to do this… I promise I won't be the guy who runs off when things get tough. Even if I have no idea what I'm doing, I won't run."

She let her smile fade and met his gaze with somber eyes. "If we're being serious… I've spent some time thinking about this, Max. The truth is that I like you. Too much. Or just the right amount, maybe. But you're living a lie, and I've already done that with one guy."

"Shit," he muttered, dropping her fingers so he could run both hands through his hair.

"You said it was killing you."

"It is."

"I don't want to wake up one day and find that you've left everything behind and faked a plane crash because you can't take it anymore."

"Even if I'm running to a house in the suburbs and the nine-to-five grind?"

"Yeah. I want you walking right up to those things, out in the open. Like a man."

"Jesus, Chloe. I didn't see that blade coming."

Pressing her lips together, she refused to offer an apology.

After a few sips of his beer, Max rolled his shoulders. "I've been living this way for thirty years. It's going to take me a little while to untangle myself."

"I understand. I can give you time. And the reason it's easy to forgive you? Because you were actually trying to do the right thing when you walked away from me."

"For myself," he clarified.

"Well, I was trying to keep you there for myself, so I don't begrudge you that. Much. And you know what? I think long-distance dating might be just the speed of dating we both need right now. For a little while."

"Can't handle all of Max Sullivan at once, Chloe?" He laughed along with her at first, but when she kept laughing, his expression turned to insulted. "Hey."

"Sorry. So now that we're going steady—"

"Oh!" a woman gasped from close by. "It's really you!"

Chloe jerked upright as a young blonde leaned into her personal space.

"You're Chloe Turner!"

"Um…" The woman didn't look like a reporter. She looked like a college student.

"Oh, my God, I love you so much. Can I take a picture of us together?"

Chloe met Max's eyes, but he looked just as confused as she was.

"I can't believe how much of an ass that Thomas turned out to be. Stealing from his own mama! What a loser. I'll bet you're glad he jumped out of that plane now, huh? Say cheese!"

Chloe smiled weakly as the girl held her camera at arm's length and pressed her cheek to Chloe's.

"Thank you! Y'all have a great night. Max, you're so cute!"

"Er, thanks," he said as she walked off.

"You are cute," Chloe offered.

"Wait a minute, what was that about Thomas stealing from his mom?"

"The D.A.'s office must've sprung a leak."

"That's the embezzlement charge? Jenn wasn't—"

"No." Chloe watched the blonde slide back into her chair and show her phone to her squealing friends. "Jenn," she murmured. "None of it's really sunk in yet. I'm relieved it wasn't Jenn. Anna is a friend, but she's not like a sister."

"Still."

"Yeah, still. And Jenn…"

"She knew?"

Chloe started to nod, then shook her head. "How did you figure that out?"

Max shifted, glancing around the room as if he were hoping for another interruption. None seemed imminent and he was clearly disappointed as he faced her again. "Look, Jenn was a little upset that last night on the island. She and Elliott…talked."

Chloe gasped. "He told you about that?"

He winced. "Yeah."

"Oh, God. Poor Jenn!"

"'Poor Jenn'? What about my poor brother?"

She waved a dismissive hand, confident that the Sullivan brothers could handle a good battering to their self-esteem. "So how did you know?"

"Elliott said she was pretty torn up about being a bad friend to you. About being a liar. That's why she was crying."

"She knew he was sleeping with Anna, and she was going to let me *marry* him. That's what happened."

"She knew before the crash?"

"Yes. She knew three months ago. How am I supposed to get over that?"

"I have no idea, but you have to, because she's your best friend and she loves you, Chloe. This has been killing her. Even I can see that."

He was right about that, at least. Angry as she was, she could see how miserable Jenn had been for the past month, and jumpy and pale for weeks. She felt a surge of sympathy and shook her head against it. "How can I forgive her? She betrayed me."

Max's warm hands close over hers. "You know she didn't mean to hurt you."

"I guess."

"So you'll do it. You'll forgive her. Maybe a little long-distance dating will work for you and Jenn, too. Time to get yourself together. A few late-night phone calls."

"Just a few?"

His smile was like a balm on her wounded heart. "I was talking about Jenn, *not* me."

"We'll see. Maybe. Right now, I just... Well, I don't know what to do now."

"I've got two weeks free for a shore-leave affair. You know any promising candidates?"

"Depends. How do you feel about a crazy girl who'll likely be called as a witness in an upcoming criminal trial?"

"You had me at 'crazy girl.'"

This was not a promising start. Her life was complicated enough without adding a long-distance relationship with a man who had serious issues of his own. So why in the world did Chloe feel so damn happy?

CHAPTER TWENTY-TWO

JENN BIT HER LIP NERVOUSLY as she pulled into the alley behind Chloe's apartment. She'd passed the point of worrying that she'd scrape all her lipstick off. Now she was worried about the state of her actual lips. But she couldn't bite her nails while she was driving, so her options were limited.

She hadn't seen Chloe since the day of the hearing, but they'd talked twice in the month since then. The first call had been tearful and halting. The second call had been a bit easier. Now they were going out to dinner. A real date, as Chloe had put it, and Jenn definitely had that level of jitters.

She'd changed her life in the past thirty days. Oh, she wasn't loud and wild and bold, but she'd shored up some of her self-confidence. And she was being brave. Things with Elliott had progressed, and she was actually…hopeful. Hopeful that the relationship with him might progress, and hopeful that he might actually be a man who would live up to her expectations. Her *new* expectations.

That thought gave her a little boost of confidence,

enough to get her out of the car and through the tall wooden gate.

A ball of fur and teeth and claws barreled toward her, snapping and snarling. "Oh, God!" she shrieked, scrambling backward so quickly that she hit the gate and shut it before she could escape. "Help!"

"Brutus!" an ancient female voice called, and the dog stopped in its tracks.

Jenn kept one hand out and pressed the other to her pounding heart.

"You'd better get on outta here, if you know what's good for you," the woman snapped.

Jenn tore her eyes from the beast for a split second to locate Mrs. Schlessing in the backyard. She was lounging in the shade of a tree, wearing gardening gloves and holding a cocktail glass.

"Mrs. Schlessing," she panted. "It's me. I'm Chloe's friend, Jenn."

The old woman tipped down the sunglasses that were half the size of her head. "You sure? That Jenn hasn't been around in a while."

Chloe's door squeaked open somewhere above her. "Is everything okay?" she asked as she jogged down the stairs.

Mrs. Schlessing frowned at Jenn. "There's an intruder."

"Jenn!" Chloe gasped when she finally caught sight of her. "Brutus, you leave her alone. You should be ashamed of yourself!" Brutus slunk away, but Chloe aimed a glare at Mrs. Schlessing, as well. "How can you not remember Jenn?"

The woman shrugged, nudged her glasses back up, and sipped her drink.

"Are you ready?" Chloe asked. Jenn nodded, hoping her legs would hold her when she pushed away from the gate. They both slipped through, and then, miracle of miracles, Chloe put her arms around Jenn and hugged her tight.

"I've missed you," she said.

Jenn hugged her back, too choked up to respond.

"Come on. Let's go to dinner."

"Chloe... I'm so sorry. I hope—"

"You've already apologized a hundred times, Jenn. Let's not go there. We're going to be okay, all right? I know you were trying to protect me."

Jenn swallowed back the sob that wanted to escape and nodded.

"Even if you went about it in a completely screwed-up way."

When Chloe smiled, Jenn finally let out her tears in a half sob, half laugh mess. Chloe pulled her into another hug. "We're okay. But for the record, I want to know if my man is cheating on me. In fact, there's a whole list of things I expect you to report—seeing him at dinner with another woman, catching him in my underwear dancing around my apartment...the list goes on."

"Okay. I promise."

Jenn hopped into the driver's seat, feeling lighter than she had in months. Maybe even her whole life.

She had her best friend back, and she was never going to put that friendship at risk again.

CHLOE SNAPPED HER SEAT BELT into place, and gave Jenn's hand one last squeeze. Max had been right. She'd needed to forgive Jenn, and it had been surprisingly easy. Not that she wasn't going to keep an eye out for any signs of strange nervousness in the future, but it wasn't as if Jenn had protested that she'd done nothing wrong. Regret was clear in everything she'd said or done.

"So," Chloe said after a deep breath. "I'm sorry I didn't run out to rescue you earlier. I was on the phone."

"With Max?"

"No...with Thomas."

The car jerked a little when Jenn's foot banged against the brake pedal. *"What?"*

"He called me."

"To try to get you to lie?"

"No, his mom kept leaving me these saccharine-sweet messages, but she's stopped calling. There's rumors of a deal with the prosecution."

Jenn glanced over, her eyes wide. "What did he call about then?"

"He wanted to apologize. Finally. Actually, he said he was going to send a letter, but with the charges…"

"Seriously? He didn't want to leave *evidence?*"

"Well, he needn't have worried. It's not like he said much at all. He just said he was sorry. That he'd panicked, and it wasn't my fault, and he didn't expect me to forgive him. Then he paused like he wanted me to forgive him."

"Oh, God."

"I know. Anyway, I asked him if it had all been a lie from the very start, and he said…" Chloe frowned at the dashboard. "He said, 'I think we both wanted it to be more than it was.'"

"What an asshole!"

"No, I'm pretty sure he's right. I *know* he's right. It wouldn't have worked. Maybe in a few years, I would've been the one jumping out of a plane. But I'd have done it with more flair. I'd have gone to Europe. If I were on the run, I'd want Interpol after me, because I'm just awesome like that." Chloe laughed, but when Jenn took her hand, she squeezed it hard, then held on for the rest of the drive.

As soon as they slid into the booth at their favorite

brunch restaurant, Chloe leaned forward and put her chin on her hands. "So, how's it going with the other Sullivan brother?"

"Good. Really good. We see each other every weekend. And when he comes here, he doesn't even bring his laptop."

"Really? That's not very nerd-sexy."

"I know. He's making a big effort to try to leave work at the office, but honestly… I like watching him work. Last weekend I was at his place, and I woke up to see him sitting at his desk in the glow of his laptop. And it was so sexy. Like I was watching him save the world with no shirt on."

"Wow, that's really interesting…"

Jenn nodded.

"…because the last time I talked to you, you said were taking it slow, and there was no sex going on."

"Oh." Her cheeks blazed red. "Um…"

"You're doing it with Elliott Sullivan!" Chloe crowed.

"Shush," Jenn scolded past a smile. "We got carried away."

"So did you cry?"

Jenn clenched her eyes shut. "That story is never going to die, is it?"

"Nuh-uh."

"No, I did *not* cry." She opened her eyes, and

they sparkled with joy. "Unless you count my cries of wild passion and crazed need."

"Oh, my God!" Chloe squealed, reaching across the table to slap her arm. "You're a dirty girl!"

"Maybe," Jenn answered with a cheeky smile.

Chloe grinned at her so hard it hurt. "I'm so glad to see you. But I don't want to talk about this anymore. Not while *my* Sullivan brother is four thousand miles away."

"Are you sure? I was going to tell you about Elliott's amazing—"

"Stop it!" Chloe covered her ears. "I am a lonely wretch of a woman."

"Aw. When's Max coming back?"

"Six more weeks."

"And then what?"

She should've felt uncertain as she pondered the question. But Chloe felt nothing but anticipation. Even if Max spent the next year going back and forth, working out his issues, Chloe Turner was going to be just fine. She looked down at her Lucky Charms T-shirt with a little smile. "I have no idea. Things are good between us, and I think they'll only get better. Right now, we're taking it slow. Some of us know how to be patient."

"Liar," Jenn said.

And she was right.

CHAPTER TWENTY-THREE

MAX NO LONGER FELT the roll of the sea beneath his feet, but a glance toward the horizon made him aware that the boat was bucking pretty hard. He scanned the water with a hard eye, waiting for the last diver to surface, but he didn't move forward to assist.

Instead, he wrapped his hands around the railing and let Kailie hunch over the water as it began to bubble. This hands-off technique made him sweat, even in the constant sea breeze, and his stomach wasn't exactly happy with the training, either.

The diver, a twenty-year veteran who still faced every day with excitement, emerged from the water, holding his net bag high. It was the last planned dive at this site, so even though the bag held only a tiny pottery shard, the diver shouted in triumph. The crew hated to leave even a fragment of treasure behind.

Greedy bastards, Max thought with total affection. They worked hard and partied harder and drove him mad every step of the way. But tomorrow he'd be on a flight to Virginia, and that was enough to keep his anxiety under control.

Chloe. Just the thought of her made him smile, though he turned serious again when he watched Kailie handling the last of the tanks. He'd check her work when she was done. So far, he hadn't discovered any mistakes. Kailie was thorough, but she was young and way too nice to boss these hard-headed daredevils around. Maybe after a few more seasons...

By the time he finished double-checking the equipment and the logs, the galley was deserted, so Max made a quick sandwich and retreated to his cabin. As he shut the door, his mind raced, anticipating the soft thrill of hearing Chloe's voice. It was Saturday, so they'd share a few hours of conversation, at least.

Damned if he wasn't giddy as a teenage boy at the prospect. And just as fucking horny. Two months was a long time to go without Chloe's touch. He was only mildly appeased by her willingness to describe in great detail just what she missed about his body. And what she wanted him to do to hers...

"Tomorrow!" she squealed as soon as the line opened up.

"Tomorrow," Max agreed. "Are you sure you're ready to put up with me in person?"

"Oh, God, I'm gonna put up with you so good you won't be able to walk for two days."

"Jeez. Maybe I should be afraid."

"You should definitely be afraid. I'm going to… Oh, Max, I've missed you so much. Jenn and Elliott are so annoying, always holding hands and *looking* at each other. It's sickening."

"You mean the way we're going to hold hands and look at each other as soon as I get there?"

"Yes, it's awful!"

"I'm sorry." He was smiling as he said it. Jenn and Chloe seemed nearly back to normal. And Jenn was all Elliott ever talked about. Life had moved on without Max, and he was acutely jealous.

Suddenly, he couldn't hold it back any longer. He'd wanted to wait until he saw her. Maybe he'd wanted to be sure. But there was nothing doubtful in him when he said it. "I love you, Chloe."

Her breath jumped, spiking his blood with a quick surge of adrenaline. The moment drew out, stretching his pulse thin, until she finally inhaled as if she'd speak.

"Max Sullivan," she breathed, "I love you, too."

Max stretched out on his bunk with a sigh. He let her words sink in. Women had told him that before, of course, but he'd never believed them. They couldn't have loved him, because they hadn't known him.

But Chloe… Chloe knew all his secrets. Except one.

"I'D REALLY PLANNED ON TAKING you straight to my apartment, you know."

Max couldn't help the big grin that stretched across his face. "Half an hour," he answered.

"In case I'm being too subtle, I want to have sex with you. Right now. I'm desperate. Horny. I've been horny for two months." Her hand slid up his thigh. "I need your huge—"

"Hey!" he barked as the tires of his rental car thumped against the grooves in the highway shoulder. "Come on. That's just mean. I have a surprise for you. Aren't you excited?"

"If the surprise isn't an erection, then no. No, I'm not excited. I'm sullen."

He tugged her hand over and put it back on his thigh. "Come on, don't pout."

"Where are we going? We're not even in the city anymore!"

"Almost there."

"Max," she groaned. But after a few seconds, Chloe seemed to forget her pouting and her hand moved in friendly little circles against his knee, edging up beneath the hem of his shorts. The skin of his thigh tightened until he couldn't feel anything except the electric sizzle of her fingertips stroking him. "Oh, Max, I didn't know I'd miss you this much."

Strange how a heart could feel joy and pain at the same exact moment. Pain that he'd left her alone for two months and sheer, prideful joy that she'd missed him. When she leaned close enough to press her lips to his neck, Max nearly purred. The scent of her shampoo… Jesus, it seized hold of his soul with a nearly audible snap.

Her mouth felt so good that it took him a full thirty seconds to realize the problem. That snap hadn't been his soul at all. "Holy shit, Chloe. Get back over there and put your seat belt on!"

She did as he asked, with only a little grumbling.

Despite the horror of Chloe without a seat belt, Max was hard as a rock now, and they were almost to their destination. Hopefully, there would be no one else around.

He pulled off the highway and turned onto a road that wound around the side of a hill.

"Where are we?"

"Here," he said, slowing the car as the road ended at a small A-frame cabin.

"What's here?"

He got out of the car and met her in front of it. Five feet away, a Realtor sign swung in the breeze. "It's a house," Max said, "for sale."

"You want me to buy a house?"

"No, I..." He turned toward her, suddenly worried about her reaction. "I turned in my resignation last night."

"You did?" When it hit her, she jumped into his arms. "Oh, Max, you *did?*"

He held on to her, closing his eyes so he could savor the moment. She pulled away way too soon.

"But I thought you said it would take a few trips to get the new girl trained."

"Well...she was the dive supervisor on another ship for five years, so it turns out she's pretty well trained already."

"But...but you said she was so young!"

"Yeah. Twenty-eight."

"Max!" She slapped his shoulder. "You big... dork." When a tear slipped down her cheek, Max shook his head.

"What's wrong?"

"Are you buying a house here? In Richmond?"

"Maybe." Was she happy? Was she freaked out?

Did she think this was moving too fast? "I haven't seen anything but pictures yet, but I need to make an offer soon if I like it. Want to go inside?"

This time, when she threw herself into his arms, she was crying. Loudly. All he could do was hold on and hope that she was overcome with happiness and not horror. "Chloe?"

"Yes, I want to look inside," she said into his shirt, her words muffled and watery. Then, "Do you have a tissue?"

While Chloe blew her nose and got herself in order, Max figured out the key safe on the door and then stood there quietly with the key in his hand. He'd never owned his own home. He hadn't even owned a car for the past decade. But this place could be his.

"Ready?" she asked from close behind him.

Max turned the key and stepped in It wasn't fancy, but he'd already known that from the pictures. It had been built as a getaway cabin, so even though the living area was a big two-story room with a huge fireplace, the kitchen to the left was small. Still, it had been recently remodeled, and everything in it was shiny and new.

The kitchen led to a mudroom with a back door beyond that. As he walked toward it, Max noticed that every window he could see was filled with green. Trees surrounded the house, and just the sight of them left Max feeling more peaceful than he had since he'd left Richmond two months before.

He took Chloe's hand and pulled her through the mudroom to the door beyond.

"You haven't even looked around yet. Where are we going?"

He opened the door and there it was. At some point it had been a garage, but now it was a workroom, complete with lights on pulleys and an elaborate system of shelves to hold every tool he could ever want.

"Whoa," Chloe breathed.

Max went straight for the garage door and pulled it up to reveal the edge of the driveway and beyond that…more trees. The scent of leaves overwhelmed him as fresh air blew in.

"I think I'm gonna buy this place," he whispered.

"Maybe you should look upstairs?"

"Screw the upstairs."

Laughing, she curled her arms around his waist. "You have to at least *look* upstairs."

"All right, fine." Just to make Chloe happy, he raced upstairs and quickly toured the two bedrooms and one bath. "Perfect," he declared, then obligingly followed Chloe back downstairs to look around the little hallway off the living room. Another bathroom and a small den. "Still perfect."

"The carpets are a little worn."

"Sure, sure. New carpet. Come on."

"Where?" She laughed.

"One last place." Max stopped in front of the long curtains on the far side of the living room. "Ready?"

"For what?"

He swept the curtains aside and reached for the handle of the sliding door before he was tempted to look through it. He slid it open and stepped outside. "For this."

Outside was a deck. It was weathered and needed sanding and painting. Some of the boards might even need replacing, but that was nothing. Nothing at all. Because from the deck, you could see for miles.

A green expanse of hills and valleys stretched out before him like an emerald carpet.

He took a deep breath, and when he exhaled, the last of his life at sea fell away from him.

"It's beautiful," Chloe whispered.

He walked to the railing and put his hands on the peeling wood. He could see a dozen houses, but not one person. Oh, they were probably out there, obscured by the trees, but he couldn't see them. They weren't his problem. Out here, the only thing he had to worry about was himself.

And his girl. He put his arm around her shoulder and pulled her body against his. "Notice anything else?"

She glanced down toward his groin, but he shook his head. "What?"

He nodded toward the view. "No water. Not one lake or pond or stream or river. And no goddamn ocean. Isn't that the most beautiful thing you've ever seen?"

Shaking her head, she leaned her back against the railing.

"Wait. Don't lean against that until I've made sure there's no rot."

She didn't even roll her eyes, she just pushed off it and moved her weight back in Max's direction. Chloe knew full well that he was a mess of anxiety and control issues, and she didn't care.

"Chloe?"

"Yeah?"

Max opened his mouth. He took a deep breath, then shook his head. "Maybe we should walk the house again. Look at it more carefully."

"Why? It seems perfect for you. The shop, the view…"

"I want to be sure you like it, too—"

"Yeah, it's—"

"Because if you're tired of the haunted house, I thought you might need a place to stay. With me. Here. Together."

Heart thundering, he waited for the confusion to clear from her eyes. It was too soon. Way too soon. But they'd practically lived together for two weeks before he'd left. And then they'd talked every night. Maybe...

"I'll be working," he added before she could say no. "I talked to a guy who does custom furniture for big mountain cabins, and he needs someone to do side work..."

"If I move in here with you, it might hit the gossip sites."

"It might."

"And we won't be taking it slow anymore."

"No, we definitely won't."

Chloe gazed up at him, her eyes searching for something in his. She looked so damn *serious*. "So..." she finally said. "If you get the workshop, can I have the downstairs den?"

"Yes. God, yes. You can have anything you want. Except a pool."

She laid her head against his chest and squeezed so hard that he could barely breathe. "I love you, Max. And yes. Yes, I want to live here with you."

Hell, he didn't need air. He had Chloe Turner. In that moment, Max was certain that normal, average girls were completely overrated. Chloe was just screwed up enough to love him, and he could live with that kind of craziness. "Thank you," he whispered.

Eyeing the ten-foot drop to the backyard, Max edged her another inch away from the old railing. Once she was safe, he kissed her until he forgot all his worries. Every single one.

* * * * *

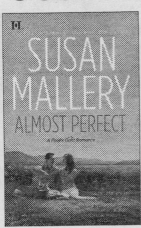

REQUEST YOUR
FREE BOOKS!

2 FREE NOVELS
FROM THE ROMANCE COLLECTION
PLUS 2 FREE GIFTS!

YES! Please send me 2 FREE novels from the Romance Collection and my 2 FREE gifts (gifts are worth about $10). After receiving them, if I don't wish to receive any more books, I can return the shipping statement marked "cancel." If I don't cancel, I will receive 4 brand-new novels every month and be billed just $5.74 per book in the U.S. or $6.24 per book in Canada. That's a saving of at least 28% off the cover price. It's quite a bargain! Shipping and handling is just 50¢ per book.* I understand that accepting the 2 free books and gifts places me under no obligation to buy anything. I can always return a shipment and cancel at any time. Even if I never buy another book, the two free books and gifts are mine to keep forever.

194/394 MDN E7NZ

Name _____ (PLEASE PRINT) _____

Address _____ Apt. # _____

City _____ State/Prov. _____ Zip/Postal Code _____

Signature (if under 18, a parent or guardian must sign)

Mail to **The Reader Service:**
IN U.S.A.: P.O. Box 1867, Buffalo, NY 14240-1867
IN CANADA: P.O. Box 609, Fort Erie, Ontario L2A 5X3

Not valid for current subscribers to the Romance Collection
or the Romance/Suspense Collection.

Want to try two free books from another line?
Call 1-800-873-8635 or visit www.morefreebooks.com.

* Terms and prices subject to change without notice. Prices do not include applicable taxes. N.Y. residents add applicable sales tax. Canadian residents will be charged applicable provincial taxes and GST. Offer not valid in Quebec. This offer is limited to one order per household. All orders subject to approval. Credit or debit balances in a customer's account(s) may be offset by any other outstanding balance owed by or to the customer. Please allow 4 to 6 weeks for delivery. Offer available while quantities last.

Your Privacy: Harlequin Books is committed to protecting your privacy. Our Privacy Policy is available online at www.eHarlequin.com or upon request from the Reader Service. From time to time we make our lists of customers available to reputable third parties who may have a product or service of interest to you. If you would prefer we not share your name and address, please check here. ☐

Help us get it right—We strive for accurate, respectful and relevant communications. To clarify or modify your communication preferences, visit us at www.ReaderService.com/consumerschoice.

MROM10R

VICTORIA DAHL